Fort Mill Ti...

Matthew [signature]

MW00427367

For information, contact Caldera@thebookcaldera.com

CHAPTER ONE

Waking suddenly from her sleep, Loeau grabs the amulet on her chest. Between short gasps of breath, she looks up and a small beam of moonlight illuminates her silver eyes, like a sunrise dancing on the ripples of a winter brook. Her long black hair hangs wildly over her shoulders, and she clenches her necklace tighter. She looks through the walls of animal skins, through the forest, and in the darkness she sees what is coming for her.

She blinks and with a wave of her hand, candles ignite throughout the small hut. An amber glow flickers against the skin of her twin boys. Still grasping her necklace, she stares at her boys, who have survived just one year in this world. Panting, Loeau gently caresses each of their small heads. Never taking her eyes off her young, she reaches above their blankets and takes down her sword.

Loeau rustles the furs of their bed, waking her man Noe. He groggily wakes from his deep slumber, and Loeau ignores him while she gathers supplies from around the hut. He grabs her arm. "Why have you woken? And why do you carry the Namid in your hand?"

With a deep-seated sigh, Loeau tells Noe of her dream. She tells him of a temple in the darkness, strange foreign men, and the eyes, white eyes that have haunted her dreams before. She looks deeply at Noe and tries to hide her fear. "They will soon be at our door. You must arm yourself, my love."

"And what of you? What of our children?"

"I will take our sons to a clearing where a stream crosses a tree whose roots have grown wild. There I must find a way to save them from a fate we cannot escape."

From the day Noe saw Loeau roaming the forest he has been consumed by her. She was naked and wild, but graceful and majestic like a forest Doe. Her mystical aura and unmatched beauty were like nothing he had ever witnessed, but when he looked into her eyes, his soul was hers. He knew when he left his people, to live a nomad's life in the deepest parts of the Black Forest, a night like this could come.

Noe dresses, stringing together his loincloth. He stares at Loeau with a heavy heart, knowing these moments will very likely be their last. Noe's eyes glaze over as he watches Loeau put on her traveling cloak. A strange and powerful enchantment surrounds the cloak, hiding her in darkness, but it does little now to calm Noe's fears. Loeau tightens her sword belt, and for this moment the Namid is quiet and at peace.

Loeau's face, which usually shines like light flickering on water, is darkened with doubt and sorrow. Noe embraces Loeau and rests her face against his chest. She takes his hand into hers as he says his good-byes. He rests an intimate kiss on Loeau's forehead and whispers to her. "Do not fear what must be done this night...my love...for you will soon be in my arms again."

Loeau picks up a candle and hands it to him. She glances around the home that they have made together. "Only we should have the right to destroy what is ours." Loeau takes a knife from Noe's belt and cuts a lock from her hair. "Be brave and without fear." Noe looks down at his sons and kisses each of their foreheads and rests his head against hers before Loeau quietly slips out into the night.

Standing alone in silence, holding his lover's hair, Noe closes his eyes and breathes deeply to calm himself. Noe begins to feel the distance between his family grow, understanding that he must survive as long as possible to help them escape.

Still holding the candle, he picks up his axe. Noe walks out of the hut and into the cool night. Without looking back, he tosses the candle onto the roof of the hut. Noe picks up a stake and pounds it into the ground. He unties his loincloth and uses it to tie his foot to the stake. Although banished from his home as a young man for loving a stranger, tonight he will die like a true Meno warrior. Like his ancestors who knew death was close, he will bind himself to the ground, showing his enemy his courage. Noe stands up and faces the darkness, waiting, as his home burns behind him.

Loeau hikes farther away from the only man she has ever loved. Her destination is a place that she has never been, but has seen in a fading dream. As Loeau hastily hacks through the thick forest brush, she hears movement and stops. She crouches, hiding within the cover of the forest. Her eyes reflect the moonlight as she spans the darkness to see what has made the noise. Loeau prays that her babies continue to sleep near her bosom, unaware of the darkness that she has foreseen. Loeau sees warriors approaching and lowers her head.

The warriors are spread out and moving swiftly through the bush. Loeau curls into a ball, clutching her cloak tightly around herself, disappearing in a veil of darkness. The men carry sticks whose tips have been dipped in crushed forest mushrooms and glow an eerie blue. She hears the rattling of bones and jewelry of one warrior. She knows the tribe he belongs to. He is a Yosemite from the west. The other two warriors are like no men she has ever seen. They are dressed in foreign clothes and have chest armor forged from ore. They carry strange weapons and move awkwardly in the forest.

Loeau looks out from behind her cloak and watches as the warrior passes her by. Loeau's nostrils sting as the faint smell of smoke rides on the night air. Akelou, one of her sons, hiccups in his sleep, and Loeau hears a warrior stop. The mercenary begins to speak in a foreign tongue, and Loeau grips her sword, ready for action. A reddish glow seeps into her cloak, and she hears the men turn and run away. With a breath of relief, Loeau stands holding her babies tightly and breaks into a run. Loeau moves quickly through the forest for a short time. As she journeys further into the night, Loeau grabs at her necklace, hearing her name echo in the forest.

"LOEAU!"

The piecing cry of her love brings Loeau to her knees. It is Noe calling her name as death takes him. In the darkness she looks up through the trees at the sky with tears falling down her dirtied face. Loeau whispers a lament for her lover and takes out a small pouch from under her cloak.

"Your father rejoins the soil that bore him, my sons, with no shame or fear for himself."

Loeau quickly opens the pouch from her cloak and dips her finger inside. Her finger now covered in glowing ash, she dots her sons' foreheads. Loeau wipes her tears with the same finger, leaving glowing streaks down her face. A horrible roar fills the air, shooting her to her feet.

Her trail has been found. Time is now her enemy. Staggering and clutching her children tightly, Loeau runs as fast as the forest allows. Closing in is a doom that Loeau cannot escape but one that she must delay. Loeau breaks through a thicket of thorn bushes that tear at her cloak as she stumbles down a gravel bank. Loeau stops abruptly as she recognizes what is now before her. Loeau shivers as she stares at the tree whose roots have grown wild.

"And so it is."

This will be the place of her death, and Loeau knows it. She walks over to the tree, whose roots have grown wild, and falls to her knees, splashing in the shallow stream. Grabbing her necklace Loeau tears it from her neck, breaking the chain that binds it to her. Holding it with both hands, Loeau shuts her eyes and speaks out into the night.

"My end is near, take whatever life still beats in my heart and save my loves and our last hope."

Her hands begin to shake as the amulet radiates with light, illuminating the forest around her. Loeau tries not to yell out, but the pain is too great. Her desperate cries echo against the trees and the light from her necklace bounces off the waters surface like brilliant white spears. Then in a flash and with a thunderous crack, she is knocked to her back. Loeau slowly gets up, choking on blood. She looks around for her sons, but they have vanished. She wipes her mouth and cries for a moment as she walks over to the tree with winding roots. She looks down at her dark, cold necklace and knows that her fate has been sealed. She can feel her life force beginning to fade. Loeau slides her sword from its sheath and holds it to her face. Closing her eyes and speaking softly, Loeau whispers to the ancient steel in the tongue of the Delar.

"Long have you been in my family...but tonight...another shall take you as theirs. May we bring fear to those who stand against us." Then there is only silence as Loeau waits for those she knows will come.

Behind her, warriors approach with weapons drawn for violence. They stop once they see Loeau's back facing them. The native from the western tribe signals for the others to move around and flank her. Once the other men fade into the bush, he raises his stone tomahawk and lets out a battle cry as he charges. Listening to the forest, she knows the moment has come. Loeau grips her sword tightly and open her eyes. They are consumed in a blue light, the last of her fading power. She spins and opens her arms, the Namid blazes to life, cutting down the charging warrior. Seeing only a brilliant flash before his death, the warrior makes no sound as he falls. After striking her attacker, Loeau raises her sword behind her head, lowering the blade, pointing it towards the forest, and caresses the tarnished steel against her cheek.

The quickness and skill of the woman stuns the other two assailants, and they falter, confused by this new enemy. Loeau senses their hesitation. She opens her eyes and charges the closest warrior. As Loeau attacks, the conquistador watches as a light surrounded by caped darkness slays his comrade. He raises his weapon and pulls the trigger. The unnatural crack of his shooter disturbs the forest. Through the smoke of his weapon, he sees the Namid gliding towards him, like a ship coming through a morning fog in a trail of blue light. Mesmerized by the magical sword, the warrior has no time to dodge the blow. The Namid drives deep into his chest hanging there for but a moment before, unseen from above, Loeau lands and grabs the Namid. With her back facing the warrior, she lunges forward, powerfully kicking the warrior against a tree, taking the sword from his chest. Loeau raises her blood-stained weapon and sees a new warrior emerge from the trees to face her. He is calm and dressed in an ornate breastplate. He has seen Loeau's skill, but is unafraid. He draws a pistol and his sword, a long flexible blade, and slowly approaches Loeau. With his sword drawn and his pistol aimed at her head, the warrior slowly circles Loeau. Loeau stands in the shallow stream, sword raised and ready for her attacker. The light from her eyes has gone and her body is getting weaker. The man speaks in a foreign tongue, gruffly and without fear.

"You are well trained, savage, but death calls your name this night."

The man maneuvers quickly, and Loeau says nothing as they circle each other, skulking in the shallow stream. They both strike, their swords clashing, shaking the forest floor below them. The warrior's pistol fires grazing Loeau's shoulder, he swings for Loeau's head, but finds only her sword waiting. Locked in battle, they push towards each other. They continue their banter, realizing that their skills are closely matched. Their faces are close, swords crossed at neck level, eyes piercing into each other. The soldier's strength becomes too much for Loeau, and he begins to push her to her knees, smirking at his conceived victory. Loeau screams, for the killer's smirk burns her soul as the dying voice of her lover echoes in her mind. Loeau breaks the standoff, shoving the soldier, striking him as he stumbles backwards. She spins, and the Namid spits in blue fury and the soldier's head separates from his neck, falling to the ground with a thud.

Panting, Loeau leans on the Namid and hears a noise behind her. Then three needle-like objects pierce her back. Her teeth clench, severing part of her tongue, and her eyes roll back into her head. Loeau wails and falls to the ground, her face splashing in the water. Her flesh burns as a toxin seeps into her bloodstream. The world is muffled as she is submerged in the water. Loeau can sense a great power around her. The water erupts, and she is thrown into the air and forced against a tree. She looks out and sees the white eyes that have haunted her dreams, and she whimpers in fear. The beast that was hidden in the forest roars at Loeau with its long rodent-like teeth and grotesque body. Loeau knows what this beast is. It is one of the ancient warriors of the darkness, a Daboon of legend. It stands taller than any man, its body covered in coarse black hair and like the trees of the forest its arms are long and powerful. On the beast's back poisonous spines rattle as it moves. The beast tosses something at Loeau, and it strikes her hard, falling and rolling into the mud. Loeau looks down and sees Noe's dead eyes staring up at her.

"No!" she yells.

Loeau looks up and sees a man approaching her. Her eyes go wide as she looks upon his face. It's the man she saw in her dream this very night. He was deep within a mountain, surrounded by worshiping men and a rising

6

fire. There was a blade and a sacrifice, and then she saw the eyes. He is the one, the foreigner from a distant land that possesses something ancient, dark and powerful. The man kneels before her dressed in his strange clothes and shining helmet with large feathers. His skin is fair and his decorated facial hair gives him a look of arrogance.

The man rubs his mustache and speaks in a foreign tongue, "be gentle General Ush-Ka we do not want her dead yet. My name is Christopher Columbus, Indian witch, and I am here for your," but before he can say another word Loeau lunges forward grabbing his head with both hands. His memories begin to flash before her in a chaotic blur.

Standing aboard his vessel, the Pinta, Columbus speaks to a short man dressed in long dark robes, "I am getting tired of your excuses Father and am wondering why I trusted a priest with a map written in pagan symbols. I did not risk my reputation and financial future, lying to the Crown of Castile speaking of trade routes to sponsor this voyage, only to be made a fool because of your faith in blasphemous artifacts."

Father Juan stares out into the ocean thumbing his rosary beads. "Patients master Columbus, the Lord guides us so have faith. It will not be long now, and soon you will be the wealthiest man in all of Europe. Just remember our bargain: I show you the way to the undiscovered lands filled with wealth and you escort me with your soldiers to the stone tower where I must perform a ceremony that will reveal to me the weapon I need to save our lands from an ancient evil. When you return to Spain, you will be a hero with enough wealth to buy yourself a crown."

"LAND HO!" shouts Rodrigo De Triana.

Memories flash forward and Loeau sees the Yosimite guides waiting for Columbus at the shore. She watches their journey through the forests where they plunder small villages leaving a trail of devastation to the Whispering Canyons, where they come to a tower rising above a great lake. They enter the tower and ascend to the lower depths of this ancient structure. In the darkness of the tower they come to a door carved with symbols of dark Gods and tortured men. Juan reads from his map and the door opens.

They enter a chamber and the Yosimite warriors kneel before a wooden bridge that leads into darkness and begin chanting. Their shadows flicker in the torch light and Columbus' Conquistadors become anxious as the ceremony continues. The Yosimites' praying gets louder and faster, and the chamber is getting hotter and hotter. Columbus, holding a rifle tightly in his hands and nervously close to his chest, follows Juan to the bridge that leads into the nothingness of the chamber. They begin to cross the bridge disappearing into a dot of light that rises from Juan's torch. Juan steps off the bridge onto a small platform and raises his torch. It reveals a stone alter carved from the tower's rock, and he places the black map on it. He reaches into his pockets and dips his finger in a pouch of ashes, and marks his forehead. A red mist rises from the abyss, and Loeau sees a crudely chiseled statue of a grotesque beast. Columbus lowers his rifle and takes the torch from Juan, shining the light on the map. All the old navigation markings fade and new symbols begin to appear on the parchment. Juan begins to read the pagan symbols, and the chanting from the Yosimites echoes louder and louder in the chamber. The rising mist gets thicker, and Juan's voice grows louder and deeper. His arms begin to wave franticly as he nears the end of the symbols. The ground shakes, and Columbus cautiously steps back. He looks to his side and sees a small, black blade carved from a reflective stone laying on a smaller alter. He stares at the blade, and his heart begins to pound. He hears a voice speak to him in a language he does not understand. The words chill his spine and tears of black begin to drip from his eyes. He looks to Juan than back to the blade. Columbus tosses the torch into the depths of the tower as Juan finishes his reading. The chamber goes quite, and Juan looks back towards Columbus. A crimson light erupts from below, and through the chaos, Juan sees Columbus with his black tears, holding the blade of Kaah.

"Christopher! No! You do not know what you are doing you will release him." he shouts.

Columbus lunges the blade into Juans' belly, grabbing him by his shoulder and pulling him to his chest. Juan's face convulses, and his veins contract with the darkness that sucks the life out of him. Loeau sees the marking on Juan's forehead. It is the symbol of the Delar, and it ignites in flames burning into Juan's flesh. Columbus releases Juan, and he falls to the ground. Columbus watches as his blood begins filling grooves carved in the stone that lead to the statue. He looks down at the blade and hears it whisper to him again. Columbus begins to laugh as a wind from the darkness circles around him and the grotesque statue crumbles to pieces; everything goes dark and Loeau releases Columbus as she sees the beast within. Both her and Columbus are breathing deeply and she can see the blade in Columbus' hand. She looks up to the moon and speaks in the tongue of the Delar. Then there is a flash of light, and everything goes dark.

CHAPTER TWO

The cries of a freighted baby searching for his mother disturb the calm southern forest. His tear-filled eyes reflect the moonlight sneaking through the leafless canopy above. The child quiets as he tires from crying. He coos into the night and starts to crawl. He comes to a tree and playfully pounds it with his hands. He grabs a twig and starts to gnaw on it, oblivious to the eyes that have been watching him since he appeared.

The creature leaps from the branch and soars to the forest floor. It lands on a twisted root and snaps its beak. The large bird sways its head back and forth, jumping up and down and confronting the stranger in its territory. The baby laughs and starts to crawl curiously towards the black bird. He sits and points at the creature's head. The bird lifts its head, responding to the movement of the child. Around the bird's neck, colors seep into its feathers, warning the child to stay away. The mysterious bird lifts its wings, exposing feathers that glow and reflect the moonlight. The child stares at the light in awe. The necklace that dangles from his neck begins to glow with life. The light from the necklace fills the eyes of the bird, and it lowers its wings. The bird steps down to the child and inspects the necklace closely. The motherless child touches the bird's soft magical feathers. The forest creature opens its wings and takes to flight, leaving the child beside the root.

A dying fire illuminates a slumbering figure. A plump, homely women who has seen many, many seasons come and go. Her face is so carved by age that her eyes can barely be seen. Her skin hangs loosely from her bones, and her back is bent from a lifetime of traveling. Her name is Mia-Koda, and she is a Bruhaa of the forest. A mystical noise wakes her suddenly. She jumps from her bed, grabbing her walking staff. She is blinded by a light and tries to shield her eyes from its power. Through the cracks of an outstretched hand, she sees the bird, which stands tall with outstretched wings that shine like a fallen star. The bird lowers its wing and closes its beak, and the forest goes dark and quiet.

"Wake, you lazy mound of smelly flesh. There is an Uluani here in our camp!" Mia-Koda says with amazement to her small companion who is still asleep.

Tib, a Wicker, a small, one-eyed, humanoid creature, wakes and blinks in confusion. He scrambles out of bed at the sight of the Uluani and hides behind Mia-Koda. The Uluani turns and looks at Mia-Koda.

"What is it? What do you want?" she asks. The bird opens its wings and takes to flight. "No, Broomay!" she shouts, and a horse comes running into her camp. She bends over with the agility of someone much younger and grabs Tib, lifting herself and the small Wicker onto the horse. She tries to keep up with the rare Uluani that appears and disappears into the night, shimmering through the forest.

Mia-Koda sees the bird land on a branch and slows her horse. She dismounts and cautiously approaches the tree where the bird is now perched. A baby cries, and Mia-Koda stops. She sees a baby boy sitting on the forest floor reaching for the Uluani. Confused, she cautiously walks to the child and kneels down beside it. She has never seen a man-child of this breed. The child's necklace begins to shine, and a woman's voice fills Mia-Koda's mind.

"To the one who hears my voice. This child's name is Akelou, and he is the last of the Delar." The amulet darkens and becomes cold. Akelou's chestnut eyes stare innocently up at Mia-Koda. Tib emerges from behind the tree where he was hiding. He comes to her side and tugs at her clothes.

"Yes, Tib, we ride tonight and leave for the city of Menoli. There, I must convince the chiefs to let this child into their city. Then we must travel to the jungles of the Wahone and tell them of this child." Mia-Koda picks up Akelou and mounts her horse. She gives Broomay a kick, and they begin the 10-day journey to the city of two chiefs.

Mia-Koda, Tib and Akelou have traveled for nine days on their quest to the forest city. They have made camp near the edge of a forest meadow covered in thick grasses and moon flowers. Mia-Koda hums as she rocks the babe with a pipe in her mouth. With each puff she contemplates her counsel with the Chiefs and how she will convince them to let the child stay in their city.

Tib stares at Mia-Koda, and the markings that cover his skin begin to glow. He sits scheming as he eats a large beetle. The necklace he saw glow has consumed him since they found the baby. Mia-Koda stands and speaks to Tib as she stretches, "Tib, watch the child while I step into the woods. Make sure he does not eat anything he is not supposed to." She gives Tib a knowing look, so he avoids her eyes. Tib shakes his head and wobbles over

to the child and sits down. Waiting until his master is out of sight Tib hunches over the baby. Now face-to-face, Tib stares at Akelou coldly. The child stops playing with his feet and looks up at the Wicker's large reddish eye.

Tib grunts at Akelou and glances down at his mysterious necklace. He takes the chain into his hands and looks for a clasp to untie it. Akelou begins to cry, and Tib puts his hand over the baby's mouth. He tries to slide the necklace over Akelou's head, but the chain is too small. Frustrated, he grabs the amulet in his hand, shakes it, and pulls. Tib begins to feel a warmth run through his body, and a lustful look rises over his eye as the necklace begins to shine. He squeezes the necklace tighter and pulls harder, desperate to claim the amulet as his own. The light of the necklace goes red, and the comforting warmth is starting to burn.

Now frightened, Tib tries to release the amulet, but his hand is cramped shut. His markings begin flashing and he becomes increasingly alarmed. Pain shoots up his arm and squeezes at his heart. The baby's screams echo like trumpets blowing in Tib's ears. Tib yells out in pain, frantically trying to free himself, but a blinding light followed by a thunderous crack throws him into the air. He lands on his back, skidding across the damp grassy meadow, twitching in an uncontrollable fit.

Mia-Koda rushes from the forest toward the sounds of the screaming baby. She scoops up the child and rushes over to Tib, whose spasms have become worse. In a quick motion, she waves her staff over his body and whispers a chant. His markings cool as the curse lifts and his spasms calm.

"Get up!"

Tib, trying to catch his breath, looks up at Mia-Koda. He raises his hand to defend himself from a strike. When nothing happens, he looks up from under his arm and sees Mia-Koda looking off towards the other side of the meadow. She quickly gets to her feet and walks into the higher grasses, pointing her staff outwards towards the darkness. Tib rushes to Mia-Koda's side ready for a fight.

"Here they come, take the child and go back to Broomay!" She hands Akelou to Tib and shoves the Wicker towards their camp.

Mia-Koda walks farther into the meadow, and Tib rushes to Broomay, clutching the child in his arms, and ducks behind some tall grass. Tib parts the grass with his small digits and sees Mia-Koda's staff pulsing with light. The tall grasses sway, and her staff illuminates dark objects soaring towards her. They land steadily, surrounding her in attack positions. Tib knows what these creatures are. They are the Salali, tree gliders of the forest and night guards of the Menoli. Once small, soft-furred tree dwellers, now they are large defenders of a great city.

Six Salali surround Mia-Koda. The last of the guards lands with authority in front of her. He is larger than the others, and unlike the grey and silver Gliders his fur is a deep earthy color. He wears an ornate helmet with thick arm and leg braces. His thumb claws are black and exaggerated compared to those of the others. As he stands on his hind legs, his arms barely rise above the ground. He speaks in the common tongue.

"Why are you lingering outside our borders, Owaga?"

Not appearing intimidated or amused by being called a witch, Mia-Koda answers with a calm face. "There is no need for insulting words, Black Claw. I must say the guard of your city is far more aggressive than last I remember."

"The forest is dark these last nights, and there are outsiders walking its floor...a small band of men were spotted near our northern borders. I imagine your footsteps travel a similar path." Mia-Koda lowers her staff, and the Salali relax. "Where is the child I saw?" barks Black Claw.

"He is in the arms of my traveling companion."

"You mean that filthy Wicker that I saw the child attack?"

Hearing these words of insult, Tib lays the child on the ground and runs out towards Black Claw, kicking up dirt and spitting at the ground. Mia-Koda stops him with her staff. Tib snarls at Mia-Koda, but after seeing her face, he turns and scampers back towards Akelou.

The other Salali seem to be uneasy at the sight of Tib. They do not trust outsiders, and begin clicking and snorting to each other. Mia-Koda signals for Tib to bring her the child, and Tib quickly obeys. Holding Akelou in her arms, Mia-Koda looks at Black Claw.

"Here is the child you speak of."

Black Claw bends down and sniffs Akelou. He looks over the baby and lightly strokes the necklace he saw curse the Wicker. "This boy is not normal, he has no business within our borders-"

"This child has been orphaned. I would think you more than others would be understanding of his situation."

This agitates Black Claw, who glances at his men with a look of embarrassment.

"You are a clever witch, with your wicked tongue and twisted words."

"The only wicked tongue used tonight has been yours, Captain. It is with the two Chiefs that I wish to hold counsel. Now please permit us to enter the city."

Black Claw looks over Mia-Koda and her companions and snorts to his guards.

"Gather your things, we will escort you ourselves. The sooner you enter our city, the sooner you leave."

Holding Broomay by his reins, Mia-Koda follows Black Claw into the forest.

"Your mate, how is she faring?"

Black Claw looks at Mia-Koda with suspicion before answering. "I have offspring now, a boy, but I imagine you already knew this."

"Yes, I am always keeping an eye on you. Good health and a long life may he live. Word has also come to my ears of your promotion to Captain of the guard. A great honor and something you have long desired, I feel. Poeau-"

"That is no longer my name, witch! And as for that man-child, I know your mind, you mean to leave him within our borders."

Lowering her voice, Mia-Koda leans into the Captain's ear, "I know you fear what you have seen here tonight, but do not forget that I once brought you as an abandoned youngling to this very city. I named you myself, so do not tell me what is or is not your rightful name." Black Claw looks around to see if any Salali can overhear their conversation. He turns back to the road, and Mia-Koda continues, "You are right, this child is special, and only time will tell the extent of his powers. Many in the city will not trust him but the child's fault it is not. When the time comes, I hope you make the right choice as I once did, Poeau."

The morning's glow begins to fill the forest in a rising mist. Approaching the city, Mia-Koda holds Akelou tightly, concealing his necklace under his fur blanket. They come to the gate of the city and halt. The changing of the guard has begun. The Salali night guard salutes their Meno replacements. Meno are men who live on the ground and guard the city, while the Salali sleep in the trees. Both races depend on each other for survival. During the day, the men farm, tend livestock, and hunt animals while the Salali sleep. At night, the Salali gather valuable food, goods, and medicine from the trees where the Meno cannot reach. The guards exchange weapons and embrace each other with words of friendship; they look at the visitors uneasily as they enter the city.

"I must give the nightly reports to the Chiefs. Follow me," says Black Claw.

They follow Black Claw through the tree city and are met with many untrusting eyes. They soon come the Tree of the Menoli. It is a tree unlike any in the forest. It rises high above the canopy and is as thick as a hundred trees. Legend tells of a powerful mystic that grew the tree from a seed in only one season. He was the father of the Salali, the one who brought them enlightenment and gave them the tree as their home. He taught them how to speak and how to fight. It was in the first great war, when the Salali and the Meno were united in battle. In this war, many tales of courage and hardship tell of how the bond between the Meno and the Salali was formed. After the wars, the Salali invited the first Meno to live with them around the great tree. When they agreed, the city of two Chiefs was born.

They all stop, standing at the base of the Menoli Tree. "It's ok, Tib, the Salali mean you no harm, and the Chiefs will be fair in their counsel, I am sure," Mia-Koda says, sensing Tib's anxiety.

Mia-Koda is escorted up the stairs by two Meno warriors. Black Claw passes them with ease, climbing up the side of the Tree. When they reach the top of the stairs, Mia-Koda stops outside the door that leads to the two Chiefs. It is a round door made from black wood, and it is guarded by one warrior of each race. On the door, symbols of Meno and Salali are carved into the wood. The Meno and the Salali stand proudly together on each side of the Tree. The Sun shines above the Meno, and the Moon above the Salali, their arms encircling the tree signifying the unity of the races.

Two guards approach Black Claw and bow. He quickly signals for them to allow Mia-Koda to enter the hall. The guards exchange a quick glance of distrust, but obey their Captain and allow Mia-Koda to pass. Mia-Koda, with her staff in hand, walks confidently down the main aisle of the hall.

The hall is quiet this morning, with only a few Meno and Salali inside. Incense made from leaves and tree cones burns, filling the room with a pungent aroma. The dome-shaped ceiling has two windows, allowing light to shine on the thrones of the Chiefs. The path to the Chiefs' thrones is lined with fresh leaves and flower petals. Each throne is carved into the shape of a forest deer. The deer rest on the floor with their legs folded under their bellies, staring down at whomever stands before the Chiefs. The horns of the deer form the Chiefs thrones.

Both Chiefs are widely known to be wise, proud, and respected by their people. Grey Back, the Chief of the Salali, is a thick-bodied glider with silver fur. Grey Back sits proudly, wearing the hide of a Feather Runner, the natural enemy of the Salali; he also wears a Feather Runner's upper jaw as his

crown. He has become blind in his old age, but his sense of smell is very keen, and to the Salali, this is a sense more trusted than sight.

The Chief of the Meno is Red Fist. The little hair he has left is white, stringy, and long. His chest is stout and bare. He wears only a pouch filled with crushed smoking root around his neck. His pants are made of animal skin and bone, and his body is covered in tattoos of red and black. On his head he wears a crown of feathers that drapes to the ground. He is a man of few words and stern action, and he is a great commander of men. Knowing this, Mia-Koda has sought out his counsel several times. Always honest and true, Red Fist's solemn words have proven to solve many issues.

"I thank the great Chiefs for their warm welcome," Mia-Koda says.

Closing his blind eyes, Grey Back inhales deeply before returning the woman's greeting. "Long has it been since that scent has filled these halls."

Red Fist stares at Mia-Koda in silence. Black Claw leaves Mia-Koda's side and walks to Grey Back, speaking into his Chief's ear. Red Fist leans in their direction, trying to pick up their conversation, and never taking his eyes from the small child resting peacefully in Mia-Koda's arms.

"My Captain tells me you bring a child with you . . . is this true?"

"Yes, Grey Back, you have not been misinformed," says Mia-Koda.

"What happened to his family that you bring him into our borders?"

"The child was brought to me in the night by an Uluani."

Red Fist nods his head while looking at a man in a far corner of the room. His eyes then return to the child.

"I know nothing of his family, but I assume they are dead. I come to look for a foster family to raise him until he begins to walk the path of a man."

"Why, I wonder, do you not take the child?" says Grey Back. "My Captain has told me what that child did to your Wicker. Why should I permit this outlander with abilities unknown into the care and protection of our city?"

"The child is special, but a danger to you he is not . . . of this I am sure. I will come back for him when the time is right and his powers start to grow. A good and stable home is what young children need, and that I cannot give."

Grey Back points his finger, exposing his worn claws to Mia-Koda. "Why should I believe that his boy brings no danger to our people?"

Red Fist snaps his fingers, and a man brings him a long wooden pipe decorated with Salali claws and various feathers. He takes the smoking root from the pouch around his neck and packs the pipe. He takes a large puff from the pipe and signals for Mia-Koda to also take a puff. She walks up to Red Fist and hands him the child before accepting his offering. Red Fist takes the child and begins to examine him. Mia-Koda puffs the pipe, kneels down, and passes it to Grey Back.

"Captain, your brother lost his only son to sickness, did he not?"

Black Claw raises his head with suspicion towards his Chief, "Yes, he died from the black cough on a cold night last winter," he says to Red Fist.

"Word has reached my ears that Dirty Hands' wife can no longer bear children and has slipped into a depression. Your brother is a farmer and has a hut at the western edge of the city . . . Good parents you both had. Close to your adopted father I was. Good of them to take you in and raise you, considering the circumstances," says Red Fist.

Black Claw stares at Mia-Koda. Grey Back passes the pipe back to Red Fist, signaling that he supports his decision. Red Fist stands and steps down from his throne. "This child is in need and deserves our mercy. I feel that he has already seen much evil and has suffered a great loss. But I also believe this decision is not for the two Chiefs to make. His fate we put in the hands of Captain Black Claw, for it is his brother's house the child will call home, and it is the captain's job to protect this city. Either the child is taken by Black Claw's brother, or he is not welcome here."

Red Fist passes the child to Black Claw and takes another puff from the pipe. Black Claw looks down at the baby and glances up to Grey Back. "Do you agree, Chief Grey Back?"

"This child's fate is in your hands, Captain."

Black Claw struggles with the decision while the Chiefs and Mia-Koda continue to pass the pipe. Black Claw knows that a child would bring joy into his brother's life again. He nods his head in agreement, without looking at either Chief, but keeping his eyes fixed on the child.

"Agreed we are. The child will pass into the family of your brother," says Red Fist.

"Wise and merciful is the Chief's counsel," says Mia-Koda. "I will see the child to his new family and then depart." She bows to the Chiefs before turning to leave.

The early dawn has faded into mid-morning, and the city market begins to fill with goods and gossip. Children play in the dusty streets while young adults mingle in small groups. Mia-Koda passes by the market and

waves at the Menoli. No one returns her wave. Black Claw has not seen his brother in many moons and feels shame knowing why he has kept his distance. Adopted by a poor Meno family, Black Claw has worked endlessly to gain the respect of the Salali he leads. Now, he returns to the home where he was raised and finds himself lost in thoughts of his past.

"You made the right decision, Poeau. A decision that will bring joy and love to your brother's family for many years."

Stopping, Black Claw turns, "I know you have great wisdom as well as the power of will, but I have seen this child's eyes before. They have haunted me since my son's birth, and only at my end will I understand their meaning. My nephew he will soon become, so like family I will treat him, but trust him I never will for I see doom and death in those eyes."

"You are still a shadow of your parents, Poeau, Captain of the Salali. That is why I knew you would help this child. You have your mother's strength and compassion." Mia-Koda leans on her staff and looks deep into Black Claws' eyes. "No matter what this dream you speak of may foretell, in the end nothing but love will you feel for this child."

Black Claw turns and begins walking down the dirt path. He leaves the road and walks into the forest underbrush, brushing it aside as he comes to a clearing.

"His home is over there. Wait here for me to bring them to you," he says to Mia-Koda.

Black Claw walks up to the hut of his brother and calls to him- "Brother!"

There is a rustling, and a man walks out of the hut. He is a stout man with broad shoulders and thick arms.

"What brings you to my home, brother?" Dirty Hands says in his soft voice.

"I do, Dirty Hands," Mia-Koda says as she steps forward. "I come to ask you a favor."

Dirty Hands looks at Black Claw, and Black Claw speaks, "She has with her a child that has been abandoned and needs a foster home. Since your son did not survive the winter, the Chiefs thought you would be kind enough to take him in."

As soon as Black Claw mentions the child, Dirty Hands' wife, Meadow, comes out of the hut. She is a short, thin woman with long, unhealthy hair. Her clothes are worn, and her eyes have sunk into the darkness of her face.

"Is it a boy or a girl?" she asks in a quivering voice.

"The child is a healthy baby boy who needs a loving home," Mia-Koda says.

Meadow walks past Dirty Hands and Black Claw and takes the child into her arms. Her eyes tear as she smiles down at the baby's face.

"We will take him and love him as if he were our own," she says with a happiness she thought had long vanished from her heart.

"Now hold on, I am the man-this is my decision to make." Meadow gives Dirty Hands a glare that makes him take a step back. "Well . . . I mean, if you want the child I will allow it."

Patting Dirty Hands on the back, Mia-Koda speaks, "Good! Then all is well . . . but there are some things that have to be said. First, when the child begins to walk the path of a man, I will be back for him, and he will have to leave with me. Also, the child bears a necklace that is very special-never try to take it off or hold it for too long. This child possesses powers that must later be dealt with. You must hide this knowledge from him and others." Meadow nods her head in agreement, and quickly rushes back into the hut.

Dirty Hands mutters to his brother upon his wife's departure. "Maybe now she will have reason to smile again."

"I am glad for you, brother. I will have my wife come visit Meadow to see if she can help her in any way."

"We would both be thankful for that, brother. It has been too long since we all have been together for a meal."

"I must go back to the council."

"I understand . . . we both thank you for this gift for which there is no repayment." Dirty Hands bows to both his brother and Mia-Koda before turning back to his hut.

Mia-Koda grabs his arm, "Remember, Dirty Hands, I will be back for him when he begins to walk the path of a man. Treat him well and tell others only what they need to know about the child." Mia-Koda and Black Claw turn and leave.

When Dirty Hands enters his hut he sees his wife running around with energy and excitement. He grabs her before she makes her way across the room to make a warm bottle and looks into her eyes.

"Are you sure this is what you want?"

Meadow looks up at him, "This is all I have ever wanted, my love." They embrace briefly before going to the baby. Together, they look down at the child lying on some furs and laugh as he again chews on his feet and coos. Meadow wraps her body around her mate's large arms and looks up at him.

"This is your son, Dirty Hands, so it is your right to give him his name. What should we call him?" Dirty Hands looks down at his new son before answering his wife. "Taeau, that will be his name-Taeau, 'a gift from others.'"

CHAPTER THREE

A small, humpbacked creature burrows its head into a muddy puddle, feeding on shellfish. It is a Muddler, a short bottom-feeding creature that survives in the swamps and flood plains of the forest. Muddlers were once human, but in the Age of Darkness they were enslaved and transformed into hunchbacked diggers and miners. They became short, weak shadows of themselves, forced to work in the mines and dark places of the world. Once the darkness vanished, many Muddlers escaped the mines and scattered, becoming a broken species, devolving into skittish scavengers. This slothy Muddler, who calls himself Puddle, wipes muddy water from his face and bites into a clam shell with his thick molars.

Puddle continues to eat, disturbing the still water around him that shimmers with moonlight. As he sinks his teeth into a shell, a wind circles around him and in a flash he is thrown onto his back. Disoriented, Puddle tries to get to his feet wiping water from his eyes. His breaths are hard and short. Confused by what has happened, he looks down and sees a baby splashing in the mud. The baby cries out when it sees the Muddler, and Puddle curls up into a protective ball. Over the ages, Puddle's ancestors evolved a thick leathery back used for self-defense.

The child continues to scream, and Puddle shakes rapidly, cowering in his protective position. Sobbing, the Muddler cries at the child, hoping to quiet his bawling. Soon Oskeau tires from yelling and becomes calm. When he feels the danger has gone, Puddle timidly uncurls himself. He looks down at the abandoned child with his large eyes and chomps his lips at the sight of the small infant. He thinks about how lucky he is to have found such an easy meal and goggles at the child as he picks him up and holds him in the air. The Muddler swings the child upside down, holding him overhead by one foot. He opens his gaping mouth and is ready to consume him head first, but a shining light distracts him. The child starts to laugh and giggle, remembering how his father used to play with him. The Muddler's stare becomes more intense, and his breathing becomes heavier. His eyes dilate as they follow the swinging necklace that dangles before his face. A voice suddenly echoes in his head, talking to him.

"Yes!" while chomping his teeth, "a slave for Puddle . . . Puddle could be the master. Little son of the tall deceivers would have to do everything I say." Puddle jumps up and down, "Yes, yes, yes!"

Puddle moves closer to the necklace, mesmerized by its beauty.

"What must I do with the tall walker?" The necklace shines again, brighter than before and pulsing with life. "Find shelter, yes, yes, I have shelter. I will show you."

The necklace dulls as quickly as it began to shine, and Puddle shakes his head. He cradles Oskeau in his arms and runs into the forest. As Puddle clumsily trudges between the trees, he is lost in excitement. When he arrives to his shelter, a dead tree with a hollowed-out trunk, he is very pleased with himself. Puddle sits down, placing Oskeau outside the tree, and he begins to sway back and forth.

"What to do, what does Puddle do now?" Puddle says as he caresses the long coarse hairs that run down his face.

Oskeau's necklace glows, shining in Puddle's eyes.

"I have seen one, a large cave, it be a good place . . . a dangerous Long-Tooth lives inside, eat Puddle it would."

Puddle stops swaying as a thought enters his mind. His eyes blaze with light. He stands, and the light from the necklace follows him. He imagines the cave and sees himself above its opening, holding a large rock and waiting for the beast.

"Oh yes! But how I get there?-Long-Tooth would know, he would get me."

With his eyes still reflecting the necklace's light, Puddle pictures himself above the cave with a rock-he sees the baby lying in front of the cave.

"An offering to him! Leave little deceiver at the opening and when Long-Tooth comes to eat it, I CRUSH HIM WITH ROCK!" Puddle jumps and rolls around on the floor with excitement. "Puddle crush him, Puddle crush him! Yes, yes, yes."

After his celebration, Puddle runs and snatches up the infant before taking off towards the cave. Morning begins to fill the forest, and a brisk wind blows against them as they travel. His journey is slow, for Muddlers wobble while they walk, and Puddle is clumsy even for his kind. A feeling of bravery has come over Puddle. All his life he has been the prey hiding in fear, but now he finds himself seeking out a beast, hunting like a cunning killer.

The Long-Tooth he hunts is a forest monitor. The monitor's mouth is lined with many small jagged teeth and two saber-like canines. A forest monitor's most deadly weapon is its venomous, flesh-eating saliva. Puddle fears beasts like this, but not this day, no, he is on a quest to become something he has never been before-a master.

The journey has drained Puddle of much of his energy, and when the Muddler approaches the cave, he hesitates and is scared.

Puddle stands above the opening of the cave where the Long-Tooth lives. Looking down the jagged, rocky face of the cave, he sees the floor covered with the bones of discarded carcasses. Placing the child at the top of the cliff, Puddle wanders off to find the largest rock he can lift.

"Gonna kill a beast-gonna crush the nasty tooth-yup, yup, yup," Puddle sings to himself.

While Puddle searches for a boulder, Oskeau lies on the forest floor staring up at the sky in silence. He closes his eyes and pictures his mother, then he curls up and cries himself to sleep. Puddle returns with a look of satisfaction on his face. He lays the stone down and sits besides the sleeping baby. He bites his short nails and sways while thinking.

"Wait-why am I here?-Why was I searching for large stone?" Puddle looks around, his eyes falling on the sleeping child. He quickly stands and snatches the child. "You!-You the reason I here! Why?-tell Puddle why!" he says, shaking the baby.

As he scolds the child, a noise spills out from the cave below. A deep breath blows dust from within the cave, and Puddle's eyes grow wide. Puddle drops the child and curls into a ball, crying and shaking with fear. As Puddle trembles in his protective ball, a dim burning glow warms his skin. He looks out from behind his shoulder and sees Oskeau's necklace shining on him.

Puddle lifts his head, "Yesss-that right, I do it -YES!-I will do it. Gonna kill the beast."

Puddle picks up the child by his foot and dangles him over the small cliff and tosses him over the edge. Oskeau cries out as he plummets to the ground. His necklace bursts with light and stops him just above the forest floor. He hovers for a moment before he lightly floats to the ground. Lying on his back, Oskeau giggles before turning his head towards the cave.

Inside the opening he sees two yellow eyes staring out at him, and two long pointed teeth dripping with poison. Oskeau begins to wail in fear and holds his hands up, begging for help. The Long-Tooth tastes the ground with excitement, savoring the moments before its meal. Oskeau rolls over and tries to crawl away, but is blocked by a large bone covered in gashes from the monitor's teeth. The baby looks up again, searching for Puddle. He sees him high above the cave holding a stone over his head. A look of intense

fury fills the Muddler's eyes, and a burst of light shines from Oskeau's necklace towards Puddle. Puddle throws the large boulder over the cliff. The Long-Tooth senses something and snaps its head upwards. The beast sees only a shadow before the boulder crushes him. The speeding stone bounces off the monitor's head and rages towards Oskeau. His necklace bursts with life, and the boulder explodes, followed by a thunderous crack that echoes through the cave.

Puddle dances on the hill, yells, and stomps the ground in victory.

"I did it!-I-ME-am the master now! I am the beast slayer, I am the thrower of stones!-Master of all!-Me, Me, Me. All will fear Puddle, the great stone crusher! No, OGDEN, yes, Ogden the stone crusher, yes, YES, Ogden, not Puddle!!" Puddle beats his chest and continues his dance as he rolls around joyfully on the top of the hill. Oskeau has not moved and looks at the dying monitor, watching the life leave the creature. The Long-Tooth takes its last, short breaths before its eyes roll back into lifelessness.

Blood from the slain monitor begins to run like a river, drowning Oskeau's legs in a pool of black reflective liquid. Oskeau stares into the blood, seeing a mirror of himself surrounded by the dead beast. He reaches out his hand and touches his reflection, creating ripples in the small pool. Oskeau's hair blows in the chilling air, and he touches his face with his blood-stained finger. He looks back into the pool of blood and sees Puddle staring down at him. Ogden, as he now calls himself, has formed a crown out of plants and sticks.

"Come, slave." Ogden grabs Oskeau by his foot, dragging him past the dead beast and into the cave. So begins the enslavement of Oskeau.

CHAPTER FOUR

It has been ten years since Mia-Koda brought Taeau to the Menoli City. These past years have been a time of peace and growth in the forest. The early evening moon shines through a window, illuminating Black Claw and his family as they sit down to breakfast. They eat their usual helpings of fruits and nuts, except for Little Claw, who licks a twig covered in wood bee honey. Little Claw, a newborn, spends most of his time in the comfort of his mother's pouch. He curiously watches his older sister, Whispers, follow their mother, holding onto her tail. Ven, the oldest of the Black Claw's offspring, is busy trying to finish his food.

"Slow down, Ven. You will get cramps and fall to the forest floor. Would you like that, hmm?" asks his mother.

"Stop it, Ma, I'll be fine, I'm done, can I go-"

"NO! Your bothersome cousin will still be waiting outside our door after you eat your food. Now finish your breakfast ," says Black Claw, giving Ven a stern look.

Half Moon, Ven's mother, gives the door a tired glance. "Is Taeau out there already? Black Claw, let the boy in-"

"No, he will wait until your son is finished with his food," bellows Black Claw with authority. His wife shakes her head and gives Little Claw another helping of honey.

"Why are you always giving him a hard time?" snaps Ven.

Ven's father stares down at him, and he quickly looks back to his food. Quiet fills the room as everyone finishes their breakfast, until three long scratches interrupt the meal. Everyone looks at the door.

"Hmm, it is strange to hear scratching this early," says Half Moon, as Black Claw gets up to answer the door. As Black Claw begins to open the door, a small boy darts into the room. A Salali warrior stands at the entrance saluting Black Claw. The room erupts in commotion as the two younglings,

THE BOOK OF IXKIN

Ven and Taeau, wrestle and greet each other. Usually Black Claw would put a quick stop to this, but at the moment he is distracted with the visitor.

"Captain, I have orders from the Chiefs . . . they request your immediate presence in the hall."

"What evil shadows the city tonight? Why do the Chiefs request me so early?"

"I do not know, sir . . . but news that a wounded Meno warrior came to the hall is circulating around the guard. I have heard that many pipes have been smoked. I was sent straight away to find you. This is all I can report."

"Report to the chiefs that I will be in the hall swiftly. Let me gather my things and say goodbye to my family."

"Yes, sir," says the glider as he bows to his Captain.

Black Claw walks back into the room with a serious look on his face. "What's wrong? What is happening?" asks Half Moon.

Black Claw goes to his room, followed by Half Moon. When he returns, Taeau and Ven are throwing seeds at each other, while Whispers yells at them to stop.

"Boys! Leave Whispers alone!"

They both sit up straight at the sound of Black Claw's voice. "Taeau . . . as for you, I do not appreciate your barging into my home uninvited. A talk with your father is needed." Taeau looks down at the floor as he receives the scolding. "Mind your mother, all of you. I will see you at the end of my shift-be well."

With these words Black Claw leaves his home. Walking out the door into the early night, he takes a deep breath, then turns his shoulder and leaps into the air, gliding down through the cool night air.

"Mother, can we go, me and Taeau? We have important stuff to do," pleads Ven as he bounces in his seat on the floor. His mother looks down at him with a smile.

"Important, huh? Is this true, Taeau?"

"Yes, Mother Claw, we have almost finished our fort-" Ven shoves Taeau, putting his fingers over his mouth. "Ahhh, ya, we got important business, but I am sworn to secrecy until death," says Taeau as he stands up and puts one hand over his chest and the other in the air.

"Well, I must not keep such important people from such important things. You both go, have fun, and tell your mother I have some seeds for

her garden." Both boys run for the door, and Ven shoves his sister on his way out.

"Ven!!" whines Whispers, but the boys are gone before Half Moon can scold them for their mischief.

Once Ven and Taeau close the door, they run down the stairs that wind around the Menoli Tree. On the steps, Taeau looks back to talk to his cousin, but he is gone.

"Ven, where are you? Stop playing around."

Taeau looks up and sees Ven leap from above, head first, right for him. Taeau is not able to dodge his cousin before he plows into him, and both boys go tumbling down the stairs.

"Ouch!-you know we could get hurt that way!" yells Taeau.

"Still fall for that trick."

"Ya, well now what are you going to do?" Taeau asks, lunging for Ven, grabbing him and pulling him back down to the stairs. Ven punches his cousin off of him, and they both begin to laugh.

"Ok, Ok, truce, let's go . . . did you get the stuff we need for today?"

"Ya, I got it all, it's at my place. Let's go get it."

"Then there's no time to loose!-Come on, let's go."

"Ok," Taeau says, and he grabs Ven from behind, holding his back tightly. Ven scampers to the edge of the steps among the high branches. He leaps into the air, opening his arms, and the boys scream with excitement as they glide through the forest towards the setting sun that engulfs the world in its dying radiance.

Black Claw steps up to the hall. "Sir, the Chiefs have been waiting for you, but you must be searched before you enter."

"What! I am your Captain, and I will not tolerate such an insult."

"Sir, we mean no disrespect. The Chiefs have commanded that we search all who enter, no weapons are permitted in the hall this night."

Black Claw glares at both guards but submits. He stands proud, raising his arms and tail into the air. The guards pat his coat, making sure he has no weapons hidden in his fur.

"Sorry, sir-you may enter."

Both guards grab the handle of the door and open it. The guards lower their heads in respect as Black Claw walks past. Black Claw is surprised

to see so many Meno and Salali standing together in the hall this early. They all seem to be locked in serious conversation. Broken Wrist, Captain of the Meno and good friend of Black Claw, walks up to him and greets him softly.

"Sir, let me inform you of the events that have unfolded. Two outer guards were ambushed by a band of soldiers led by the beast general Ush-Ka."

"Ush-Ka! Here, inside our borders?"

"Yes-they murdered one of our guards, Runs-With-Speed, and beat the other badly, sparing his life only so he could give a scroll to the Chiefs. We buried Runs-With-Speed facing the setting sun in the graveyard of his forefathers. As his family mourns, word has spread and the men have become angry and vengeful. We must calm the men and keep this quiet. We do not want to alert the city, causing fear and rash action." Black Claw looks towards his chiefs and sees Red Fist reading the scroll to Grey Back. Black Claw walks up to them and bows.

"Great Chiefs, I am here and await your orders." Red Fist looks down from the scroll and signals for the hall to become quiet by holding a stone in each hand and striking them together three times. The sound echoes throughout the hall, and everyone becomes silent as they find their seats. Grey Back, Chief of the Salali, speaks first.

"You all know of the strangers that now gather at our borders. They have surrounded our city and have given us this scroll . . . they await our answer."

"What question do they beg be answered?" cries a soldier from the rear of the hall.

"They demand our allegiance to their king, dominion over our lands, and payment for the right to live on them." These words spark an uproar of shouting and insults as the meeting quickly becomes chaotic.

"They murdered one of our own without provocation and than demand our allegiance?"

"We must protect the city-"

"Gather your weapons, we must fight-"

Red Fist raises his hands and strikes the stones three more times. The hall quiets, and he takes smoking root from his pouch, packing his pipe.

"Powerful forces threaten our city." The pipe clinks between the Chief's teeth as he speaks. "We, Salali and Meno, have lived here in peace for some time . . . we have kept wars away from our borders before, but we have been lucky. Now a war has come to us, and we can no longer hide. We must negotiate with General Ush-Ka and his master Columbus or chance losing everything."

The room is quiet as the pipe is passed among the warriors. A Meno soldier asks, "What are Grey Back's words on this?"

Grey Back rises from his throne and blindly stares at the warriors. "Red Fist is wise and speaks the words of a man who has seen the sun set and the moon rise many more times than most in this hall . . . we will prepare for an attack on the city, but negotiate with Ush-Ka before any action is taken." Grey Back takes the pipe and puffs from it. "Go to your posts. Tell no one of this news and await your orders."

Grey Back sits in his throne, and the Chiefs become silent.

Soldiers slowly shuffle out of the hall. The two Chiefs and the two Captains stay behind to smoke one last pipe and take counsel.

"Taeau, why do we need to stop at your hut?"

"Because today I found something, and I have to check in with my mom before we go to it."

Ven gets very close to Taeau and looks around to make sure that no one can hear him. He lowers his voice to a whisper. "What did you find?-Is it something that will help us defend the unspeakable from them?"

Taeau stops and looks into the eyes of his cousin. "The treasure I have found will make us invincible."

Ven starts to rub his paws together in anticipation of this treasure, letting his mind run wild with images of what it could be. "I hope it is as good as you say becau-"

Ven suddenly snaps his head around, his ears perk up and he starts sniffing rapidly.

"What is it, Ven? What do you smell?"

While Ven tries to make sense of the conflicting smells in the air, two young gliders and a Meno youngling sit in a nearby tree, scouting Ven and Taeau below.

"Now," whispers the leader of the group, and before Ven can make out the scent, two gliders jump from the canopy.

Ven is the first to spot the gliders and yells, "ENEMIES!" warning Taeau of the attack. There is no time to run. Both Ven and Taeau put up their hands and fists, ready for the assault. The younglings land and surround them. One of the Salali gliders exposes his claws aggressively, while the

Meno has his fists clenched. The largest of the three, named Stripes, stands only steps from Ven. He is large for his age and stronger than both Ven and Taeau combined. He has a white strip of fur crossing his left eye, which has been blind since birth. His father is Black Claw's second-in-command, the Captain of the city's gate.

"Well, Ven, I see you still like to hang out with this freak instead of us," sneers Stripes. The other two start to laugh.

Ven looks at Stripes, "Hey, Taeau . . . is he looking at you or me? I can never really tell. I find it rude when someone can't look you straight in the EYE!"

"You got a smart mouth, runt, for the son of an abandoned big-clawed freak." Everyone looks back at Ven, who takes a step closer to Stripes.

"Yeah?-well, I'd rather be the son of a Captain than the son of a doorman any day, Stripy."

Stripes opens his hands and starts to move towards Ven. "I've been waiting to prove to you whose family is better for a long time. Boys, show our other friend here what we think of freaks."

A Salali grabs Taeau from behind while the Meno youngling attacks from the front. Stripes and Ven begin to circle one another.

"Should I only walk to your one side to make it fair, Stripes? I wouldn't want to be known for beating up the blind youngling, now would I?"

"You're dead!"

Stripes lunges, claws open and ready to strike, but Ven is too fast and he dodges the attack. Ven kicks Stripes in the back and he falls to the ground.

"You're gonna pay for that, runt!" yells Stripes as he gets up. But before Stripes can follow through with his threat, they all hear a yelling voice. Turning, the five youngsters see Dirty Hands coming up the road, signaling for Taeau. Taeau's nose is bleeding and his eye is bruised. He quickly wipes away what blood he can, and tries to look as if nothing has happened.

"Ha, look-the farmer boy got his daddy to save the day," taunts Stripes.

Dirty Hands reaches them, panting as he tries to catch his breath. "Boys . . . I have been looking for you . . . Taeau, what is wrong with your nose?-Why is it bleeding?"

"I . . . I fell while playing with my friends."

"Oh . . . well, let your mother have a look at it when you get home." Stripes and his gang start to snicker behind Taeau.

"Ya, Taeau, go see your mommy, she'll make everything alright." Taeau spins, trying to leap at Stripes, but Dirty Hands grabs him from behind and holds him back. Dirty Hands pulls his son behind him, bumping into Stripes as he moves to separate the younglings.

"Taeau!-control yourself, son."

Stripes stares at Taeau and brushes off his fur. "Just look at my fur. It'll take the rest of the night to get this filth off-not to mention the smell." Stripes' companions all start laughing. The glider then snorts and runs off with his pack.

"Why did you let him talk to you like that, Father?"

"Like what, son?"

"Like you're beneath him or something, just because you're a farmer, huh, why? You should have crushed him." Dirty Hands smiles at his son and gets down on a knee. He puts his hands on both Taeau's and Ven's shoulders and looks into their eyes.

"If we grownups started crushing all the younglings that talked back to us, there wouldn't be a single one left, now would there?" Both cousins look at each other, and Taeau speaks first, "You're right, I know . . . but it still would have been nice."

Dirty Hands laughs at his son, for he knows how it felt when he and Black Claw were once in the same situation as younglings.

"Ven, your father, did he leave for work yet tonight?"

"Yeah, he left early . . . there was something important going on in the Great Hall." These words fill Dirty Hands' face with a look of concern, and he chooses his next words wisely, not wanting to scare his son or nephew.

"Yeah . . . I was afraid of that. Well, you two, don't travel too far into the forest tonight . . . and you, Taeau, the moon had better not be setting when you come home. Your mother is still fuming about how late you came in last night. Ven, I think I will visit your mother this evening. Is she home?"

"Yes, she should be, uncle."

"Good, then you both have a good night."

"You alright, Taeau?" asks Ven.

"Yeah, I'm fine, let's go. I still gotta check in with Ma, then I'll show you what I have been doing all day." They both run off towards Taeau's hut with a new excitement, knowing that a treasure awaits them.

Out of breath from climbing the stairs to his brother's home, Dirty Hands tries to scratch the door, but his nails are too short and raw from working in the fields. The door opens, and to his surprise Half Moon is smiling at him. Her daughter holds onto her tail and also looks at him shyly. Black Claw's youngest son, Little Claw, nudges his head out of his mother's pouch to see who is at the door.

"Dirty Hands, what are you doing here? This is a surprise-"

"Yes . . . I do not mean to intrude, but I would like to have a word with my brother. Is he in?"

"No, he had to leave early for work. Would you like to come in and have some honey water?"

"Yes, thank you." He looks down at his niece and says, "This must be Whispers. I have not seen you in a dog's life, and who is this little one?" Dirty Hands tries to get close to the infant, but Little Claw quickly disappears into his mother's pouch. They both begin to laugh, and Dirty Hands walks into the room. Talking about family and local gossip to fill the space, Dirty Hands works up the courage to tell Half Moon he thought he saw a Feather Runner in the fields. Right away, she looks concerned. She explains to him how strange it was for a guardsman to call for her husband so early in the evening. They sit and stare at one another in nervous silence, both pondering whether there is a connection between the Feather Runner and Black Claw's early beckoning to work.

Dirty Hands tells Half Moon that he is sure it is nothing to worry about. He then takes his leave, asking Half Moon to tell Black Claw that he stopped by.

"Of course, Dirty Hands. Say hello to your wife and tell her that I have seeds for her." Half Moon opens a pouch and it gives to Dirty Hands as he steps out the door. They wish each other good health, and Dirty Hands leaves Half Moon alone with her children.

Taeau and Ven continue their evening journey to Taeau's hut, bantering playfully. When they break from the edge of the woods and enter the boundaries of the farm, they notice that Taeau's mother is outside in the yard tending to the livestock and enjoying the evening's cool air. She has gained weight in the years since Mia-Koda brought Taeau to her. The dark circles under her eyes are gone, and her hair has once again grown thick and long. She sings to herself with only happiness in her heart. When she looks up from her chores, she spots her son and nephew running across the clearing. She tries to put on a stern face to scold Taeau.

"I thought I told you to be home by sunset."

"Hello, Mother Dirty Hands, good to see you," greets Ven.

"It is nice to see you too, Ven-TAEAU! What is wrong with your face?-Why are you bleeding? You got in a fight again with those younglings, didn't you?" She takes a rag from her waist and starts to wipe his face.

"Ma, stop! I'm fine-Why do you always do this? It is not a problem"

"Don't you tell ME what is or is not a problem!-Look at your eye, it's already starting to change color."

"He took on two of them at once, Mother Dirty Hands," says Ven, trying not to laugh as he watches Taeau's mother clean him up.

"Two ... you fought two at once. Who do you think you are, huh?-some kind of tough, strong Meno warrior? I have had it with this fighting. I will have to talk with their parents."

"What?-Are you crazy! Don't you dare! If you think I have it bad now, see what happens if you do that. I'm fine, really. I'm ok."

Meadow stares at her son, "Ok, since you're such a big boy now, I won't interfere . . . but if it gets worse ...," she warns as she shakes her finger at Taeau. "How late do you plan to wander the forest tonight, I wonder?"

"Well, since Ven just got up, and I have been doing my chores all day, I was wondering if I could be home as the moon sets."

Meadow grabs her hips and looks at them both, closing her eyes tiredly, then nods her head. "You can stay out 'til the moon is almost high. Take Carn with you. Your father said he saw some animals roaming in the woods, so be careful." Taeau's mother turns her back and notices that the wood has still not been piled. "What chores did you do today, Taeau?"

Taeau does not wait for her to figure it out, "Thanks, mom, see you later." Taeau calls Carn, and they race off into the forest.

Taeau runs as fast as he can through the forest with Carn at his side. Ven, as usual, follows from the treetops. The night is dark, but with the full moon there is enough light for the two boys to see. Ven, being nocturnal, has natural night vision, but Taeau's uncanny night vision is not as natural. His differences were noticed early when he was playing with the other younglings. At one of the Menoli changing-of-the-season festivals, at which both Salali and Meno were celebrating, a youngling noticed that Taeau's eyes reflected the moonlight. They teased him constantly, saying his mother mated with a deer, and they refused to play with him after this. Taeau's parents became

isolated as well. Dirty Hands was rarely invited to meetings, and Meadow was excluded from gatherings of the women.

At first, Taeau thought that he should try and play with the older younglings, hoping they might be more likely to accept him. Unfortunately, they only used him to do things that always got him into trouble. They teased him as well, and what was worse, Taeau didn't understand how they were mistreating him. Once, older Meno younglings had Ven cornered, and they were roughing him up. Ven was on the ground covering his face, when one of the older younglings told Taeau to kick his cousin. Taeau hesitated as he walked up to Ven. Until that day, he had rarely seen his cousin. He crouched down and whispered in his ear, pretending to taunt him. Taeau told Ven to run when he stood up and not to look back. Taeau grabbed a stone from the ground, making sure Ven saw him pick it up. When he turned around, he threw the stone at the leader of the younglings and hit him in the head. Ven jumped to his feet, climbed a nearby tree, and was able to escape.

The younglings beat on Taeau after that, and warned him never to show his face around them again. Ven watched what they did from inside a tree. After the children left Taeau on the ground bleeding, Ven helped his cousin up and carried him home. They had been best friends ever since. Ven lost many of his friends after that. They made fun of him for associating with the city outsider. It only brought Ven and Taeau closer.

Taeau stops and stands at the wooden walls of the city. Ven lands to his right. "I found it just beyond these walls," says Taeau.

"You know that younglings are not permitted to go outside the walls of the city." Taeau looks at Ven and smiles, spins, and begins to sprint along the wall.

"Where are we going?" shouts Ven, who is trying to keep up with Taeau, who is running faster than Ven has ever seen him before. Ven can usually jump circles around Taeau, but tonight he can't keep up even while leaping at full speed. As Ven struggles to keep up, he sees Taeau's necklace beginning to shine and he stops. He has never seen his cousin's necklace do this before, and he stands there, confused.

"Here!" yells Taeau.

Panting, Ven lands and stares at Taeau's necklace, which has gone dark, "Wha . . . what are we looking for, cousin?" Not listening to Ven, Taeau kneels on all fours and crawls through a crack in the gate. Carn whimpers and sniffs the spot where Taeau disappeared through the gate. Ven looks around and hesitates for a moment while looking at the crack. Ven knows how angry his father would be if he knew his son was breaking one of the most important youngling rules.

"Come on, Ven," whines Taeau, "we won't be outside the walls for too long, I promise. The treasure is right over here." Ven looks back one more time, shakes his head, and sneaks through the crack. Once on the other side, he spots his cousin standing only a short distance away.

"It's just over here-come on," urges Taeau.

They both struggle as they walk through the choking underbrush that pulls at their clothes and fur. It's not long before Ven notices something hanging from a tree. As they near the tree, Ven sees something flapping against the bark, slapping the tree as the wind blows. Ven becomes confused as he recognizes a pair of his cousin's pants.

"What is that doing here?"

"Well, when I found the treasure, I needed to mark the spot with something, now didn't I?"

"So what did you wear when you left?"

Taeau scratches his head, "I ran home with no pants on, of course." Ven looks at his best friend for a moment before he breaks out into an uncontrollable laugh.

"Ha . . . how did you get past your . . . mom . . . with no pants on?" gasps Ven between giggles.

Taeau shrugs and turns away from his cousin, not understanding what is so funny. Not letting his cousin distract him, he whacks around the tree, brushing plants out of his way. Ven continues laughing, and Taeau answers his cousin's question in exasperation. "Well, I just waited 'til mom was out in the yard, and then I ran inside our hut and quickly put on another pair of pants. Ha, here it is, come look."

Ven comes to Taeau's side and peers over his shoulder at what he has uncovered. Nothing could have prepared Ven for this. On the ground is the decayed corpse of a foreign soldier. All that is left of the warrior is a skull and a few scattered bones, but that is not what is so interesting. Although his body has long become dirt, his armor is still intact along with a broken sword and helmet. They are all worn by weather and time, but they are weapons of war all the same.

"Quick!-grab the shield and the helmet. I'll get the sword," says Taeau. They pick up everything they can carry, and run back to the gate. Ven and Taeau crawl back through the crack and into the city. They both are breathing heavily as they lay down their treasure and inspect it. The helmet, made by a foreign blacksmith, is simple, with a few roughly carved symbols. The shield is rusted and filled with many small holes made by burrowing

forest insects. The sword is cracked and broken, but is the perfect size for a youngling. Ven starts to circle the found treasure with desire in his eyes.

"Who gets what?" asks Ven.

"Well . . . I was thinking I should get the sword and the helmet."

"No, you do not get both the sword and the helmet!-I get the helmet and the shield, and you get the sword."

Taeau looks it all over and agrees. "Fine, let's get this to the unspeakable for safekeeping."

"Agreed."

They both pick up their treasure and run towards the unspeakable, with Carn barking at their sides. They reach the fort and crawl inside. The unspeakable is a large mound of earth that has been hollowed out by some forest creature. The two cousins came across their fortress during one of their adventures, and they dug further into the mound, making it larger. They also made a gate at the entrance like the one to enter the city. They even figured out how to create light by harvesting forest mushrooms that glow from a nearby stream.

"Ok, we will store everything here and tell no one about it," declares Taeau. "Finally we have what we need to defend ourselves against our enemies-"

"What does that mean, Taeau?-We can't use this stuff on them, or let anyone catch us using it," says Ven with a stern look on his face. He takes a cautious step back away from his cousin as he looks at the sword in his hand.

"I know, I know. If our enemy ever attacks us at our fortress, we will use the treasure only to scare them off, and then we will just deny we have it. I mean, who will believe them over us?"

Ven does not like the idea. His father is too intimidating, and he fears him too much to lie to him. Ven does like the new helmet, though. It makes him feel like his father, who wears the helmet of the city each day.

"Tomorrow can you sneak out and meet me here? There is so much to do, and I have to get home before mom goes crazy," Taeau says, putting his hand on his cousin's shoulder.

"Yeah, sure, I will see you here tomorrow. Let's go." With this, they both leave the fort and start home. When they get to the crossroads that leads to each of their homes, they wave goodbye and run off in different directions. When Ven arrives home, his father is already there, sitting at the table and talking to Ven's mother. Ven's sister hangs onto her father's back, and his younger brother watches from his mother's pouch.

"What are you doing home so early?" Ven asks his father curiously.

"I will be in and out all night as well as tomorrow. Come to the table and sit down. So where have you been all night?-Out with your cousin at that unspeakable place again?" Ven senses that his father is only playing nice while baiting him for information, so he answers the question vaguely.

"Ya, well, we were all over the place tonight, is that ok with you?"

Ven's mother lowers her head in an unbelieving look. She puts her hand on Black Claw's and gives him a look before leaving Ven and his father alone. "Come on, Whispers," she says, "I think it is time for us to get dinner ready."

Now Black Claw and Ven sit alone, and Ven can feel his father's glare.

"Look, son, you are getting older . . . so I am not going to lie to you." Ven looks up at his father with a puzzled look in his eyes. "Today we had a meeting in the Great Hall about an enemy that will be coming here to the city tomorrow." Ven is shocked to hear his father talk to him about important matters relating to work. "You see, if tomorrow does not go well, I may have to leave for a while and help protect the city. When I am gone, or if anything happens to me, you will be the oldest male and will have to take care of the family." Ven freezes in his chair. His head begins to spin and his eyes swell up.

"But, Father, I am only a youngling. What can I do if you don't come back?-I am not strong and big like you."

Black Claw smiles at his son and puts his hand over his son's smaller hand. "I was once young and small too . . . but I had to prove myself, and one day so will you. I am proud of you, son, and when I leave, I will not worry about my family's safety if you promise to take care of them."

Ven speaks as tears slide down his face, "I will do what you say, Father. I promise."

"I know you will . . . Now help me pack my things."

They get up, walk into Black Claw's room, and together open a chest in the corner that contains Black Claw's armor, fighting claws, and the helmet of Eel. When Ven sees his father's armor, he can only think about getting his own helmet from the unspeakable. He knows it will anger his father if he sneaks out, but all he can think of is his father's words about protecting his family.

"Son, tomorrow I do not want you and your cousin going to your fort . . . there will be a curfew in effect, and I do not want my son getting into trouble for breaking it. Also, I heard about your little scuffle with Dark

Water's son, Stripes. I would like it if you got along with them and the other younglings, and stopped spending so much time with your cousin."

Ven looks up angrily and tries to control his voice, "What?! Why?-He is your brother's son and my best friend."

His father breathes deeply, "I know this. It was Dirty Hands who told your mother what happened. I just don't see why you can't get along with the other younglings."

"Taeau is family and not a stinking dung-sniffer like Stripes."

"Look, boy, I am just trying to make it easier on you if you want to be something important one day. You need to gain the respect of the other younglings, younglings like White Stripes. Think about it." Black Claw taps Ven on the head and leaves.

Ven stays in the room staring at the floor. He knows what his father says is true. He also remembers the lessons of loyalty and honor his father taught him, and the thought of betraying Taeau turns his stomach. Ven punches the floor and decides he must sneak out and meet Taeau, so he can get his hands on the helmet and come home and protect his mother and siblings.

Taeau creeps up to the family hut, and Carn begins to bark at the sight of his home.

"Sshhh!-boy, you'll wake them and get me in trouble!"

But it is too late, because his mother's silhouette becomes visible in the doorway.

"Trouble you are already in-now get inside," she says, glaring down at her only son. Taeau scampers inside and sits on the floor. His mother joins him, and they both sit staring at each other.

"Well, what time did I tell you to be home tonight? Do you think you can just do what you want?-not to mention all that is going on in the city. You are lucky your father is already asleep, or I would tell him to take you into the woods, find a switch, and use it on your backside. Taeau looks up and begins to shift back and forth uncomfortably. His mother sees this, and a small smirk crosses her face.

"Well, since your father is asleep, we will just have to keep your misbehavior to ourselves, ok?" Taeau smiles. "Give your mom a hug before bed. Your father will be going to that big meeting tomorrow, so be up early for your chores to say goodbye."

"Yes, mom . . . ahh, I love you." Taeau gives his mother a hug and stays in her lap until he falls asleep.

Meadow sings to her son until his eyes roll back, and he enters the dream world. Once he is asleep, she lays him down in his bed, pulls the animal skin blankets over his sleeping body and moves the hair from his face. She stares at Taeau for a while and kisses his forehead. Her face begins to wrinkle with apprehension as she looks down at her adopted son, shaking her head at how much he has grown. She begins to think of the words spoken to her by Mia-Koda.

"I will be back for him when he begins to walk the path of a man." Meadow knows the time with her son is limited. She dreams about stopping the seasons or defying Mia-Koda when she comes, but she knows she will have to face that fear one day. Meadow lies next to Taeau and falls asleep still playing with his hair.

CHAPTER FIVE

Dirty Hands wakes to an empty bed. He turns over and sees his wife sleeping next to their son. He smiles because no matter how many times she falls asleep by Taeau's side, it brings joy to his heart. He gets up, puts on his clothes, and approaches his wife and son. He kisses his wife and wakes Taeau.

"Come, son, let us leave your mother to her sleep." Taeau gets up and throws on his clothes before leaving. The sun is just beginning to shine through the trees, lifting the morning's mist. "Taeau, did your mother tell you about what I am doing today?"

"Yes, Father, why have they asked you to join the meeting? They have never done that before."

"They have never done that before," Dirty Hands says, as he puts his hand on his son's shoulder. "Yes, I was surprised myself, but I hear that there were a few other farmers asked to attend as well. This is why I am worried. The last time I heard of farmers attending a big council was when my father was summoned to fight in the Border Wars."

Taeau looks up at his dad, "Wasn't that when you lost your dad?"

"Yes, your uncle and I grew up quickly after that-we had to take care of both our mother and ourselves at around your age. Black Claw joined the wars, and I took care of the family farm. It was a tough time for the both of us." Dirty Hands kneels down to his son.

"The future is never clear, son. Sometimes you must stand for what is right even when it means hard times and sacrifice. I want you to stay here with your mother today, and not go to your fort in the woods or play with your cousin. Stay here the entire day and evening, do your chores, and keep your mother company."

"Ok, Father-whatever you say." Taeau knows he is lying.

"Good boy . . . I am off, then." Dirty Hands rustles his son's hair, and Taeau watches as his father walks away. Once his father is gone, Taeau runs off to find Carn and begin the morning's adventures.

"Come on, boy, we have to get away now while we still can."

Carn licks Taeau's face, and they set off towards the unspeakable. Just before they are out of sight, Meadow catches sight of her son and runs out the door. She moves quickly despite her plump figure and begins to scold Taeau.

"Where do you think you're going?-Your father said for you to stay and do your chores!"

Taeau looks at his mother and does his best to fake a whine. "I am, Mom!- Father just told me to take Carn to get firewood. We're all out, you know."

"Oh . . . okay . . . well, don't be long now, you hear?" Meadow turns back towards the hut, but she notices that the woodpile is already full. She stares at it for a moment and realizes she has been tricked.

"Taeau!" Meadow yells as she spins around, but her son is long gone.

At the same time, Ven has just pulled a similar trick on his mother. She awoke from her sleep to check on her children and found her oldest son's hammock empty. She runs to the door and bursts it open. Blinded by the morning sun, she is barely able to see Ven scampering away.

Taeau and Carn reach the unspeakable first. They stop and wait a moment behind a tree to make sure that no one has followed them.

"Come on, Carn! To the fortress so we can arm ourselves against our enemies," exclaims Taeau, as he skips towards the fort. Taeau approaches the fort as Ven lands on the ground behind him, breathing heavily and looking tired.

"Ven, you made it!-I didn't think you were going to . . . ohhh, this is great!" But he looks into his cousin's eyes and knows there is something wrong.

"Cousin, I am going to be in so much trouble for this. I know my mom saw me sneak out."

"Yeah, mine did too, but it is worth it. I have not been able to stop thinking about the treasure all night." Ven brushes past Taeau and heads to their fort's opening as his cousin speaks.

"What's wrong with you?"

"Look, Taeau, I don't care about Stripes and his crew . . . there are much more important things going on."

Taeau looks at his cousin with a blank stare, "Well, what do you mean? What could be more important than this?"

"Look . . . there is a meeting today at the hall, and there might be a war. My dad is going to need my help. I am going to take my half of the treasure to protect my family if my dad leaves."

Taeau walks over to his cousin and puts his arms around him. "Look, you are my family and your fight is my fight-I will help you and your dad. My father is going to that meeting too, so you're right. We should get our stuff and help out our dads." Ven nods his head as they walk into the unspeakable, leaving Carn behind to stand guard. Ven feels slightly better knowing that his cousin understands how he feels. They both sit in the fort dividing the treasure, and a new courage builds inside each of them with the understanding that there is nothing that could ever keep them apart.

The Hall of Eel is filled with both Meno and Salali. Most of the adult males in the city have gathered together, speaking to each other with suspicion and apprehension. They were instructed to attend this council unarmed a sign of peace to their enemies, but in the minds of both the Salali and the Meno peace will not last. Both Chiefs sit in their thrones dressed in their ceremonial attire, smoking and watching the men in the room. Black Claw stands between the chiefs. He wears the helmet of Eel and passes out orders to his captains and various warriors. The Meno farmers, the Salali gatherers, and city warriors converse with each other, renewing old bonds as the dark cloud of war gathers around them. It is always like this when the days seem darkest; old grudges are forgotten, and new, stronger alliances are formed.

Dirty Hands talks to a fellow farmer about the strange things that he has seen, and he catches a glance from his brother and nods his head in response. Dirty Hands knows that his brother is glad that he is attending the meeting, and Black Claw's small gesture in front of the others makes him feel like a member of the city once again, a feeling he has not had since his first son died.

The door opens slightly and then closes again. A Meno guard swiftly walks into the room and approaches Black Claw. The hall becomes silent, and all eyes are on the guard and Black Claw. The guard softly speaks to Black Claw. The Captain nods his head and signals for the guard to go back to his position by the door. The hall remains silent as Black Claw raises his hands and speaks loudly.

"Columbus is at our door and requests admittance into the Hall of Eel. Does anyone object to his admittance?" Silence reigns, and Red Fist rises in response.

"Admit our guest, and may this council bear the fruit of peace and not the thorns of war."

Everyone in the hall stands shoulder to shoulder on either side of the path leading to the Chiefs; farmers and gatherers behind the warriors who proudly stand like walls to the thrones. They stand together united as brothers as they create a lane through which Columbus and his men walk towards the thrones. All eyes settle on the doors as they open, letting daylight into the hall. Columbus walks in followed by Ush-Ka and two body guards.

His bodyguards are men of the Nossa, castaway barbarian Vikings whom have no home. These Nossa bodyguards are dressed in only loincloths and have covered their bodies in red war paint, with white paint splashed over their heads.

Ush-Ka walks up to the Chiefs and bows his head in respect. Through his long rotten teeth, he spats his first words with a sneer. "Such a grand turnout. I am pleased to see you honor your future king with such respect."

The room erupts in anger as Black Claw steps down from between the Chiefs and approaches his enemy shouting and pointing to Columbus. "Tell me Beast . . . by what right does your King believe he has ownership over our lands? Did he bleed with our ancestors as they fought and forged our great city?"

The room again begins to echo with talk as the men nod their heads and point towards Ush-Ka, agreeing with their captain. General Ush-Ka looks to Columbus who yawns with boredom.

"I do not speak to lowly tree rats," he hisses. "I ask the Chiefs to swiftly punish this rodent's insolence and without mercy. Anything less I will take as a personal insult."

The room erupts in shouting and fist-shaking. Red Fist is the first Chief to speak. "This is the Captain of our city whom you insult, General. You will show him respect while you are inside our borders."

Ush-Ka chuckles, "Captain? This is your Captain? Well, if this is the greatest warrior you have, then you are in greater need of our King's protection than I perceived." Ush-Ka turns and points to all the Meno and Salali in the hall. "Those who swear allegiance to the greatest and most powerful King in this world will be under his protection. They will be allowed to work on his majesty's lands that he will generously provide to his loyal subjects. Those who prove their worth will receive his blessing, but

those who oppose him will burn in the ashes of his fury. This is not a threat but rather an offer and a DEMAND! Do not be so foolish as to let courage fill your chests . . . my Lord has the means to destroy your city, and I will do as my King commands. My new brothers, submit to Columbus and live under his rule . . . in peace . . . or oppose him and die."

Black Claw opens his hands and flashes his large thumb claws. "We do not need your protection, nor do we need permission from your farce of a king to work our own lands." The hall erupts in yelling in support of Black Claw. The men stomp their feet and the Salali scratch the ground and brandish their claws towards Columbus and his men. "And as for his fury, it is you who should be worried about ours, Dog!"

Ush-Ka turns towards the chiefs, lifting his shoulder to Black Claw so as to ignore him. "Chief Grey Back, you have been read the terms. You will bind your allegiance by signing the scrolls with the ink of your own blood. This act will prove your oath to Columbus and allow your people to live."

Grey Back stands proudly and points his aging finger in Columbus's direction. "And after we have given you everything we possess, including our sons and our daughters, what then do we have left? I will tell you . . . nothing . . . we will have nothing. Take our lives if you must, but you will not take our honor or our freedom without a fight."

Ush-Ka walks up and down the aisle, purposefully looking into the eyes of both races. "Hagur, Leaf, show these peasants what true warriors are." With these words Columbus's bodyguards begin to perform. They shout out in the Nossa cry of war. They begin to do a war dance showing all in the hall their skills of combat while chanting and slapping themselves violently.

This demonstration brings uneasiness to the room, and fear begins to fill the hearts of the men and the Salali. Ush-Ka can smell their distress, and he begins to smile.

Black Claw tries to bring courage back to his men. "The only thing we need protection from is Columbus, your black-hearted king who orders you to slaughter the innocent and steal what is not yours. We will never become slaves working our own lands or in your cursed mines."

"Do not dare insult the King in my presence, you powerless rat. You will accept the terms that are given or feel his wrath," threatens Ush-Ka.

In defiance, Black Claw waves his claws in Ush-Ka's face. The hall echoes with the men's shouts, and the line begins to close in on Columbus and his men.

"SILENCE!" shouts Red Fist, and the hall becomes still.

Grey Back rises from his throne and speaks. "You can tell Columbus that it was not with his fathers' lives that these lands were secured. You can also tell him that these lands will run red with your men's blood if you do not leave our borders now and never return."

The Meno and Salali start to chant and dance around Columbus displaying to him that they are also ready for war. Dirty Hands stays on the outside of the circle and looks around the room in fear. Ush-Ka turns and looks at Columbus and Columbus walks to his side.

Columbus begins to speak in Italian and Ush-Ka translates, "I am Christopher Columbus a son of Italy. I traveled across the great sea a feat that none before me has ever accomplished. I come from a land very different from yours. We worship the one true God and live a civilized life unlike you and your savage ways. I am offering you chance to join me and convert from you pagan beliefs. If you do God will show you his blessings and I will guide you on a path towards a great civilization. Defy me and all my power and knowledge will rain down upon you like the fires that destroyed Sodom and Gomorrah. Because for you and your people there can be no victory as long as I am guided by the hands of God. So I ask you one last time savage chiefs, join us and bend to my will embracing the glory of God or be destroyed by my might."

The hall does not settle down. The walls of Meno and Salali begin to close in on Columbus. The Nossa guards and Ush-Ka surround their King and slowly walk towards the door. Once outside, Ush-Ka nods in the direction of the Nossa bodyguards before starting down the stairs following his master. The Nossa do not follow, and the men standing guard look at each other in alarm.

"You are no longer welcome here . . . leave with your general now!" yells a guard as he lowers his spear at the backs of the barbarians. The guards look down, hearing screams from below. They see Feather Runners approaching the stairs to the hall. The Runners are chained at the neck and are being whipped by Ush-Ka's men who force them to attack anyone who comes close.

"WE ARE UNDER ATTACK! WARN THE OTHERS!" yells a Salali guard from the ground, just as a Runner overtakes him from behind and tears at his body. The Nossa warriors then attack the guards and the two sides battle for control of the door. A Meno guard manages to open the door to the hall and quickly yells a warning to the Meno and Salali inside.

"The city is under siege, arm yourse-," a Meno spear pierces his stomach, and he falls in a pool of blood.

"Protect the city! Arm yourselves!" Everyone looks blankly at Black Claw, for all the men in the hall are unarmed. A Salali reaches the wounded guard and checks to see if he is dead, when suddenly the door opens wide and Feather Runner's bursts into the room. The Salali who crouches over the slain guard is helpless, as a leaping Runner tears him to pieces. The rest of the hall watches in horror as he desperately cries for help beneath the teeth and claws of the bloodthirsty beast.

The door then slams shut behind the intruders, and the room becomes silent. The Runners and their Nossa masters begin to creep slowly towards the Meno and Salali. Both sides are eyeing each other, waiting for the first move to be made. The soldiers standing behind the Runners smile in anticipation of the blood that will soon be spilt. One of them raises his whip high in the air and brings it down with a hard crack. A Runner lunges forward, and the massacre in the hall of Eel begins.

Two Meno farmers fall to the ground, helplessly crying out for aid. As a Runner roars with the blood of the fallen farmer dripping from its teeth, Black Claw lands on the Runner's neck and drives his thumb claws into the beast's eyes.

"Their eyes! Go for their eyes!" yells the Salali Captain as his thumb claws gouge out the Runner's eyes. The Runner roars in pain and squirms out of control, trying to free itself from Black Claw's grip. Black Claw is thrown to the side as the Runner falls to the ground, mortally wounded.

Chaos takes over as the battle continues. Many of the Menoli's best and strongest are slain; the barbarian soldiers strike down unarmed farmers and gatherers as they whip their Feather Runners. Grey Back is the first Chief to fall in the onslaught and as he dies, two Salali desperately defend his dead body. At the loss of Grey Back, Red Fist takes control of the men and gliders.

"Take the slain soldier's weapons and kill the beasts!" yells Red Fist in a final attempt at victory. "Black Claw!-Out the window! Open the door and save the city!"

Black Claw and a few gliders crawl up the walls and exit out a high window. They crawl around the tree to see the entire city under siege. The guards at the gate have come back into the city and are trying to fight their way up to the hall door. Black Claw yells out orders to his soldiers.

"I will take the leaders! Kill the soldiers by the door and save our trapped brothers. Now, MOVE!"

They all jump into the air and dive down towards the steps. The soldiers near Black Claw dive first, attacking the Runners and their masters, while Black Claw assaults the Nossa bodyguards who first accompanied Ush-

Ka into the hall. Black Claw lands on a warrior's back and drives his claws into both sides of his neck. He jumps from the slain Nossa's back and rolls down the stairs. Black Claw lunges for the other bodyguard, and they both fall to the ground, wrestling down the steps. Rolling down the stairs though the chaos of the battle, they come to the last step. Now only Black Claw stands, his fur covered in blood. Black Claw turns to the hall doors and leads the remaining guards back up the stairs. In a quick assault, he and his guards are able to slay the remaining enemies and open the door to the hall.

Inside, Red Fist is mortally wounded, and only a few Salali and Meno remain to guard him. The injured and dead lie in a lake of blood on the floor. One Runner and two warriors survive, and they surround Red Fist and his men.

"The end is at hand, you weak old fool," spats a soldier as he whips a Runner to attack. The Runner's jaws clamp shut around a Meno's arm, and Red Fist creeps backwards, preparing for the end. Behind the cries of the Meno who has just lost his arm, a wounded Dirty Hands rises from the ground with a Nossa sword and slices off the Nossa's arms that hold the Runner's chains. The warrior screams, and Dirty Hands grabs the Runner's chains. Dirty Hands pulls on the chain, and the Runner slips and falls onto the bloodstained floor. The remaining Meno and Salali jump upon the runner and slay it with ease. The last rider retreats to the door, only to be killed by the Menoli guards who have fought their way in. Dirty Hands goes to Red Fist's side.

"Are you alright? Can you walk?" Red Fist nods his head as Dirty Hands helps him to his feet.

The door opens, and Black Claw enters with a few other men. Those who were not in the hall during the first attack look around in shock at the sight of the dead and wounded sprawled across the floor. Black Claw quickly approaches Red Fist, "The city is lost, we cannot defend against this onslaught-they are too many and we have too few warriors left. The dog Ush-Ka has outmaneuvered us. We must retreat."

Red Fist lifts his dying head, "You must lead our people to safety . . . gather what soldiers you can, lead the women and children to safety. Our children must survive." Red Fist then collapses into Dirty Hands's arms and stops breathing.

Taeau and Ven pretend to defend their fortress from unseen foes, as they stand side by side with their fathers. Absorbed in their fantasy battle they do not realize Stripes and his gang have followed Ven to the hideout and have been spying on them from the trees.

46

From the canopy above, Stripes snickers to his two followers. "When my father hears Black Claw's own son has been playing with forbidden weapons with the dirty, freakish son of a worthless farmer . . . oh, the shame on his family!" A large grin forms on Stripe's face as he pictures the fall of the Claw family and the rise of his own. "Come on," says Stripes, and the crew jumps from their branch and floats down towards Taeau and Ven.

Taeau and Ven battle imaginary warriors on the top of the hill, dramatically pretending to fight a last stand, when Carn suddenly begins barking at the open forest. The two cousins look out into the forest, wondering what Carn is barking at. As they stare into the woods, Stripes and his gang suddenly land behind them.

They both spin and see their attackers. "Back, you three! I am warning you," yells Taeau as he points his weapon at them.

"Smart farmer boy, use a junky, broken, old sword on one of us. Your filthy family will be exiled forever, so go ahead and do it." These words make Taeau back down and rethink what he is doing-he did not consider that Stripes would be so brave with a sword pointed at him. He looks at Carn, who is snarling at the woods surrounding the hill.

"As for you, when I tell my father about what you are doing, he will-"

Stripes stops talking and stares into the forest. Taeau takes advantage of this and attacks his enemy. "You won't tell on us, you coward! Because if you-"

Stripes eyes become wide and terrified as he looks over Taeau's shoulder; he quickly turns around and runs away in a crazy fit.

"Yeah, you run, you stinking coward!" shouts Taeau at Stripes' back.

"Taeau, look out!" yells Ven.

Ven pushes Taeau to the side and catches a flash of teeth before he is knocked off the hill and lands on the ground, hitting his head hard on a rock. A young Feather Runner has appeared from the forest, his mouth and face covered with blood. It turns towards Taeau and snaps at him. The other younglings run away in fear, leaving Taeau alone to defend his friend. The young Runner moves closer, drooling and snapping while keeping his eyes fixed on Taeau. Taeau stares at the beast, frozen in shock. The beast attacks, and Taeau closes his eyes, swinging his sword. He feels the weapon strike the Runner, and he hears it roar in pain. The noise scares Taeau, and when he opens his eyes, he has to shield himself from the blood pouring from the Runners' snout. The Runner retreats into the woods, shrieking in pain. Taeau then drops his sword and runs to Ven. Carn is still barks loudly at the Runner but stays by his master's side.

Taeau kneels next to his cousin. "Ven!-are you hurt, can you hear me?" He grabs Ven by the arm and shakes him in panic. "Ven!"

Ven's eyes flutter open, and he looks at his cousin in confusion.

"Taeau, what happened? Why are you covered in blood?"

"It's not mine, Ven . . . are you alright?"

"Ya, just got knocked out, who knows what would have happened if I hadn't had on this helmet." He takes off the helmet and rubs the bump that is starting to form on his head. They hear screaming in the distance over Carn's barking.

"Quiet, boy!" yells Taeau.

Carn comes to his master obediently, but continues to stare into the distance as he licks Ven's forehead.

"We'd better get back home, something big is going on. And I need to tell dad what I saw, no matter how much trouble I'm in."

"I agree, let's run to the crossroads and then split up. Come on, Carn, let's go."

Taeau helps Ven up, and they run back to their homes. Taeau can't believe what he did, it happened so fast, and Ven is beginning to dread how much trouble he will be in when he sees his father. They reach the crossroads and face each other. Through short breaths they say their good-byes.

"Well, this is it. I imagine I won't be seeing you for a while," says Ven.

"Ya, well, they can't punish us forever. I'll see you again as soon as I can."

Ven looks up and starts to thank his cousin for saving his life. Taeau cuts in before he can say a word, "You're the closest thing I have ever had to a brother. If you would not have pushed me out of the way, we both would have been a meal for that beast." With that, they give each other a punch on the shoulder and go their separate ways.

They both start running home, but Taeau does not get far before Carn stops and begins growling loudly. Taeau turns and looks down at his dog, "What is it now, boy? What do you hear?" Carn darts back the way they came, and Taeau shrugs his shoulders, turns around, and runs, trying to catch up to Carn.

"Wait up, boy!-not so fast!"

Taeau follows the dog through the woods and stops in his tracks. His body stiffens, and he stands rigid behind a bush in terror. Carn is still

running and barking towards the most frightening creature Taeau has ever seen. It is hideous: a beast that stands so tall that Taeau's neck hurts as he looks up. Carn has gone up to it, and is barking and growling more fiercely than Taeau has ever heard him. Taeau stares at the beast and sees that the creature is clenching Ven by the neck. His cousin is squirming violently, and the beast is whispering to him. Carn tries to jump and bite the monster, but the beast swipes at Carn, slaming him to the ground. Carn looks up at Taeau with blood pouring out of his snout and whimpers softly before his eyes shut and his breathing stops. Taeau stands horrified, disbelieving what he sees. Taeau then hears a bone-chilling crack, and Ven stops squirming and his body goes limp.

Taeau collapses to his knees. Tears streak down his face, but he feels nothing. A bloodcurdling scream wakes him from his trance. He sees a large figure diving down from the treetops. Taeau recognizes his uncle, who soars towards the beast and lands behind him with his outstretched claws.

"USH-KA!!"

The beast tosses Ven to the ground like he is an insect.

"NO! NOT HIM! I'LL KILL YOU!" screams Black Claw, as he jumps towards his son.

Ush-Ka steps in his way and sneers at the captain. Now clad in his battle armor, Black Claw faces Ush-Ka. Ush-Ka lowers his head and arches his back showing Black Claw his many deadly spines. He roars, contracting his muscles and rattling the hollow, poison-laced quills. Black Claw charges, and in a blur of teeth and claws their death struggle erupts. Urine begins to trickle down Taeau's leg as he watches, terrified by the fury and the viciousness of the battle. Black Claw digs his claws into Ush-Ka's thigh and wraps his teeth around his calf. Ush-Ka roars then slashes Black Claw across his body, cutting him deeply with his claws. Black Claw falls, crying out as blood blankets the forest floor. Ush-Ka then picks up Black Claw and holds him over the body of his son.

"The mighty Black Claw, time to join your rat son in the darkness!" sneers Ush-Ka as he slams Black Claw to the ground.

Tears stream down Taeau's face as he helplessly watches his uncle crawl towards Ven. Taeau can't move as Black Claw struggles to drag his broken body closer to Ven. Black Claw reaches for his son and pulls Vens' lifeless body close to his own. He lays his bleeding head on his son and stares through the brush, and sees Taeau looking at him. Black Claw smiles, remembering the day Mia-Koda brought the child to the city. He remembers the words he spoke to Mia-Koda after giving the child to his brother. How the child's eyes had haunted his dreams. Black Claw had foreseen this moment and only now at the end does he understand his vision. Black Claw closes his eyes and snuggles with his son. Ush-Ka puts his foot on the back of Black Claw, raises a spear over his head, and chuckles loudly, "The great captain of the Salali, ha," and slams the weapon into the back of Black Claw. Black Claws' head lifts as the spear is driven through his torn flesh. His eyes open for just a moment before closing again and landing on his son's soft fur. Taeau falls to the ground, and the world around him goes black.

Everything is dark, but Taeau can feel the warmth of blankets around him. There is whispering nearby, voices he does not recognize. Taeau sits up and opens his eyes. Through his blurry vision he sees the unfamiliar face of a stranger. She is an old woman, older than he has ever seen. Her face is carved by time, with a few strands of brittle hair dangling across her face. Taeau looks into her eyes and senses something familiar. Her pupils have lost all their color, but there is a light, an aura of energy, that raises the hairs on his neck. A small, dark, one-eyed creature rushes to his side and begins rubbing his arms and back. The miniature, man-like creature is half his size, dirty and wild looking. He has markings on his skin that flash as he pets Taeau.

Taeau looks around and can tell that he is outside of the city gates. The trees grow close here, creating a quiet, eerie darkness that he does not like. Taeau begins to breathe more lightly now and lies back. As he closes his eyes, flashes of the violent deaths of his best friend and uncle jolt him up with a gasp.

"Shhh...it's ok, there-don't be afraid," the stranger says. For some reason, he trusts this voice, and when he looks up at the old woman with strange clothing, he feels safe. She holds a staff and reaches into a pouch folded into her robes.

"Here, chew on this, it will help with your stomach," she says.

"Taeau!," yells a voice from behind him. His mother runs out of the dark woods and collapses onto him, smothering him with hugs and tears.

"Are you alright?-Let me look at you," she gushes as she begins to pat him all over, inspecting his body for injuries. He can see his father from within his mother's grasp. He is talking to the older woman. His father is covered in blood and seems to be injured. The two are arguing, and Taeau overhears the old woman telling his father that "he knew this day would come!" The old woman keeps stating that "Taeau is not safe" and that "he must start his training."

Taeau's mother stands up and blocks Taeau from the old woman.

"I won't let you!-He has been through too much, and he needs time to get better! He needs his mother-I am the only one that can help him." His mother's broken and desperate voice only frightens Taeau, who is confused and weak.

The older woman walks up to Taeau's mother and stares into her eyes. In a calm but stern tone she speaks. "You have no say in the matter, Meadow. Now say your goodbyes, time is short."

The old woman bows her head and disappears into the forest with the tiny one-eyed creature straggling behind her. Taeau's parents kneel down and take their son into their arms. Dirty Hands is the first to speak with a quivering voice.

"Son . . . you must leave with Mia-Koda tonight for your own safety. She is wise and powerful; she will teach you many things and help you grow into a man. I wish . . . I wish I could be there to see the man that you become, but it is not to be. Know that I will never forget you or stop loving you, son."

Taeau glances at his mother, searching for reassurance or some hope. He is met only by his mother's uncontrollable tears, and his heart begins to sink, his throat starts to close, and the tears fall.

"Bu . . . But I don't want to go with her!" Taeau gasps between sobs. "Why can't I stay with you? I'm sorry about everything, I didn't mean it . . . please don't send me away."

Meadow breaks down, clenching her heart as she grabs her son with her other arm. "You have done nothing wrong, child, nothing at all-your father and I love you very much . . . never forget that." She hugs him, squeezing him tightly as she convulses in sorrow. She whispers to him her last words to him as a mother.

"I will always be with you, Taeau . . . every night when you look up at the sky, know that I am looking at the same sky and thinking of you . . . and remember, my son, that I love and miss you very much. You must be strong now, and do what Mia-Koda tells you, she was the one who, who-"

Meadow does not have the strength to continue. The thought of losing another son is too much, and she begins to fall apart. Between his own sobs, Taeau grabs his mother as she quickly kisses him on the head and runs into the forest.

"MOM!" screams Taeau, as he reaches in the direction of his mother.

His father grabs him by the arm and speaks to him lovingly. "Let her go-this is the second time in her life she has had to say good-bye to a son. I never told you this, but we once had a child before you. He died of sickness at an age younger than you are now. It was you who brought happiness and hope back into your mother's life. I am thankful for the time we have had, and you are a better son than I could ever have hoped for. We will see each other again one day . . . I promise." Dirty Hands then picks up Taeau and carries him to Mia-Koda's wagon.

He lies in the back of the wagon, staring up into the forest. Mia-Koda begins to walk, pulling Broomay, her horse, as Taeau watches his father fade away into the distance. The day grows late and the threesome has been traveling with no rest. A small storm cloud has come in from the West, and a light drizzle begins to dampen Taeau's hair. Tib clumsily slops through the muddy forest floor while covering his head with a large leaf. Taeau has not said a word since their journey started, and he has been falling in and out of consciousness in the wagon. When his eyes close, he is assaulted with the images of Black Claw, his cousin, and the monster that took their lives. He cannot escape his uncle's stare or the image of him lying helplessly with Ven. The dream repeats itself over and over, and soon Taeau cannot erase the vision even with his waking eyes. His body becomes numb, and nothing seems real to him as the rain continues to fall, echoing in his mind.

The storm finally passes, and Mia-Koda decides to make camp. She finds a small clearing where she sets up their things and starts a fire. Tib moves around, preparing their beds and gathering kindling as Taeau sits staring at the ground. Mia-Koda senses that the boy will not be hungry, so she puts a pot of water over the fire to make them all a warm drink before they sleep. She takes a root from one of her satchels, grinds it up, and pours the powder into Taeau's drink.

"Here, child, this will help you sleep through the night without dreaming."

Taeau looks up at her and nods his head while reaching for the cup. Mia-Koda notices that he has a black eye and is still wearing blood-soaked clothes. She tells him to take them off, and she gives him new ones. He stares at the bloodstains in the dark and begins to drink, choking on the liquid for a moment.

"You soon will be asleep-things will look better in the morning."

Taeau stares into the cup with a distant gaze and answers the strange woman's comforting words. "Nothing will be the same."

She looks down at him with understanding. Tib yanks on Taeau's pants as he points to his bed. Taeau finishes his drink and crawls limply into the warm furs. Mia-Koda sits by his side and speaks to him in a soft, storytelling voice. "I have not seen you since you were an infant. You have

grown well. Tib here has been waiting a long time to see you again-he is pleased that you are healthy."

"Again?" mumbles Taeau with confusion in his voice. "I have never seen either of you in my life."

Taeau is beginning to feel the effects of the drink. His eyes begin to feel heavy and his mind becomes light.

"You did when you were a young child. You do not remember, I imagine. That is a story I will save for another time. Close your eyes, child . . . fall asleep."

Barely conscious, Taeau garbles, "What will happen to me now?-Where will I live? How will-"

Mia-Koda looks down at the young boy and waves her staff over his eyes, and Taeau falls into a deep, dreamless sleep. His necklace dimly glows for a few moments, and Mia-Koda takes it into her hands. A light blinds her, and she falls back breathing heavily as she clutches her wrist. Tib runs to his master to see if she is injured. She looks down at him and between gasps she mumbles, "He . . . he is not . . . the last."

CHAPTER SIX

The moonlight creeps through the treetops, blanketing Taeau's cheeks as he falls into a deep, dreamless sleep beside Mia-Koda. Far away under the same moonlight, Oskeau, Taeau's twin, stands staring at the sky, lost in thought. Oskeau takes his eyes off the moon and walks back to his master's cave. He comes to a small clearing and approaches the cave where his master killed the forest monitor those eight years ago. He enters the dark, damp cave with food he has gathered during the day. The wetness of the cave glistens reflecting Oskeau's malnourished figure as he moves deeper into his master's lair.

Oskeau, having never been given a proper name, answers only to "slave," "thief," "worm," and other various insults from his master Ogden, as Puddle now calls himself. Ogden has been a cruel master, and Oskeau has become weak, his thin hair has grown wild and knotted, and he now smells nearly as foul as his master. Oskeau lays out Ogden's dinner of shells and fish on the floor beside his master's throne. Ogden, who has become fat while he has not had to hunt, lifts up his arm and throws a shell, striking the child in the head. Oskeau falls back, holding his head in pain.

"What this I find in cave, slave? You hide it from master, huh?"

The boy looks up at Ogden in shock, shaking in fear. "S-Sorry master . . . I di-i-i-id not m-mean it, let me have it b-back I-I need it."

Oskeau's stutter only brings courage to Ogden. He jumps on top of the boy. "You dare keep secrets from me?" he sneers as he grabs the shell from the ground and crushes it in his hand with a smile.

"Noooo!" cries Oskeau as he watches his master destroy his secret possession. Tears now streak down his dirty face, "Why, ma-ma-m-aster, I have been good, why-"

"Because you mine! And I do what I want with you."

Ogden then chases the boy out of the cave and away from his meal. Oskeau can hear Ogden laughing, and he falls to the ground weeping, his face

in his hands. He stares at the moon and lightly cries until he has no more tears, then lies down on the cool earth and closes his eyes.

Late in the night he wakes to a soft noise riding on the wind. He sits up and stares into the forest. His eyes reflect the moonlight, but he hears nothing but the rustling of the trees. He hears something again, and this time he stands up and moves closer to the trees. He stares into the forest, scratching his face with curiosity. The calm silence of the forest begins to unnerve him, and he thinks about his rock. Oskeau turns and runs to its hiding place. The child shivers in the night as he digs up his most beloved companion. He is not as careful as he should be, and in his carelessness he forgets to wait until his master is sleeping. His heart pounds, and he mumbles to himself, "It has to b-b-be here, I nee-e-ed it, I will l-l-leave m-master," he says, crying while he digs. When he spots his stone in the hole, his hands stop and his eyes fill with relief.

"I found you," whispers the young boy as he brushes off the dirt from the stone's smooth face.

But Ogden has been watching from inside the cave. He has become increasingly angry as he witnesses his slave's disobedience, and at the moment that Oskeau bows his head in relief, his master stomps to his side.

"More secrets you keep from me?" he growls as he kicks the boy in the face. There is a sharp whimper, and Oskeau tumbles backwards from his master's blow. Ogden then snatches the stone from his slave's hand while Oskeau is doubled over, coughing up dirt and blood.

"I keep this for myself, you deceiving worm!-I make a necklace of my own with it, and you will stare at my rock."

These words pierce Oskeau's heart, and anger begins to burn inside him. His chest begins to smolder in rage, and a faint red haze now emanates from his necklace. Oskeau lunges at his master in anger, and he begins screaming and grunting while trying to grab the stone. "Give it back to me!" he yells clearly.

Ogden jumps back, his voice becoming angrier and louder, "What? What did you say?"

The boy stands up and harnesses the power coming from within him. He again hears a noise whispering on the wind, but this time a strange voice echoes in his ears. While he does not understand what this voice is saying, it gives him courage and strength.

"Give it back to me now, Puddle," he says in a voice that is no longer timid but commanding. Its power makes Puddle hold the stone to his chest and take a step back. Puddle is shocked to hear the boy speak his old name, and he tries desperately to regain control.

"Teach you a lesson I will slave." Puddle looks directly into Oskeau's eyes and tosses the stone into the forest.

"Nooooo!" the boy screams, watching the stone vanish into the night. His body is ablaze with a rage that he has never felt before. His blood feels like it is on fire, and the world starts to glow red. Oskeau closes his eyes; he feels all of his anger condense into a small ball inside of his chest. The anger wants to leave him. It pushes against his chest, burning for freedom. He stops fighting it and expels the anger with a deafening, thunderous crack. He is thrown to his back, and the forest around him goes dark.

He sluggishly wakes, opening his eyes to the night sky. He is on his back, and everything is silent. He sits up and slowly comes back to his senses. First, he notices Puddle rolling around on the ground and holding his face. He looks pathetic and childish, and this makes Oskeau giggle. Next, sound begins to re-enter his mind, and he is shocked to hear his master screaming and crying in pain.

"Ahhhhh, it burns. So much pain!-wicked boy hurt me, ahh." There is blood squirting out of Puddle's hands, and when the Muddler takes his hands from his face to wipe away the blood, Oskeau is able to see what he did to him. A deep, bleeding gash is slashed across his master's face. Oskeau's heart begins to pound with fear and excitement after he sees what he has done. Puddle desperately tries to escape from the boy by running back into the cave. Oskeau takes a deep breath, looks at the cave, stands up, turns and runs into the dark forest.

Frightened, the young boy runs as far as his feet will take him. He does not know where he is going, but the air feels good to Oskeau and he enjoys his newfound freedom. He continues running until his chest burns with each short breath he takes. The cold night breeze cools his wet skin. Oskeau sits down at the base of a tree and begins to shiver from the cold. The forest is dark here, for deep in the woods the canopy allows little moonlight to penetrate its leafy thickness. As he huddles against the tree, anxiety and apprehension of his new unfamiliar surroundings begin to play with his mind, and he starts to see things all around him. He holds his necklace tightly for comfort and closes his eyes as he hides from the forest's trickery.

Oskeau is nearly asleep when he feels his hands warm against the stone of his necklace. The amulet begins to glow dimly in the darkness, and the small boy opens his eyes wide in wonder. He stares in amazement at his necklace, clenching it tightly, absorbing all of the metal's warmth. A noise then startles him, and he turns his head, peering into the forest. A rustling from above catches his ear, and he snaps his head to look up to the canopy. His large reflecting eyes follow a small beam of moonlight that has begun to

gradually penetrate the forest, casting a blue hue from the heavens to the ground.

It is not much light, but he is able to make out most of his surroundings. Oskeau is intrigued by the light's sudden appearance, and he slowly walks towards it, reaching his hand inside the light. Playfully, Oskeau smiles at the shadows his fingers create in the streaking light, and as he stares at his hand, he hears the same voice as before, but this time it seems much closer. He spins around, but sees nothing in the forest. The deep, chilling voice speaks again, and Oskeau stumbles backwards into the light. He loses his footing, falls back, and crashes through the forest floor. He feels a sensation he has never felt before, as if the wind is blowing up from below him, and his stomach begins to turn from the sensation. He starts to kick his legs and arms but he can't find anything solid. Oskeau reaches up, watching the light slowly dim away to nothing.

Oskeau wakes to the feeling of cold sand against his skin. He opens his eyes to total darkness. Alone, cold, and blind, Oskeau grasps his necklace and it begins to glow. With the soft light from his chest, he explores this dark world. He digs his hands into the soft sand and tries to climb the steep incline before him. The farther he goes, the steeper he climbs. His muscles ache as he struggles to continue his ascent. His necklace pulses with every step, keeping him warm in the cold emptiness. Oskeau can see a beam of light that shines down from the dark abyss above and falls onto a narrow door carved into a stone wall. Oskeau reaches the top of the summit and slowly reaches into the light. It warms his skin and he stares at his hand as it manipulates the heavenly beam. Oskeau walks into the light and looks up into the brilliance that shines from above. He closes his eyes and embraces the warmth, breathing heavily and smiling at the peace he feels. Oskeau opens his eyes and faces the great door. Squinting into the light, he can see nothing beyond the doorway. He looks down and sees markings carved into the stone around his feet. Oskeau does not understand the symbols, but as he looks at them he grows fearful. He hears behind him the whisper that drew him into the forest, and he turns to the darkness.

Afraid, Oskeau creeps backwards into the doorway. Once he is inside the doorway, the light from above vanishes, and the floor begins to shake. Boulders fall behind him with such force that he is thrown to the ground. He scampers farther into the darkness and curls into a ball, waiting for the violent shaking to stop. Once the world calms, he stands up and waves his hands blindly in the dark. "A wall," he mumbles in relief, and drags his hand along the wall.

He feels an indentation, flat on the bottom but round on the top. There is something inside, small and smooth, with a type of hair sticking out of its top. He takes the unfamiliar object from the hole and smells it. It has no odor, so he licks it, but the object tastes like nothing. He plays with it for a while, but becomes bored and drops it. He continues his journey and comes across many similar indentations.

Oskeau reaches a gap in the stone that is unlike the others. He moves his hand inside the gap and grabs at something he has never felt before. It has a strange square shape and does not feel like stone. He runs his palm along its brittle surface and makes out the shape of a hand. His own hand fits inside the indentation, so he presses against it with an inquisitive smile. As soon as his palm presses firmly into the object, he feels a wind blow against his face. Startled by the warmth, he tries to pull his hand away. Struggling to free himself, Oskeau begins to wave the object violently. Then, a flare of pain shoots through his hand and up his arm. His hand goes cold, and the object releases him. He takes back his hand and throws the object into the cave's darkness.

The room begins to shake, and more stones fall from above. He puts his hands over his head, and when the shaking ceases, he opens his eyes. A dim light glows from behind him. Oskeau turns to see what it is. He looks to the ground and spots a single flame. The object he found and discarded casts dark, contrasting shadows on the floor. He stares in awe as many more of these lights begin to ignite, lining the walls of this hidden chamber. His eyes settle on the strange object that he threw from his grasp. The boy remembers the pain this object caused and looks at his hand that is now dripping blood. His glance returns to the object, and he notices it is changing. It has opened itself, becoming bigger, and its insides are flapping from one side to another.

What Oskeau does not understand is that he is staring at the flipping pages from an ancient book that is bound in the flesh of his murdered kin. The boy sits down in front of the book, gazing intently at the pages while carefully touching them with his fingers. Markings begin to bleed onto the open page, and he stares at them for a long time. He doesn't know what to make of the symbols, but the longer he stares at them, the more they rearrange themselves on the paper. His necklace glows, and a voice speaks to him from inside his head. The voice resembles his own, and unbeknownst to him, he is beginning to read his first words.

"Who opens the book of Ixkin?" he hears. He does not know how to answer, so he speaks out to the empty room.

"Ah, I-I do."

The markings fade from the page and are quickly replaced by new ones. As he looks at them, he hears his self-voice. "I have tasted your blood, child of the Delar. How have you come to this place."

As the boy knows nothing of his lineage or of himself, he says with a true innocence, "I am nothing but a slave with no master. I was l-l-lost when the forest attacked me and I fell into the dark."

The books slams shut, and the boy stares at the handprint on the cover. He feels more alone now than he did before and yearns to read more. He continues to stare at the book, and then an idea enters his mind. He knows it will hurt, but his curiosity is too great to resist, so he puts his hand into the indentation and waits.

Nothing happens, and Oskeau slumps his shoulders in defeat. Then a new sensation raises the hairs on his neck. The boy's head snaps up, his eyes close, and his jaw clenches shut. Pictures flash through his head with great speed. He watches images of his life pass him by. The flashing pictures begin to slow, and he sees images of this very night. His body becomes hot, and he clenches his fist, breathing in quick, short breaths. He sees Puddle throw his stone into the woods. He sees a brilliant flash of light and Puddle squirming on the ground. He sees himself running through the forest and then the beam of light from above, just before the forest floor vanishes under his feet. Everything goes dark again, and his hand is released. The book opens, flipping its pages, and when the pages stop shuffling, the markings appear again.

When he reads the page this time, he hears not his own voice but that of another, deep and calm. "You should be the slave of no one, my child. You have great power inside of you. Bind yourself to me, and I will teach you to use this power. I will teach you about the world and all the creatures in it. I will grant you limitless power, so one day you will be the master."

Oskeau is filled with excitement, as he likes the idea of learning very much. "Y-y-es, I will bind myself t-t-to-o-o you. Will you be my new master?"

"Place your hand upon me, my child."

Oskeau places his hand on the book. The same feeling of pain returns as the book pierces his flesh, and blood rises around his fingers. The book's light ashy cover grows dark, and Oskeau watches as the book's skin changes from brittle and broken to healthy and smooth. His eyes become heavy, and he soon falls asleep next to the book.

Oskeau wakes feeling very hungry. He looks at the book, and there is an apple beside it waiting for him. He pounces on the offering and devours it with a ravenous hunger. The apple warms his belly, and he feels fuller than he can ever remember. A strength fills his aching arms as he stretches and rubs his belly. He does not know whether it is night or day, for the only light he can see is that of the candles flickering on the walls. He looks next to him and feels comfort at the sight of the book. He crawls to it to see if there are markings on the page waiting for him. He looks down at the book's pages.

"My fallen son, now begins your new life. Take me into your hands and embrace your destiny."

Oskeau takes the Ixkin onto his lap and eagerly begins to read the markings that appear.

CHAPTER SEVEN

Waking suddenly, Taeau gasps for air. He rubs his swollen, bloodshot eyes and wipes the sweat from his forehead. He looks up at the moon, and his eyes shimmer, reflecting the moonlight. Taeau pushes himself to his feet and wraps his bed furs around his shoulders. Making sure not to wake Mia-Koda, the boy slips out of camp. He shivers as he steps on cool leaves filled with their payment of dew from the night. Taeau stands taller now than the day he left his home in the Menoli city nine years ago. His body has grown lean and strong, and his hair has become wild and confused like his spirit. Walking away from camp, he comes to a small stream in the forest and takes a drink of the cool water. He stares at his reflection as droplets from his lips ripple through his image. Taeau sits down against a tree and stares numbly at the moving stream. Taeau has always liked the sound of gurgling water and the way it clears his mind.

As Taeau lingers, the darkness of the night fades and the moisture of the coming dawn gathers on the plants and trees. A tugging on his blanket shakes him from his mindless wondering. Tib is trying to get his attention and bring him back to camp.

"Oh, ok, Tib, I'm coming," Taeau manages through a yawn and stands up to follow the Wicker.

Back at camp, Taeau notices that Mia-Koda has started cooking breakfast. Tib goes to work cleaning, and Taeau follows him and starts his morning chores. The silence of their morning routine is interrupted as Broomay begins to stomp and snort at the ground.

"Whoa, boy, settle down," says Taeau as he strokes the horse's neck in reassurance. Taeau combs Broomay's thick, knotted hair with his fingers to calm the animal. He looks up over the horse's mane and stumbles backwards, startled at the sight of a young woman. She is dressed in strange clothes and stands beside a horse with patch-colored fur. She lets down her hood, revealing her face and long black hair. Motionless, Taeau stares at her and does not move.

"Mia-Koda!" yells Taeau, but the old woman's hand is already on his shoulder, reassuring him all is as it should be.

"Do not be alarmed, child, for she is here on my invitation. Good morning, Leotie. I hope your trip was safe and without trouble."

Leotie bows her head before speaking, "Yes, Abokswigin, it was . . . is this the boy you spoke of in your writings?"

Taeau looks at her strangely, for he has never heard another person call Mia-Koda by a different name.

"Yes, dear, this is the boy. Taeau, this is Leotie of the Enopay people." Taeau gives her a small smile and nods his head.

"Is he of a sick mind, Abokswigin?-I saw him staring at a stream, whispering to himself."

"You were watching me?"

Leotie pays no attention to Taeau. "I hope you do not mean to bring a boy with a lost mind into our tribe."

Mia-Koda chuckles, "The teachings of Alo, your shaman, is why he goes to your tribe."

Taeau has become annoyed at how everyone seems to be speaking about him but not to him. He glares at both Mia-Koda and Leotie. "What is going on? Where am I going, and why do I not know about it?"

"Oh, now you decide to talk to me? . . . well, since you have been so quiet and lost in your own thoughts these past few seasons, I did not want to disturb your solitude to tell you." Leotie snickers at Mia-Koda's words.

"What is so funny, huh? Who are you anyway-"

"I am the one who was watching you all night. I could have taken your head at any time, and there was nothing you could have done about it."

Taeau's blood heats with anger. "You think so? Well, why not try it now?" he asks as he reaches for a wooden staff in the wagon. Leotie smirks at Taeau, chuckling again, which only makes the boy angrier. She takes from her robes two short, finely crafted blades. Staring at her weapons, Taeau suddenly feels silly standing alone with just a wooden stick.

"Put your staff back, Taeau, before you get yourself hurt again," dismisses Mia-Koda.

Taeau's face flushes with embarrassment. His necklace dimly glows red, and he slams the end of his staff into the ground with such power it creates a shockwave, causing Leotie to step back in alarm. She lifts her eyes from the ground and peers at Taeau with suspicion.

"Leotie, mount your horse, and we will follow you out of the forest."

"Yes, Abokswigin," she says, and swings her leg over her horse and begins to trot off into the forest with Mia-Koda, Tib, and Taeau following close behind in their horse-drawn wagon.

The morning passes quickly, and Taeau remains silent with a clear scowl on his face. He refuses to speak, trying to wait for Mia-Koda to apologize to him for keeping such secrets. But as the sun rises higher in the sky, Taeau becomes impatient with Mia-Koda's quiet humming.

"Why did you not tell me about this?" Taeau asks with a hint of sadness. His mentor looks up at her student, who has grown taller than her over the last two summers, and answers him clearly.

"I am sending you to live with the Enopay tribe and into the teachings of the tribe's Shaman. The Shaman is wise, and he will help you find yourself and your vision. I have taught you many things over the time we have spent together. Alo will complete your training and help you better understand yourself and the power inside you. I have kept you away from others for too long, which may have been a mistake . . . I think. You have become too solitary, and your mind wanders to a past that you should have long ago accepted. You must take the journey that all boys must make and become a man. Alo, I have chosen to guide you on this path."

"Have I not been a good student?" whispers Taeau as he tries to fight back his emotions.

"Yes, child . . . you have. You learn quickly and do not argue, but there is more to life than just doing what you are told and following instructions. You still have much to overcome, and I cannot teach you how to become a man. I have chosen a better teacher than myself for this part of your journey."

Taeau has never understood Mia-Koda's many speeches about the man that he needs to be. He sits silently, staring out at the landscape as it passes by, and wonders when the time will come when he can make his own decisions. Tears well up in his eyes, but he dares not let one fall, especially with this strange woman so close.

"You will understand soon . . . when we depart you will be a boy, but when we meet again, a man will stand before me."

Taeau, sulking and wanting to make his teacher feel as badly about this as he does, brushes her hand from his shoulder and stares off into the forest.

The Black Forest has been the only home Taeau has ever known, and now in the company of a stranger Taeau and his companion's reach its western edge. They have arrived at the plains of Ora, a flat land of rolling hills and tall grasses. Taking his first steps out of the forest, Taeau raises his arms to block the bright light of the sun. He stands still, watching the grasses sway against the quiet prairie wind. Lifting his face to the sun, Taeau takes a deep breath, inhaling the perfume of the plains. The smell of the grass and dirt fill his mind with thoughts of his father. He wishes his father was by his side, so together they could listen to the soft songs of the golden grasses. Taeau knows it would be something his father would like very much. Taeau is startled as Mia-Koda rests a hand on his shoulder, smiling at him as they move on towards the setting sun.

That first night in the plains while sitting by the fire, Taeau is mesmerized by the night sky. It's as if he is looking at it for the first time. Free from the confines of the forest, he has never seen the moon or her children stars with such clarity. Overwhelmed by the majesty of the celestial heavens, he realizes how little of the world outside the forest he understands. It is nights like these when he feels most alone, and memories of his mother are the only things that bring him comfort.

As they travel deeper into the prairie, Taeau becomes more curious about Leotie and her people. Each night, Leotie arranges her bed in alignment with the moon's path, and when the moon is in a specific position, she grabs a handful of dirt and sprinkles it on herself. She then sits silently, watching the moon with a strange peace that Taeau is sure he has never felt. When he asks Mia-Koda about Leotie's strange nightly rituals, she explains that the word "Enopay" means "people of the great night star." The moon is sacred to Leotie's tribe, and everything in their culture revolves around its movements and cycles.

When the four travelers come within a day's journey of the Enopay camp, Mia- Koda explains to Taeau what he should expect when he meets the Enopay. "You will have to build your own hut and tame a horse . . . you will-"

Taeau's head perks up, "I will be getting my own horse?"

"Yes, you will learn to become a fine rider, among other things. The Enopay are great horsemen, and anyone who wishes to become a man in their society must have at least one horse."

Taeau has never imagined having his own hut. He has never lived alone before, and a deep feeling of excitement comes over him. "But how will I pay for all of this? I have no precious stones nor valuables to trade."

"True, you have no real possessions to barter, but I have secured your apprenticeship with Alo. He will give you a horse and supplies for a hut.

In return, you will obey him without question and become his student. If you do not, it will be a great insult to me." Mia-Koda smiles warmly at Taeau. "This is not going to be easy Taeau . . . many Enopay will not like you. They do not take to strangers easily; it took me a long time to gain their trust. Do not ruin that for me."

"I will not shame you, Mia-Koda. I promise."

"Hmph, I doubt you will, child."

The night's sky is especially clear, and Tib is trying to play with Taeau, waving around a burnt stick like a sword. Leotie sits outside of camp staring up at the moon. Taeau watches her as the thought of being left with strangers turns his stomach. Taeau thinks back to his parents and his old home in the Menoli. He has no idea where his parents are or if they are still alive, nor does he know the road home. These thoughts weigh heavy on his heart. He remembers his mother's sobs the day he left and the warmth she always brought him. Taeau grabs a handful of dirt and touches his clenched fist to his forehead. With his eyes closed, he swears an oath to himself that he will see this journey through, no matter how hard the path, so that if he is ever to see his parents again he can do it without shame. He opens his eyes and stares up at the moon, and slowly lets the dirt filter through his fingers. Taeau looks back to Leotie and walks over to her. He sits down besides her and tries to think of something to say.

"You come over here for a reason, or just to make stupid faces?"

Taeau, looks at her and begins to regret his decision to talk to her. "Are all the Enopay as warm to strangers as you?"

"Not many strangers come to our tribe unless it is for war or trade."

"What is it like where you are from?-What do people do there?" Taeau says in the friendliest voice he can muster.

Leotie sits silently, and Taeau can see her contemplating her words. She continues to look up at the moon as she speaks.

"We travel with the seasons, following the great herd, so you had better learn to break down your hut quickly. We don't wait for stragglers, and we will leave you to the beasts and the sun if you fall behind. We are the greatest hunters and warriors in the land, we are feared by all others. I am a tracker and an archer, the best the Enopay have. I imagine you will be Alo's pet while you stay with us."

"Yes, I am to become his apprentice . . . do you know him well?"

Leotie chuckles, "I do, and when you are finished cleaning his hut, you can come to mine and do the same-now leave me alone."

"Fine! Enjoy staring at the moon like a useless bush," Taeau says before he stomps back to his bed.

He covers himself with his furs and falls asleep. Taeau does not sleep well, and throughout the night he has the feeling he is being watched. His dreams keep repeating the same images. A rocky cliff and a high pitched screeching, then the sky goes white, blinding him until he opens his eyes. He does not mind the dream, for any dream other than his usual nightmares are welcome. A gurgling noise startles him, and when he turns to see what it is, he notices Tib snoring and choking on his own saliva. Taeau shakes his head and tries again to fall asleep.

In the morning, Taeau wakes to find Leotie missing. Mia-Koda is preparing their meal, and he asks her where Leotie has gone.

"She left right before dawn to tell the Enopay that we would be arriving today . . . I suggest you ready yourself for the day ahead."

Taeau lowers his head and gathers his things. He loads the wagon and takes a seat next to Mia-Koda. They do not travel far before men on horses surround their wagon. The men do not speak or make eye contact as they escort the wagon to the tribe's camp. The men sit proudly on their horses and carry their spears close to their chests.

"Who are they?" asks Taeau.

"The warriors of the camp . . . and the heads you see popping up and down below that small hill, not far ahead, are Enopay children trying to catch a glimpse of you."

Taeau sees the children look up at him and giggle; they watch his every move with great curiosity. Taeau sees the silhouette of the tribe's huts and smoke from the morning fires. The huts are small, and he can see they are not made to be permanent. They look, as Leotie said, as if they could be broken down and moved in a very short time. In the middle of the camp there is a large hut that rises high above the others: ornately painted, it must belong to the Chief, Taeau figures.

The Enopay people gather around the entrance to their camp and watch in anticipation as Taeau and Mia-Koda approach. The warriors gallop towards the camp, shouting and screaming, kicking up the dusty plains beneath their horses. Taeau grows more and more anxious, not having been around a gathering of people this size since he left the Menoli city. Mia-Koda watches as Taeau squirms in his seat, and she smiles as she sees the sweat drip down his forehead.

"When we enter the camp, you will get down from the wagon and walk straight to the main hut. You will bring nothing with you, and you will not look back . . . if you do, Taeau, you will show Alo that you are not yet

ready for his teachings. I have watched you grow up from an infant, and we have been together a long time. It is time for you to become the man that you need to be. I believe in you, child . . . as I always have, but I cannot help you walk this path, you must do it alone."

"I know there is a path in front of me, but I do not see it. I feel like I am trapped in the dawn, yearning for the rising of the sun to warm my skin but it never comes. You say there is a path and I must walk it alone, and so I will . . . again, alone."

"No, never alone, and one day you will understand that. Besides, Tib will be staying with you. I have tried to tell him he cannot stay, but a long time ago in a dark, cool meadow, he swore an oath, and Wickers would choose death over the disgrace of breaking such a vow. Taeau protect Tib from others in the camp who might want to buy or steal him for a slave. He has been a good Wicker, and I will miss him greatly."

"I promise," says Taeau.

Halting at the outer edge of the camp, Taeau steps down from the wagon and stands in the tall grasses.

"It is time, Taeau. Do as I have told you, and do not let them break you. Become a man your parents would be proud of."

Taeau nods his head and begins to walk to the camp. A group of Enopay stand like a wall between him and the huts. He fears what will happen if they refuse to move out of his way. When he reaches the Enopay, the crowd opens and lets him through. He takes a deep breath as the crowd surrounds and follows him. The swarming Enopay slowly trail behind him in an unsettling silence.

A young girl charges at Taeau and tears away a piece of his clothing. She raises it into the air, shrieking loudly. The crowd turns wild, ripping off his clothes and shouting at him. He struggles to move forward, shoving through the suffocating riot. A rock strikes him on the back of his head, bringing him to his knees. Blinking and kneeling on the ground, he can feel blood streaming down his face. He grabs the back of his head and feels the wet wound. He looks up, but has to squint to see through the cloud of dirt. He chokes on the dust-filled air as he struggles to his feet. The Enopay continue to abuse him, yet he pushes on and moves closer to the center of the camp. He is focused and determined to make it through the attacking Enopay and not to shame Mia-Koda. A female grabs his necklace and tugs on it hard, trying to rip it from his neck. Taeau and the stranger begin to struggle, stumbling into the crowd.

"No! Stop! Don't! That's mine!" screams Taeau as he tries to free himself from her grip. But it is too late. His necklace is already glowing, and the woman's hand starts to burn. She screams in pain, pulling harder on the necklace and trying to escape. A loud crack pierces the air, and both Taeau and the woman are thrown to their backs. The woman is left squirming on the ground, holding her nose that is gushing blood.

The crowd grows quiet, staring from the wounded woman to Taeau in confusion. The Enopay tribe steps back. Their mood has now changed from excited to fearful. Taeau sees the mistrust and anger in their eyes. He preferred the shouting and the beating to the cold, heartless stares of the people now.

Moving quickly away from the stalled crowd, he walks up to the main hut and ducks through the doorway. Taeau's face is caked with coarse soil that has mixed with his sweat and blood. His head throbs, his ears ring, and when he enters the hut, Taeau notices an older man in fine-looking furs staring at him. The man holds a long spear ornately decorated in many colored feathers. On his head he wears the scalp of some beast with two curved horns. The man continues to sit, and he examines Taeau from the far end of the room and raises his hands. The few elder warriors that have followed Taeau into the hut lower themselves to their knees. Taeau looks around and does the same. The man, whom Taeau has concluded is the Chief, waves his spear at the Enopay. They rise and quickly leave the hut.

The Chief then motions for Taeau to approach him. Taeau obeys and tries to appear proud as he limps towards the Chief. The Chief points at the place where Taeau is to sit. Taeau makes no attempt to start conversation, so they both sit and wait in silence. Finally, the flap to the outside opens, and a man enters the room. He is older, but not as old as the Chief. He wears no shirt, and around his neck are many necklaces with small pouches attached to them. He walks with a large staff that is curved at the end. His nails are long, and his eyes dark and reflective. He has a clean face, and long black hair tied back like a horse's tail. Following him into the hut is Tib, who sees Taeau and quickly runs to his side. The Chief then stands and approaches the black-haired man, while Tib pats Taeau on the leg and brushes at the dried blood on his face.

"I'm fine, Tib," Taeau says softly.

Taeau believes that the black-haired man is Alo. He seems wise, and he has a presence about him. The man begins to argue with the Chief, and Taeau suspects that the Chief does not want him to stay. Alo then hands the Chief something that makes his eyes open wide, and Taeau has a sinking feeling that the Chief has just been bribed. The Chief walks back to his place and sits down to examine the gift. He raises his hand and nods his head, but never takes his eyes off what he holds. Alo lowers his head to the Chief, walks up to Taeau, and motions for him to follow.

Relieved, Taeau leaves the hut, while the Chief continues to rub the object with lust in his eyes. They walk through the camp to its southern edge, and no one pays any attention to Taeau as he follows Alo. They stop in front of a pile of sticks and furs laying on the ground.

"Mia-Koda, as you call her, has secured you a place with the Enopay. Here is everything you need to build your hut. I will come by in the morning. Be ready."

"Yes, thank you-"

"Here is some dried meat for your meal and a water bladder." Alo then abruptly turns and leaves Taeau there, confused, with Tib by his side.

Taeau stands over the scattered materials for his hut, looking at them with confusion. He stares at Tib who is looking up at him with his one large eye. Tib's markings begin to flutter, and Taeau can tell Tib is as bewildered as he is about how to build the hut. Yet Taeau is relieved to have something to do that distracts him from the anxiety of his new life. Tib is good help to have, and he seems to know more about building a hut than Taeau thought. When the hut stays up for more than a few moments, they decide its strong enough to sleep in it.

Taeau feels a sense of accomplishment as he sits outside his hut watching the cerise sun slowly set, engulfing the sky in a rage of color. When the sun has gone and the moon starts its climb, Taeau enters his hut. There are a few leftover furs that he makes into a bed. Taeau wraps the furs around him and notices that most all the furs used by the Enopay come from the same type of animal.

Like most nights, he struggles to sleep, but tonight with the constant teasing from the Enopay children it has become impossible. Taeau can hear the children creeping close to the hut, then running away yelling and screaming. He does not mind the children because he remembers playing similar games as a child with Ven. Taeau lies in bed and notices that the camp has become strangely quiet. He looks outside his hut to see what is going on. Taeau observes everyone in the camp sitting outside their huts gazing at the moon. Small children sleep in their parents' arms as their mothers sing to them. He watches young lovers kissing and holding each other close, and elders staring at the moon lost in the memories of their youth. Everyone is at peace, and it makes Taeau feel utterly alone.

The darkness of night gives way to the rustic rising of the morning sun. The wet, life-sustaining dew that covers the coarse golden grasses now begins to fade. Taeau wakes to loud noises and movement all around him. He opens his eyes, but everything is still dark. He feels a weight on top of him, and hears Tib thrashing and grunting close by. The hut must have collapsed during the night, and Tib is trying to escape. Taeau tries to get up, but he is tangled in the furs. He hears laughter coming from outside as someone lifts the furs off of him. Taeau looks up to see Alo and Leotie glaring down at him. She has a nasty smirk on her face as she turns, shaking her head and walking away.

"Does she enjoy seeing me make a fool of myself, so she can give me that look?"

"I asked Leotie to walk with me to your hut so she could tell me of your travels. She does not understand why I have taken you into our camp, or why I will be teaching you the wisdom and secrets of our people. She distrusts strangers more than other Enopay . . . I think because she was once a stranger to our people herself. Come, leave your Wicker behind to rebuild your hut," says Alo.

"Where are we going?"

Alo turns to Taeau. "You will call me 'Gahano.' The word means 'spirit guide' in the Enopay tongue. You have not yet earned the right to call me by my Enopay name. You will also learn when and when not to ask questions. This is a time not to ask but to follow."

"Yes, Gahano," Taeau says, with his head down.

"Mia-Koda has told me of your past and of your troubles. Fear and guilt are powerful emotions that can destroy a man. You blame yourself for the deaths of those who were close to you, yet what could you have done differently? You must learn to accept loss and sorrow, stand up to fear, and wash yourself of the stink that is guilt."

"What do you know about what happened? You were not there. You didn't see the life leave their eyes and me just standing there in the bushes with my mouth open and tears running down my face."

Alo stops and strikes Taeau with his staff, knocking him to the ground.

"I know plenty of death, for I have seen more than my share of it. So do not think that you are the only one in this world dealing with the pain of losing someone he has loved." Alo looks down at Taeau and kicks dirt towards him. "Has my blow killed you, child, or do you enjoy staring up at me from the ground with a dumb look on your face?"

Holding his ribs, Taeau gets to his feet, "No, I am fine."

"Can you continue to walk with me?" Taeau nods. "Then keep up, for life does not wait for us no matter the pain we feel or the horrors we have seen."

They walk together to the outskirts of camp in silence. Taeau continues to rub his ribs, and as he does, he looks up to see a few Enopay watching him, only to quickly turn away their heads. Taeau and Alo come to a weak wooden fence that encloses the Enopay horses. The fawns stay close with their mothers in the center of the herd, protected by a ring of males. Far away from the herd is a lone black male, strong and unkempt. He is eating prairie grasses and staring out at the horizon beyond the fence. The black horse has a stripe down the front of his face that flashes as he looks at Taeau. He seems different from the others, alone, out of place.

"That is a newly caught stud from the edge of the flatlands. He is of a wild breed and is not taking to captivity or to the other horses," says Alo.

"Why is that, Gahano?"

"Some animals are not meant for captivity. They may be too aggressive or too independent in spirit. He has yet to be broken, and he will not work or carry any goods. He will have to be slaughtered for food and hide by winter if he does not change."

Taeau looks up at Alo, and then back at the black horse.

"Mia-Koda has paid for you to have a horse of your own. You will need to learn the art of riding if you are to survive in our world. Go into the pen and pick out any animal that is not already marked."

Taeau walks into the pen, examining the horses. He has never seen such finely kept animals in all of his life. The markings on some of the horses' backsides indicate who their masters are. After closely looking over most of the horses, he walks away from the herd toward the lone black male. The horse is still eating, staring beyond the fence. Taeau feels a strange connection with the outcast creature. He knows how the horse feels, being different and separated from the herd. He too has felt isolated and left feeling he belonged somewhere else.

Taeau approaches the black horse, and as he comes closer, the animal looks back at him and walks away. Taeau slowly follows the animal around the edge of the fence. The horse becomes annoyed and turns aggressively to face Taeau. He stomps his feet and flashes his marking as a warning. Taeau stands his ground, glaring into the eyes of the horse. Taeau starts to feel lightheaded but continues to stare into the soul of the animal. Time slows through his blurred eyes, and he hears each breath the beast takes through its wet, flaring nostrils. The horse senses Taeau's glare and stands on its back legs, swinging at Taeau with his hooves. Taeau falls to the ground, never taking his eyes off the creature. His necklace burns as he continues to peer into the eyes of the horse. Taeau senses great anger, frustration, and a longing to be free in the black stallion. The horse becomes more enraged and begins to jump in a circle, kicking his hind legs high in the air as he tries to show Taeau his dominance.

The loud noises have disturbed the herd, and they move closer together to protect the young. The other male horses face Taeau and kick up dirt as a warning to stay away from the fawns and females. The Enopay, hearing the horses' call, have come to the fence to watch. They talk among themselves and point at the horses as the chaos grows. One Enopay has taken out his bow, and grabs an arrow to slay the black horse, but Alo lays his hand on his shoulder to stop him.

Taeau's head throbs as the noise of the horse's breathing becomes deafening. The animal approaches Taeau, and with each breath dust expels from its nose like fire. The horse pushes Taeau to his knees with his powerful head, but Taeau continues to stare into his eyes, never breaking their connection. Taeau knows he must calm himself or be crushed in the beast's rage. He lets a peace fill his mind and reaches his hand up towards the animal. The horse tries to bite his hand, but Taeau keeps it steady and shows no sign of alarm. Taeau's heart begins to beat louder and louder until it is as loud as the horse's heartbeat. Then the rapidly flashing marks on the animal's forehead begin to calm. Taeau touches the horse's marking and it stops flashing; it glows bright and Taeau's necklace begins to glimmer. Their hearts begin to beat as one, and Taeau can feel a connection between them as if energy is transferring from his body to that of the horse.

"Be my companion, dark hair, and I will protect you with my life," Taeau says softly.

Taeau's strength is fading, but he rises to his feet only to stumble forward, losing his grip on the horse. The horse lowers its head and catches Taeau as he falls. Taeau looks up at the animal, and with what strength he still has, he tries to mount the creature. The horse lowers a knee, helping Taeau to his feet and onto his back. Once on top of the horse, Taeau lies down, hugging his neck.

"I will name you Akima . . . my friend. My name is Taeau, son of the Meno farmer Dirty Hands." The horse walks around the fence to find a nice spot to graze, and with a mouth full of grass it stares back out towards the horizon, with Taeau falling asleep on his neck.

Having witnessed the union between such a wild horse and Taeau, the Enopay are impressed. The calming of a horse with just his touch will bring much gossip to the huts of the Enopay tonight. Leotie, who has been watching from the fence, turns and walks away, kicking at stones on the ground. The crowd slowly disappears, and Alo soon leaves Taeau with his new companion, alone and basking in the early morning sun.

CHAPTER EIGHT

A shadowy figure strides through a fresh powdering of snow concealed by a black tattered robe with a satchel draped over its shoulder. A dark liquid drips from this satchel, melting the snow with each drop. The forest hides under the moonlight, fearful and aware of a growing darkness in the shadow of the White Mountains. This phantom walks out from the cover of the trees and approaches a rocky shore of a mountain lake. Oskeau lifts his hood revealing a matured and dark face and looks up to the moon that has begun falling behind the mountains. Standing on the shore, he dips his staff into the still water. A canoe slowly appears out of the mist that lingers over the water, hiding the far shore. The nameless youth drops his satchel into the vessel and steps inside the wooden craft. He lowers his staff into the water, and the canoe begins to glide gently towards the mountains that disappear into the fog. Oskeau lifts his right hand, and the thick mist that rises from the warm water parts to reveal a path to the mountains.

The canoe scrapes against stones polished by the ages at the base of the mountains. Stepping out of the canoe, the youth quickly swings his satchel over his shoulder and begins to climb a steep, muddy embankment towards a small stream that flows down the mountainside. As the young man reaches the foot of the mountain, he slides his hood from his head and turns back to look out over the lake. The moonlight reflects in his eyes as he assures himself he has not been followed. Once satisfied he is alone, Oskeau runs his fingers along the rocky surface of the mountain and finds three lines carved into the stone. Cutting his finger on a jagged edge, he fills the markings with his blood. The icy runoff falling beside him parts revealing an entrance into the belly of the mountain. He sets foot into the cave, and the mountain closes behind him. Here, he begins the long journey back to the chamber he has lived in for nine years.

With only the faint glow of his necklace to guide him through the choking emptiness of the inner mountain, he comes to an underground stream and steps in. Wading through the cool gurgling water, he takes a drink from its untouched purity. He follows the stream until it runs down a small crevice. Beyond the stream there are three openings with engravings over the

entrances. The youth smirks as he looks down into a doorway and sees the skeleton of a foot, long decayed by time. He sits down and crosses his legs, laying each hand on a knee. His head sways forward and backward, his lips softly mumbling an ancient chant. Small pebbles begin to strike the floor around him, and the mountain wall splits into an opening between two of the doorways. When the wall settles, he walks through the new opening.

Climbing through the roughly chiseled tear he created, he comes to a ledge hanging over a deep mountainous trench. The trench walls rise and fall into the black void of the mountain. He stands at the edge of the cliff with his necklace glowing pushing against the nothingness before him. A warming updraft rises from the cavity below his feet. The light breeze blows his tattered robes that flap noisily in the silence as he steps out into the trench. His foot lands on rock, invisible to those who were never told it exists. He comes to the far wall and runs his hand across the stone, searching for a marking. His hand finds the smooth engraving, and he steps back. He lowers his staff and places it against the wall. He whispers an incantation, and a light shines around his staff illuminating a door on the wall. He lowers his staff, and the wall unnaturally crumbles into pieces by his feet.

A thunderous bellow charges through the mountain as he enters the chamber. Inside, candles ignite along the walls of the cave he came to as a child. The cave is different now than when he first entered it as a youngling. Holes have been dug into the ground and are filled with a dark, simmering liquid. The book that cut his hand and spoke to him sits on a ledge carved from the cave's wall. The tall, slender youth walks over to the book and drops his satchel. He releases his staff, but it remains upright next to him, and he places his hand on the Ixkin.

"I am back, Master, and I have done all that you have commanded. I thank you for your wisdom and give an offering of blood as a sign of my gratitude."

Tiny blades from the book's face pierce the flesh of its servant. The youth lifts his hand from the Ixkin and watches as the book opens, turning its own pages.

"You have done well."

Bowing to the Ixkin, the young man speaks, "Thank you, Master. What do you wish of me?"

"You must finish your writings and complete the symbol of the Hhtuno."

"Yes, Master. It will not be long now."

He picks up a deer-hair brush and a skull bowl lying on the cave's floor. The youth dips the bowl into one of the puddles of liquid and walks over to the wall. The Ixkin floats by his side as its open pages fill with symbols. He dips his brush into the liquid and begins to inscribe the symbols onto the wall.

After he writes the last symbol from the book, he steps back.

"It is finished, Master . . . I have completed the incantation of the Hhtuno!"

"This is a night of nights, my servant. You have done well, and it is time that I fulfill what I have promised. You must leave this cave and become a true Hhtuno. Tonight, you will feel the power that only a Hhtuno lord possesses, and you will hear your Hhtuno name for the first time."

The young man's heart pounds with excitement, for he has wanted a name for as long as he can remember. He has been called "slave" and "servant" for too long.

"I am honored, Master."

"Kneel in front of the pool filled with the blood of the Uluani and place the satchel to the North and the staff to the West."

The youth walks to the largest pool on the floor. The Ixkin slams shut, echoing loudly in the cave. He winces as he bows his head lower to the ground. A wind blows within the cave and extinguishes the chamber candles. The symbols he has painted on the cave's floor begin to ignite in flame.

"Put your head over the pool," he hears the voice of the book echo in his mind.

Without hesitation, he obeys. A strong wind blows down from above, pushing his face closer to the blood of the Uluani. His scalp burns, and he watches his long black hair slowly fall into the pool. Once the last strand of his hair sinks into the liquid, he hears the Ixkin again. "Take the satchel and drop the feathers and beak of the Hornbill into the pool."

He does as he is told. The Ixkin rips a page free from its binding and sends it shooting into the air. Oskeau's eyes follow the page as it slowly floats down into the bubbling pool at his knees. When the page touches the liquid, it becomes still. The cave shakes, and all the pools erupt, expelling a thick vapor into the cave. The smog creates a tornado of darkness around the youth.

"RISE, MY SERVANT, AND READ THE INCANTATION OF THE HHTUNO!"

The dark cloud that circles the cave lifts him to his feet. He reads the symbols on the wall. With every word he speaks, the cloud circles faster and louder around him. A great intoxicating strength begins to well inside the

youth as he continues to read, speaking each word louder than the last. The billowing smoke continues to rise from the pools circling around him.

"Ruck-Ketsa-Ko-A." When the last words leave his lips, the dark swirling cloud slams into his chest, driving him into the chamber's wall. The darkness seeps into his flesh, changing the color of his skin and turning his eyes to darkness. He looks down and sees that the feathers from the Hornbill have bound with the cloth and the beak of the bird with his hood. He lifts his hand to his face and looks at his changed skin, and he touches his bald scalp. A laughing sound echoes in the cave, and he turns his black eyes to the Ixkin resting back in its rightful place. He opens his hand and his staff rises, soaring through the darkness of the cave. He comes to the book and places his hand on the cover.

"Open me for the first time, not as my servant but as a lord of the Hhtuno. Open my pages, and look upon your name."

He slowly opens the book and stares in anticipation as the pages shuffle. He bows to the Ixkin. "I am ready," he says as he looks down at the page with great excitement. A black murky ink begins to consume the coarse fibers of the page.

"You are the Lord of the Hhtuno and Master to the Oota-Daboon. Now read your name aloud and take your place as a true Hhtuno."

The young man looks at the book, but sees only a page veiled in darkness. As he stares at the empty page, his heart sinks in disappointment. His fists begin to clench tightly, and the thick cloud around him begins to swirl violently until a light shines from a far wall. All of the markings he inscribed on the stone glow and reshape themselves on the wall.

"UN-NABUS," he speaks out loud upon reading the newly formed writing.

The word reverberates in the cave. His necklace rises, shining in the dark; he speaks his name again, and like thunder it roars from his mouth: "UN-NABUS!"

"Now raise your hand and release me."

Un-Nabus drops the Ixkin, and the slowly rising smoke from the pools swirls around the book, engulfing it. The dark cloud that swallowed up the book surrounds his hand and rips into his flesh. There is a brief sensation of deep cold before the pain is gone. He lowers his hand and stares at what the darkness has done. His hand now bears a scarlet mark.

"You now bear the mark of the Hhtuno. You no longer need to read my pages to hear my voice, for now we are one. You can summon the Ixkin from your mark when you need to look at its pages. Before you now is a great quest. You must regain the allegiance of the Oota-Daboon and reclaim the Len of Ituha before you can sit on the throne of the Hhtuno. Alone you cannot do this. You must have a slave to serve you. Go back to the cave where you were once a captive and find your former master, Puddle. The bond you share with him is strong, for a slave and his master are always connected. You must find him and become his master."

"Yes, Master. I understand," says Un-Nabus.

Un-Nabus starts to laugh in triumph as he reaches out his arms. He slams his staff to the ground, and the darkness swirling around him obeys his every command. Un-Nabus turns, facing the western wall of the chamber, and taps the floor with his staff. The dark swirling cloud crashes into the rock, revealing a tunnel. He lowers his staff and walks through the door. He turns back to the cave with a twinkling in his black eyes, and the cave begins to collapse. Once the last stone has fallen, he turns back to the darkness and begins his new journey.

A black Hornbill flaps its wings through a cluster of Mobu trees. Spotting a sturdy tree, the bird perches on a thick branch. Shaking its hollow beak and filling the large red sacs on its neck with air, the Hornbill bellows loudly. The noise echoes through the quite marshland as the morning sun begins to rise. The Hornbill dives off the tree, opens its large wings, and explodes into a dark cloud. From inside the darkness walks Un-Nabus, pushing back his hood as he assumes his human form. Un-Nabus's feet silently slosh through the thick mud to the place he has been searching for, a place he has been before. His dark aura follows his movements as he circles the Mobu tree and lowers his head beneath its high roots. A small puddle has collected under the tree, and Un-Nabus stares at it inquisitively. Pulling up a sleeve of his dark robe, Un-Nabus catches a glimpse of his marked hand before he waves it over the puddle. The creatures below the surface frantically fight to the surface as their wet home suffocates them. Shellfish, crabs, snakes, and lizards wiggle in the muddy water beneath Un-Nabus's hand.

Un-Nabus pulls up his hood and takes on the form of the Hornbill. The black bird bellows as it flies up toward the trees; it lands on a branch, snaps its large beak, and tucks its head under a wing to rest while it waits. Life in the marshland is slowly beginning to wake from its nightly slumber when the Hornbill snaps its head in the direction of loud splashing. A small creature, face deep within the mud, grunts and snorts while it dives through the marsh in search of food. A Muddler's head rises from the marsh floor before it shakes the mud from its face. Un-Nabus can see a large scar across the creature's face.

"Ahhh, no tasties, no pinchers, Puddle so hungry."

Puddle has become a thin, wild-looking creature whose scraggly hair has turned white and thin. Un-Nabus peers down at the ground where his trap is prepared. The shellfish, crabs, and other creatures splash and make noise again under Un-Nabus's gaze.

"What? Where?" Puddle shouts as he runs over to the tree in disbelief.

"Good food Puddle has found! Puddle is great hunter!-oh yes," the Muddler cries as he quickly jumps into the buffet of small critters.

Once Puddle has eaten his fill, he collects what is left and starts the half-day journey back to his cave. Un-Nabus follows Puddle from the trees, unseen. At midday, Puddle stops under a tree to take refuge from the sun and rest. He sets down his gathered food and quickly falls asleep. Un-Nabus takes this time to hunt and swiftly catches a brown-haired forest rabbit. Un-Nabus brings the small animal back to the place where Puddle sleeps, and watches the Muddler from a branch as he tears at the flesh of his prey. After picking at its meal, the Hornbill swoops down and drops what is left of his kill next to Puddle.

Puddle wakes from his midday nap with a full stomach and renewed strength. He cannot remember the last time he felt so pleased with himself, but as he collects his food, Puddle is startled to see the half-eaten rabbit lying next to him. He slowly backs away from the dead animal; Puddle nervously looks around, sensing Un-Nabus's eyes upon him. A darkness begins to permeate the forest, consuming Puddle with fear. He runs as fast as his legs will carry him, constantly looking back, stumbling and tripping through the underbrush. As Puddle runs, he slowly drops all the food he has collected, leaving a trail of shellfish behind him. The day is fading, and he wants to return to the safety of his cave before dark.

As Puddle approaches his cave, he stops and stares at the forest floor. He bends down to take a closer look, and his eyes widen as he makes out the imprint on the soft ground. He knows the sight and smell of these tracks.

"My cave! NO, NO, NO! Not Puddle's cave," shouts the Muddler as he slams his fists on the ground and slobbers in anger.

"Won't let him!" he squeals as he runs down the side of the hill above his cave. Puddle trips in his haste and rolls down the rest of the way, landing with a loud thud on the ground below. Crouching on the floor and holding his stomach, Puddle tries to catch his breath. But before he has time to stand, he hears the hissing and slurping of a long-tooth. The creature's massive tail waves in the air as it awkwardly crawls towards Puddle. The lizard's body is all black except for its blood-stained head. The lizard keeps its face to the ground smelling his surroundings with its long, blue tongue. The beast's body is covered with scaly armor, and small tusks that contain poisonous saliva protrude from his mouth.

The monitor stops licking the ground and raises his head as it has picked up on Puddle's scent. The beast snaps its jaws at Puddle, who is still frozen in terror.

"Leave my cave, you nasty beast, or I'll kill you! Leave me alone, PLEASE!" Puddle pleads desperately with the beast, half sobbing, half yelling.

Puddle begins to beg, "Don't eat me, beast. I will give you the cave, I promise!"

Puddle screams as the forest monitor lunges for his head, ready to devour him. He cowers, covering his face with his hands. When Puddle looks up from behind his hands, he sees only darkness. The monitor is suspended in the air, desperately trying to escape. It groans as its arms and legs struggle with no success. The darkness overtakes the creature, and blood stains the forest floor. The darkness that has embraced the beast disappears, and the lizard drops to the ground.

"Do you fear what is before you, Muddler?" bellows a voice that terrifies Puddle more than the creature that was about to consume him.

Puddle scampers away from the voice, but he does not go far. The darkness that attacked the lizard forms a hand and pins the Muddler against the cave wall. It raises him off the ground, and Puddle kicks helplessly.

"Don't kill me! What has Puddle done to you?"

"What has he done indeed," says the voice.

Un-Nabus walks out from the shadow and reveals himself to his former master. Puddle's body is frozen, a fear so powerful and overwhelming his breath stops as he stares at Un-Nabus. Puddle looks at the dark one's face but can only see his eyes, and his flesh immediately begins to curl. Puddle looks away, trying to avoid the dark one's glare.

"Well, Puddle, what do you think I have come for?"

"Not to kill little Puddle . . . he not worth it, he not worthy to be in the dark one's presence. Puddle thinks the dark one wants something, Puddle will do anything the dark master wishes."

"You are right, worm, but I will give you a choice since your life I now own. Be my slave until I release you, or begin your journey to the afterlife now. What will it be?"

"Puddle will be dark one's slave! Puddle will do what he is told! He has been a slave before and he can be one again."

Un-Nabus waves his marked hand over Puddle, and the darkness follows. The darkness surrounds Puddle's back. Puddle screams in pain as the black mark slowly burns onto his neck. Un-Nabus laughs as Puddle squirms with tears rolling down his face.

"This black mark will bind you to me, and not until it is gone will you be free." Un-Nabus then releases Puddle from his grip and drops him violently to the ground.

"The name of Puddle has been stripped from you, for you are now a slave of the Hhtuno. Defy me, and your punishments will be far harsher than the pain you have felt this night. And there is no escape, for the mark of the Hhtuno will always call to me and betray you."

"Yes, Master, I will serve you without questi-"

"Yes, you will! And if you please me, in the end I will grant you the domain of a grand cave much larger than this one . . . and I will give you the power to keep it. This I promise for your servitude. From this night on, Puddle, you will be named 'Gnyok,' 'slave to the shadow.' Now bow and show respect to your new master."

"Yes, thank you, my Lord," Puddle says as he obediently bows to his master.

"Gnyok, we have a long journey ahead of us, but first go back into your cave and bring me a shell."

"Yes, Master," cries Gynok, and he runs into the cave, picking up the first discarded shell he finds.

"Here, Master, Gnyok has done what Master has asked."

Un-Nabus grabs the shell from the Muddler and walks over to the dying lizard. He drops the shell into a large open wound on the beast. His shadow then surrounds the lizard, and it roars in pain. When the darkness lifts, only a mummified carcass remains.

Un-Nabus reaches down and picks up the shell that is now stained with the blood of the monitor. Un-Nabus flips the shell over, admiring the markings, and places the shell into a pocket in his robes.

"We leave now, slave, but before we do.

Un-Nabus turns, points his staff at the opening of the cave, and summons a power that shake the ground. Gnyok watches as his dark master destroys his home with a smile. When the cave has crumbled, Un-Nabus turns and begins his quest followed by his Muddler slave that disappears in his masters shadow.

CHAPTER NINE

Taeau bends over a paw print on the floor of the plains. He picks up a small clump of hair, sniffs it, and than looks out into the night. He grabs his spear and rubs his necklace, lost in thought. This hunt has taken him far into the plains, and his shoulders ache from carrying Tib. Taeau looks up at the moon with his reflective eyes, and Tib grunts from the satchel in which he is riding. Taeau takes a deep breath and a few strides before crouching over more tracks. His ear twitches as he listens to the plains around him. Tib's head jerks forward, and his markings begin to flash. Taeau hesitates for a moment before breaking out into a sprint.

Taeau breathes heavily, and his necklace shines brighter as he runs faster and faster. The tall grasses whip against his skin and leave thin lashes across his arms. He comes to the top of a hill and skids across the dirt as he tries to stop himself. On a hill across from him stands a figure hidden by darkness. Taeau raises his spear and points it towards the phantom. He can see the stranger's arm pointing at him. Tib screams as he sees a spotted plains cat roar from behind the figure and charge towards them.

Tib wiggles out of the sack on Taeau's back, jumps, and runs off into the distance followed by a trail of bio-light as his markings flash in panic. Taeau turns to the beast and runs down his hill. He plants his feet and slides on the wet soil before leaping into the air. Soaring high above the cat, he aims his spear and propels it towards the beast. The spear whistles through the night, striking the cat on the shoulder driving it to the ground. The beast roars in pain as it slides across the plains, falling from the fatal blow. Taeau lands in a cloud of dust besides the cat and grabs his spear.

Triumphantly, Taeau looks up at the figure, but the phantom has vanished. Sensing its presence, Taeau spins, turning his spear defensively. He catches a glimpse of the specter as a flash of darkness shoots him into the air and onto his back. Coughing from the blow, Taeau gets up quickly and readies himself for the fight. He groans from the pain in his ribs. The dark creature lets out a deafening screech before it soars through the air towards him. Stumbling backwards, Taeau raises his spear to attack. The wraith grabs his weapon, and Taeau can see its bony fingers scraping the spear and driving it into the void of its body. Taeau's necklace illuminates the phantom, and he looks into the blackness of the creature as they come face to face. He sees an endless abyss, and his mind begins to lighten. Mesmerized by the emptiness of the creature, Taeau feels a bitter chill raise the hairs on his neck. A memory flashes through his mind as he remembers what Alo taught him about damned creatures like this: *"They will try to hypnotize you with their stare as they feed on your soul."* Taeau yells as he breaks the standoff, pushing the phantom back. He digs his feet into the ground and throws his spear at the creature with all his strength. The spear vanishes into the darkness of the wraith's hood.

The phantom screeches as it soars towards Taeau. Taeau stumbles backwards, defenseless without a weapon. The specter claws at him with its skeleton hands and cuts his face. Taeau locks hands with the wraith, and a coldness starts to cramp his arms. The frigid touch of the monster tries to consume him. Taeau's necklace turns red as he tries to fight the cold. Fear brings him strength that builds in his arms, and he pushes back against the bones that are digging into his flesh. His arms ignite in a flaming light fed by his necklace. The dark creature screeches as the flames grow brighter and stronger until they consume both the specter and the youth. The screams from the creature painfully ring in Taeau's ears until the wraith explodes into flames, sending Taeau soaring through the air. He lands hard on the ground.

Taeau slowly regains his senses as he sits up. He can taste blood that is dripping from his nose and the cuts on his face. He wipes his nose and stumbles forward, dazed and hurting from the battle. A light begins to warm his back, and he turns to see a lit fire. Taeau stares at Tib, who is eating an apple and watching him contently with a smile on his face.

"What, what are you doing? Tib-"

"Not bad, Taeau. Your powers have grown, I thought I would have to finish that Jee'bi myself," says a voice from the edge of the small camp.

"You, I thought I was done with. I have never fought anything that powerful before. I did not even know how to kill it," yells Taeau in a quivering voice.

"Yes, well, Tib has prepared our meal so let's eat."

Still breathing heavily and covered in sweat and blood, Taeau flops to the ground by the fire. Alo smiles at Taeau, seeing him shake his head, annoyed at how such a big event like destroying a Jee'bi, with his bare hands is being treated no differently than as if he had just collected wood for the fire. Waiting until Taeau has eaten his fill, Alo breaks the silence.

"The Enopay are only a day's journey from here. They have made camp outside the Ga-Taga herd not far from the Msa-Oda."

Taeau's eyes grow wide as he looks up at his teacher. He takes a gulp from his water bladder and wipes his mouth. "Only a day's journey . . . but I thought I was not allowed into the city or allowed on the Great Migration until I am a man of the Enopay?"

"I have discussed it with the Chief, and he will allow you to assist on the hunt. You can help butcher the slain animals and drag them to the city. As for the migration, you are not allowed to take part in that, nor will you be able to camp with the tribe. But if you prove your worth, you will be allowed into the city."

Taeau looks up with both joy and irritation. To be included in the hunt at all is a huge honor. He has heard so much about it and the heroism performed by the Enopay hunters. But to be shamed again by not being allowed to join the camp is hard for him to deal with.

"Is there something the matter, Taeau?"

Taeau looks at Tib and takes a breath. "No, Gahano. I am very pleased with this news. I am just tired from nearly having my soul sucked out of me . . . that's all."

Alo chuckles and goes to his bed. Taeau stares at the fire late into the night as he dreams about hunting with the other Enopay hunters. He pictures himself slaying a great beast and receiving praise from all the men. He is embraced like a brother into the Enopay camp, and Leotie just watches from the shadows, angry about his victory. Taeau throws his stick into the dying flames and crawls into his bed, quickly falling asleep.

The next morning, they break down the camp and mount their horses. Alo comes up behind Taeau and covers his eyes with a blindfold.

"Hey, what are you doing, Gahano?"

"I have negotiated the terms of your arrival. The Chief only agreed if you were blindfolded and unable to learn the secret road to the Msa-Oda."

Taeau shakes his head in frustration as they begin their journey. The sun begins to set, casting a hypnotic hue of crimson over the vast plains as they arrive outside the camp. Alo removes Taeau's blindfold, "Tonight, the hunters will go on a scouting party to inspect the health of the Ga-Taga herd. I must go with them and bless the upcoming hunt. You are not welcome, as you are not yet an Enopay hunter. But I will not deny you the privilege of seeing the great herd undisturbed and peaceful. You will follow the hunters from a distance and wait for me on the far side of the ridge."

"Yes, Gahano," says Taeau, surprised and excited to be included.

"Once the hunters reach the herd, they will cautiously climb the ridge to look down at the herd. Once they have seen all they need to see, they will return to camp and the ceremonies will begin. At the camp there will be a large fire, and many of the men will dress in masks and other costumes. The hunters will dance and perform rituals around the fire late into the morning. They will dance in the hopes that their spirits and the spirits of their fathers will dance above Ga-Taga, blessing the hunt. The women and children will be beating drums and singing ancient songs of past hunts. Only after a successful hunt will they be allowed back into the Msa-Oda," Alo tells Taeau as they sit on their horses on the outside of camp.

Taeau can see everyone in the tribe busily setting up their huts and preparing for the hunt. The women and children gather wood and Ga-Taga chips for the fire. The men dress and paint themselves in preparation for scouting the herd. They put on their furs and headdresses and gather at the center of the camp.

"Make camp, Taeau, and once you have erected your hut, gather your horse and follow the scouting party, but stay out of sight of the hunters. Once they climb the ridge, wait for me at the bottom."

"Yes, Gahano. I will do as you ask."

"Remember your training, Taeau. You must not be seen by the hunters, for this would be a great insult and a violation of Enopay law." Taeau nods his head as he helps Tib unpack his things.

Alo leaves Taeau to join the hunters, and Taeau and Tib start building their small hut.

"'Follow the hunters,'" he says, "'not allowed to go with them, don't be seen,'" he says. "In big trouble I will be, like I am a child or a common thief. I have learned so much these past seasons, seen many things, and still I am treated with no more respect or welcome than the day I arrived." Tib ignores Taeau and continues to work, for he has heard this rant many times before.

"She just looks at me with those eyes. She's not so great. What has she done? Ooua!" shouts Taeau, as Tib bites his calf.

"What, Tib?"

Taeau looks down to see Tib pointing at the hunters as they start to leave. "Oh, ah, thanks, Tib. You can finish here. I gotta leave." Tib just shakes his head and gets back to work. Taeau mounts his black horse, Akima, and starts to follow the hunting party's trail.

Taeau comes to the ridge and watches the hunters crawling up the grassy hill. He avoids being seen by the men and follows the ridge towards the valley. What he observes next, he never could have imagined. In the early moonlight he looks down at a herd of Ga-Taga that stretches far into the horizon. The earth shakes under their hooves as a cloud of dust rises above the creatures. He looks down to his feet and sees where the great herd walked, creating a trail like a deep scar on the plains.

Taeau watches the calves stay close to their mothers near the center of the herd, while the males proudly strut around them. He can see the fur behind the males' shoulders glow, illuminating the herd with dim bio-light. This is mating season, and the bulls can be heard fighting for breeding rights. They pace in circles around one other to display their markings until one stops to challenge the other. The challenging bull will stand his ground, scrape the valley floor with his hoof, and snort his nostrils. If the challenge is met, the bulls will charge, ramming their massive heads together, crushing bone against bone. The sound of the colliding bulls is like thunder striking Taeau's chest.

Taeau watches in awe as the bulls duel. At times, some of the bulls stumble back and fall to the ground, dazed from the blow. They become disoriented, and many sit in place drooling and breathing heavily until they regain their wits. Taeau looks upon the Ga-Tagas' world and finds it peaceful and majestic. As he stares at the herd, his nerves are calmed, and his mind clears. Taeau falls asleep on Akima while waiting for Alo. He sees himself walking through a fog. It is dark all around him. He reaches out into the mist, searching for something, and then he feels a tapping on his shoulder

"Taeau, wake, wake up."

Taeau wakes suddenly and sees Alo by his side, petting his horse.

"An amazing sight to see . . . the Ga-Taga for the first time?"

"Yes, Gahano, a sight I will not forget."

"Dismount and let us walk among the sleeping animals." Taeau does not move from his horse and stares at Alo.

"Will they not trample us, Gahano?" Alo points at Taeau for him to dismount his horse.

"You have nothing to fear . . . for my ability to calm the minds of beasts is great. I suggest you take this opportunity to hone your skills and remember your training," Alo tells Taeau, who grabs his necklace in agreement.

"Yes, Gahano."

"Good, then follow me and be silent."

Alo leads them into the heart of the herd. They cautiously walk among the slumbering beasts. The calves snuggle with their mothers who are watching Alo and Taeau with a deep maternal glare. Alo signals towards a lone bull that walks in an open circle in the center of the herd.

"He is the alpha bull master and leader of the herd. He has defeated all challengers and leads the herd when it travels or flees from threats. All Ga-Taga avoid him out of respect and lower their heads as he passes. One of his horns is cracked below the tip, and his shoulder markings are different from most of the other Ga-Taga," Alo whispers to Taeau. Alo walks up to the bull and bows, "Lord of the thunder hooves, I come to gain your blessing on tomorrow's hunt."

The bull stomps his hooves and snorts at Alo, his breath forming a white cloud in the cool night. Taeau thinks it strange that Alo would talk to the bull about the upcoming hunt, for the Enopay are going to kill some of his herd. The bull starts to kick up dirt, shaking his head at Alo.

"Please, Broken Horn, grant us your blessing, and we promise not to harm your females, for we will only take what we need and leave your herd in peace," Alo says, bowing even lower and exposing himself to the bull.

The bull digs in the ground with his good horn, picking up dirt and grass. Taeau notices other bulls beginning to gather behind him. Alo does not move as the bull displays his power. Alo reaches into his robes, pulls out a handful of yellow flowers, and lays them on the ground in front of the bull. The bull walks up to the flowers and snorts again as he sniffs the offering. Taeau, thinking Alo is going to be harmed, reaches for his knife.

"Stand down, Taeau. Make no sudden moves," Alo whispers. Taeau stops, for when he reached for his knife he felt movement all around him. After a few snorts, the alpha bull kneels down and begins to feast on the flowers.

"Thank you, Broken Horn, for granting the Enopay hunting rights to your herd." Alo reaches into a pouch and takes out a handful of dirt. He sprinkles the beast with the dirt, which sticks to his fur and shimmers when the moonlight hits it. He then takes out a knife and reaches for the bull. Broken Horn stops eating and fixes his eyes on Alo, who pets his head and grabs the long hair that hangs down from his chin. He takes the knife and cuts off this hair. The bull snorts again and returns to the flowers.

"Turn around, Taeau, and leave the way you came." Taeau slowly turns and walks back to Akima. Large bulls follow him as he walks back to his horse. Once they have left the Ga-Taga, he looks back and watches as the bulls close off the herd to the outside. As Taeau and Alo mount their horses, they can hear music off in the distance.

"Your mind is wandering again tonight, Taeau. Pondering tonight's events or the past?"

Taeau looks up at the stars, "I know there was a lesson here tonight, but I did not see it, Gahano. Tonight, what I beheld was a wonder I could not have imagined, and I am thankful to have witnessed it, but the great number and size of the Ga-Taga only made me feel smaller and less significant. Even in their countless numbers every animal seems to have a place in the herd. Even the calves are important. I do not feel like I am a part of anything, nor do I perceive my life's purpose."

Alo pulls his horse in front of Taeau's. "Even in your confusion we have made progress here tonight. As to your first question, yes, here tonight among the Ga-Taga there was a lesson. I wanted you to see the herd in all of its greatness. Taeau, even the smallest Ga-Taga walks with the herd, helping it survive. The Ga-Taga traveled this seasonal migration long before the first Enopay drew breath. Many Ga-Taga die every season on the journey, but more are born to replace them. The only thing that matters is the survival of the herd and the protection of their young. The males fight only for position and mating rights, not for wealth or other such selfish reasons. Through those battles that shake the earth a great harmony is maintained. The strongest bulls earn the most mating rights, which produces the strongest and healthiest calves that are the fittest to survive. In the hunt tomorrow we will kill a very small number of bulls, and that will help weed out the weak and the old, pruning the herd's numbers and securing its future. It is the natural order of life. With all life there will always be death. One cannot exist without the other."

"I understand, Gahano, but Black Claw was the greatest and strongest Salali, yet he was killed without mercy or reason."

"You are confusing truths, Taeau. You believe Black Claw's killer to have been an evil entity. But are the Enopay hunters evil that kill fathers and sons of the Ga-Taga tomorrow? No, we are not evil . . . we must hunt to survive, to sustain life for our people's future. We have the power to kill many Ga-Taga, but we do not. We kill what we need and use all that we take. If we were to abuse this relationship and take more then we require, the balance would be broken and both worlds would suffer. When we go on war parties, it is not to fight evil but rather to maintain our balance in this world. There will always be forces that ignore this cosmic balance. They destroy life just because they can and leave only needless pain and suffering behind them."

Alo looks at Taeau and reaches into his robes, grabbing a handful of dirt. He tosses the glittering dust into the air. Taeau watches as it forms the silhouette of Broken Horn against the star-filled canvas of the night sky. The bull dances above them, illuminating the night as its nose snorts and its hooves pound.

"That bull we met tonight is Master of the Ga-Taga. He fought and killed the alpha bull before him." Taeau watches overhead as the bulls begin to duel. Every time their heads collide, an explosion of glimmering dust falls to the ground.

Alo continues, "He is not evil for what he did, nor does he lust for blood or murder. He has great strength and vision for a Ga-Taga, as did the one he replaced. Now the herd follows him and looks to him for guidance as the herd has always done. The path of a leader is a hard and lonely road. One day, a younger, more powerful bull will take his place. The fight will likely take Broken Horn's life, but this is nature's way and it should not be disrupted. You have a choice, Taeau. There is great power and wisdom inside you. You must understand the nature of life and not let your emotions control you. Every day in this world, all forms of life die only to be reborn. You must embrace both death and life in all of its forms and celebrate them as equals. You must start believing in yourself before others can believe in you, because one day many people will depend on your guidance whether you are ready for it or not." Alo waves his hand, and the dust goes cold and falls to the ground. He takes a deep breath and turns from Taeau, galloping off towards the camp and leaving the young man with his thoughts.

Taeau rides in silence to the edge of camp and dismounts Akima. He pats his black horse on the neck, "I think tonight, my friend, I will grant you what your heart desires."

Taeau presses his head against his horse's snout. Akima's stripe glows in the dark under Taeau's touch. The horse pushes against Taeau's head, licking his face.

"You are like a brother to me, Akima, and tonight I will treat you as one." Taeau takes the reins out of the horse's mouth and removes the furs he uses as a saddle.

"Run wild and free, my friend, for tomorrow . . . I feel . . . change will ride on the winds." He smacks Akima's hind end. Akima whinnies loudly and runs off into the distance. Taeau watches as Akima's glowing marks fade into the darkness.

Taeau picks up the reins and furs he took off his horse, and walks the rest of the way to his hut. The night air blows in his face, carrying with it the noises and smells from the camp's hunting rituals. When Taeau reaches Tib, he sees the Wicker sitting up, admiring the fires and the dancers. Taeau gawks at the flames from the fire as they climb into the sky; the sparkling embers descend to the valley floor, leaving long blazing trails behind them.

The dancing men surround the fire with their spears and bows, yelling and kicking up dirt. Most of the women and children sit around the men, singing and beating on various drums. Some of the women dance around the men, flapping their dresses gracefully, but only one female dances with her long bow as an equal to the men. Taeau can make out Leotie's silhouette wildly stomping as one of the tribe. He turns his head, trying to suppress his deep jealousy.

Taeau turns his back to the tribe and looks down at his small one-eyed companion. He puts his hand on the Wicker's head and rubs his smooth skin. Tib rolls around playfully, then gives Taeau some smoked meat he stole from an Enopay child.

"Thanks, Tib," he says before getting into his bed. Taeau lies on his back and stares up at the crescent moon. He feels lonely, and thoughts of his father and mother start to flood his mind. Do his parents still think of him? Would his mother even recognize him now? Taeau closes his eyes, trying to feel a connection to his lost family. He opens his eyes in disappointment only smelling the Enopays' fire riding on a soft night's breeze.

"Good night, Tib," he says as he pulls up his blankets and falls asleep.

The sounds of the Enopay rituals echo in his dreams. His sleep is fraught with swirling fire, billowing smoke, and beating drums that chase him through the chaotic rhythms of his subconscious. The beating of the Enopay drums slowly quiet and fades, overtaken by the dark emptiness of deep sleep.

Taeau becomes uncomfortable, feeling the cold of stone against his skin. When he opens his eyes, Taeau sees he is no longer sleeping on dry ground but on solid rock. His necklace begins to shine, showing him a cliff that plummets down into an endless void. Above, he can see no ceiling, just darkness, and the emptiness pushes against his chest. He hears something creeping up behind him. The noise comes closer, very close, until he can feel its breath chilling his spine. Taeau stands stout, ready to defend himself, but there is only darkness. Light shines on his back, and he turns to face it. He steps back, seeing two eyes of light racing towards him, and he stumbles over the edge. Taeau falls screaming as he descends into the depths, followed by the small orbs of light.

The chill of stone again touches him. Taeau coughs and gets up off the floor, standing naked in total darkness. A light from a flame begins to flicker on cavernous walls. He looks at the floor and sees small pools of black liquid bubbling, with small plumes of dense black smoke rising from within them. The floor is covered in black feathers that are floating down from above. By the light on the wall Taeau sees something that seems eerily out of place. He approaches the object with caution. With every step he takes, the smoking pools ripple and the flame grows wilder. He comes to the dark item lying on a stone shelf. He looks down at it and sees an impression of a hand on its surface. Taeau reaches out to touch it, his heart beating with so much power it disrupts his breathing. His hand is close now, and his flesh begins to freeze. He closes his hand, and the object opens with a thunderous crack that echoes in the stone chamber. Taeau's heart jumps, and he stumbles back. A scorching light grows around his feet. His body burns as the floor shakes, rumbling with energy. The pools of liquid explode, vomiting a noxious cloud that surrounds him. He tries to escape the choking smog, but the floor collapses and the world around him erupts in darkness. Taeau begins screaming in pain as he sees the eyes appear again.

"Ahhhh!" he yells as he lifts himself up from his sleep. Breathing heavily, he wipes sweat from his forehead and looks around at an empty valley.

"What is going on . . . where is everyone?" he asks himself. He looks to the horizon in wonderment as the stars streak across the heavens leaving blazing trails of light behind them. Again, he feels the presence of another. He jolts to his feet and turns to see what has frightened him.

"V-V-Ven, is that you?" Taeau questions the crouching glider that has come to him. Taeau stands still, unsure of what to make of this vision. The ground begins to shake, and the stars start to fall, crashing into the valley. He turns back to the vision of Ven. The apparition looks like his cousin, but its fur has faded and its eyes appear lifeless and grey. The figure stares at him and makes no movements or sound. Then the glider scampers away, avoiding the barrage of falling celestials.

"Ven, wait, I am coming. Don't leave, wait!" Taeau yells, as he runs after the specter of his cousin.

The faster he runs, the farther away Ven gets from him. The sky continues to rain down around him. The sound of the collisions is so loud that he cannot hear himself yell. Taeau notices that the valley has transformed into a lush jungle. The jungle is like nothing he has ever seen, for the plants are brightly colored and there is a heavy wetness in the air.

"Ven, come back. I need to talk to you, VEN!!"

He runs again, fighting the jungle until his body collapses in exhaustion. He falls to his knees, trying to catch his breath.

"Why run from me, Ven? Why do you reject me? Do you punish me for your unavenged murder?" He looks up and sees Ven in a clearing, with his head raised and his lifeless eyes fixed on something.

Taeau slowly walks up to him, looking down at his tiny face. He pleads to the vision, "It is me, cousin. Do you not have anything to say? Do not forsake me, Ven." The glider looks at him and points to the sky. Taeau

glances up and sees a large rocky structure covered in vines and moss sticking out from the jungle floor.

"I have seen this before . . . in a restless dream," Taeau says as he remembers dreaming of this large protruding rock many times before. He is forever climbing it, chased by the burning sun.

"Do you want me to climb that, Ven? Why? What is up there-"

Taeau turns sharply when he hears a chilling noise from within the jungle. It is a terrible roar, and the tropical forest grows dark around them. Ven is on the ground, shaking, curled up in a ball.

"What is coming, Ven? What do you fear? I will not abandon you. This time we will face it together. I will stand by your side, my brother," Taeau yells as his voice is drowned out by the gusting winds that have begun swirling, blowing his hair across his face. Ven runs off and vanishes into the protection of the jungle. "Ven!" Taeau yells again, turning back to the oncoming terror. The roaring shadow approaches with furious speed surrounding and lifting him into the air. He fights to free himself as he kicks and punches at the darkness. The empty blackness that has lifted him fades, and his face starts to feel cool and wet. Taeau hears slurping in the distance that grows louder. He opens his eyes and sees not darkness or terror but Akima staring down at him, licking his face.

"Akima?" Taeau asks. He looks down at himself and sees that he is covered in dirt, with many scrapes and bruises over his body. He peers at the empty valley, not knowing where he is. He cannot see the camp or his bed anywhere. He brushes off some of the dust. "I must have sleptwalked during the night."

Taeau looks up at the horizon and sees that the sun will soon rise. He can still see Ven's face clearly from the dream like no other he has ever had.

"It was only a dream, of course . . . stupid to think . . . ," he whispers to himself as he mounts Akima.

"Take me home, friend, for I do not know the way. Akima snorts as he starts to trot back toward the Enopay camp. Taeau lies down on his beloved horse's neck, resting his worn and tired body. As the sun rises, it warms his back and brings him needed strength. He looks up to see smoke rising from the camp's fires. He gives Akima a kick, "Let's go, boy, we have a long day ahead of us."

CHAPTER TEN

Taeau returns to his hut and sees his bed scattered across the valley floor. He dismounts Akima and starts to reclaim his blankets. He kneels down to recover his pillow, which is still wet from his sweat, and his thoughts return to his dreams.

What could they mean? Was Ven really there, contacting me from death in some way? It was all so real. He brushes his hair out of his face. I could feel the wind . . . his eyes, I could see the overwhelming emptiness in them. Tib kicks Taeau's shin and points at the camp. Taeau stumbles as he sees the hunters riding off towards the Ga-Taga.

"No, Alo will have my hide. Tib, you have to help me get my things together." Tib looks up at him while holding Taeau's knife and butchering stone. "Thanks, Tib, you saved me."

He remounts Akima, not having time to put on a saddle, and with a whistle he is off after the other hunters. As Taeau catches up with the rear of the hunting party, he catches a harsh look from Leotie who rides next to Alo. The hunters start to spread farther and farther apart as they near the herd. Taeau watches the hunters as they dress in their disguises. Ga-Taga furs cover both the hunters and their horses as the tribesmen try to blend with the herd. Alo raises his hand at the sight of the herd. All of the hunters stop and wait for their commands.

Excitement builds inside Taeau as he badly yearns to join the hunt. Alo makes a sign for the hunters to move in slowly. Taeau stops at the top of the ridge, watching the hunters as they stalk the herd. Sensing the strange beasts that are closing in on them, the Ga-Taga grow restless. The sentry bulls begin to circle around the herd approaching the intruders to protect the cows and calves. The hunters are close now, and Taeau can see them readying their weapons.

"Remember, Taeau, you just watch the hunt from here. We don't want you getting hurt out here," Leotie whispers, chuckling as she sneaks up behind him.

Taeau stares at her as she moves down the ridge, clenching his fists and picturing the herd trampling her.

"She will get hers, Akima. Just you wait."

"I-YI-YI," Alo screams, and the hunters explode towards the herd. They toss off their furs, chasing the stampeding animals. The Ga-Taga herd springs to life, each animal following the one before it. Taeau sees how effective the markings behind their shoulders are. A great streak of color fills the herd, distorting his vision. The hunters all yell and chase the bulls as they throw their spears and shoot their arrows.

"Let's go!" Taeau yells as he kicks Akima, and they race down to the action. The energy and noise from the hunt is intoxicating. Taeau watches the hunters in amazement at their skills on horseback. Taeau finds a fallen bull and dismounts Akima. He kneels by the massive animal and marvels at its great size; he feels honored to be among such magnificent creatures. Taeau takes out his knife and butchering stone and begins to gut his first bull. The work is slow and hard, but it feels good to be part of something for a change. Taeau's arms and back begin to ache, so he sits back to take a break.

He looks up to see what the others are doing. Men dance and celebrate around their kills, while others finish off lone bulls they have separated from the herd. In the distance, near the horizon, a giant cloud of dust rises from the fleeing animals. Alo walks around blessing and honoring the hunters by splashing blood over their bodies. Akima has scampered off to graze on the ridge, and is now running around kicking his legs wildly. Taeau sees Leotie in the distance kneeling down by her kill. She looks back at Taeau for a moment, then quickly turns her back to him. Taeau just stares at her for a while, shaking his head in anger.

"Still even now she still finds it in her heart to hate me." He looks around for Akima, but he sees something that alarms him. With all the hunters' attention on their kills, no one has noticed a bull that has doubled back. It is the alpha bull Broken Horn that he met last night. He has two broken spears sticking out of his body, and foam drips from his mouth and nostrils. It looks as if the beast is ready to fall, but he stomps the ground ready to charge. Taeau gets up and yells and points at the bull. He sees what has caught the bull's attention. Crazy with anger and near death, the animal shakes its head and stomps the ground furiously.

"Leotie!" he yells, but it is no use. She is too far away to hear him.

The bull raises its head, roars at the sun, and starts to charge. Taeau has no horse to ride or weapon to carry. His only instinct is to chase the charging beast. Fear fuels his body as he races to catch up with the bull. His feet start to move at an unnatural pace until he is running at speeds greater than any normal man. No! Not again, not in front of me, I won't let it happen! Taeau screams silently to himself as his body flies across the valley. His necklace shines brilliantly, leaving trails of light behind him as he runs. The burst of light catches the attention of the hunters. They are shocked and confused at what they see: a rabid bull charging at Leotie, followed by Taeau running so swiftly his body is blurred and busting with light.

The only thing Taeau hears is the sound of the wind in his ears. His body pulses with energy as he closes in on the bull. Hearing a loud noise behind her, Leotie turns to see the giant beast racing toward her. Leotie dives to the ground in an attempt to dodge the charging bull. The bull strikes her ankle as it runs past, tossing her into the air. The bull pivots, twisting its immense body and weight to finish off his target. Broken Horn lowers his massive head, digging his hooves in the ground and snorting with large, snot-filled breaths. With a head-twisting roar, the bull lunges with the last of his exceptional strength as he lifts his front hooves off the ground. Leotie looks up from the ground to see the bull standing on its hind legs ready to crush her. She curls up in a ball crying loudly for help. Taeau leaps over Leotie and charges shoulder-first into the bull.

The energy of the collision shakes the valley and spooks the horses of the Enopay hunters who have come to their aid. Leotie watches as Taeau holds the bull by its horns in an effort to knock the beast off its feet. Light shines from his necklace, and blood pours from Taeau's mouth, nose, and ears. Taeau's mind becomes lighter and his eyes heavier as his face presses against the forehead of the bull. Taeau looks to the floor of the valley and sees a pool of blood. Taeau is losing ground as the bull pushes against him. Then he hears the bull roar, and the animal lifts Taeau into the air and knocks him to his back. Taeau hits the ground hard, landing on his side. He looks up and stares into the rabid eye of the bull. Suddenly, a spear strikes the beast's neck and brings him down beside Taeau. The Ga-Taga falls, covering Taeau with a cloud of dirt.

The smell of fresh blood and earth enters his mind with every breath. Taeau can hear the loud, gargled breaths of Broken Horn. He looks into the bull's eyes as they both lie on the ground. He watches as more spears and arrows strike the fallen bull. Taeau's eyes well up with tears, and his heart fills not with relief but with sadness as the bull is slaughtered. He was the greatest of his kind, the leader of the great herd, but now helpless and broken, the majestic beast takes his last breath. Taeau watches as the beast's eyes roll back into its head, and Taeau can only think of the moment Black Claw died.

"Taeau, are you alright?" asks Alo as he splashes Taeau with water to rouse him.

Taeau is helped to his feet and feels pain in his head and side. Holding his ribs, he says, "Yes, Gahano. I know I was not to interfere with the hunt, but I saw the beast charging Leotie and I did what I thought I should. Do not be disappointed with me."

"Disappointed! After bringing down Broken Horn, the Ga-Taga's mightiest bull, with your bare hands!" Alo grabs Taeau's arm and raises it into the air. Cheers come from all around as the hunters honor his courageous deeds. He looks down to see Leotie's head buried in her arms as a hunter dresses a splint for her ankle.

During the ride back to camp, hunters gather around Taeau to talk about the hunt. He has become a celebrity in the camp and everyone wants to talk to him. The hunting party approaches the camp, and the tribe's children run out to see their fathers. They look in awe at the animals that were killed, shouting praise to the brave hunters. Everyone is happy and excited knowing they will soon return to their beloved city. As the Enopay break down camp and ready for the trip to the Msa-Oda, the women begin to sing, raising the tribe's spirits even higher.

During the trip to the Msa-Oda, the men talk about the hunt, the children play, and the women pull wooden sleds that hold supplies and slain Ga-Taga. Each sled is pulled by six women who sing and gossip during the joyous walk to the city. Stories of what Taeau did during the hunt have passed through many ears in the camp, and the tale becomes more fantastic every time it is retold. The children no longer play pranks on Taeau but mimic his battle with the great Broken Horn as they wrestle each other to the ground. Taeau looks back to see Leotie hunched over her horse at the end of the line.

As the journey continues, the talking, singing, and laughter begin to die down. Taeau can see the excitement in the Enopay as they climb a steep grassy hill. In the fading light as the sun finishes its journey to the other side of the heavens, Taeau looks upon the city for the first time. It is more magnificent than he had imagined. The Msa-Oda is carved into the side of a wind-blown canyon that rises from the valley floor. Many torches dimly light the city, and Taeau hears drums beating and horns blowing from within it. Taeau watches as men wave torches inside the city signaling to the tribe at it approaches the city.

Alo rides up to Taeau. "It has been an eventful day Taeau. You have won the acceptance of the people, and your Gahano is proud of you. Like our mother the moon, you have come to the end of a phase, and are now empty and ready to begin anew. You, like our great mother, will shine for all to see and will be embraced. A new beginning is before you. An Enopay man you will soon be. I am sad to say that until you are a man, you are not welcome into the Ny-a-Oda, and will not be able to join in the celebration tonight. Wait for me in the city, and when the moon starts to fall back behind the stars, I will come to you for your final lesson." Taeau nods his head in understanding as Alo rides away.

The Enopay have reached the base of the formation, and they start up the Path of Silent Steps towards the city. Everyone walks in silence, listening to the men in the city singing and playing the Lament of the Msa-Oda. Horns, flutes of wood, and deep drums fill the air with hypnotic music. An Enopay woman, seeing the delight in Taeau's face, tells him what the music means.

"The song is about when our Mother Oda, 'the moon,' gave birth to the first of the Enopay. These early Enopay lived scattered throughout the lands in darkness and were afraid. They wandered for many seasons as vagrants in the world. With no home or protection, the Enopay were easy prey for many beasts and suffered from hunger and disease. It was Mother Oda who led the first of the Enopay to the city. She showed our people the Ga-Taga and taught us how to hunt them. This gave the Enopay great life and power. She told our ancestors that we must protect her city and keep it in her image. We have done this ever since, and she has blessed our people."

The travelers stop as they come to the gate of the city. Warriors dressed in elaborate costumes point spears and arrows at them. The Chief raises his hands and speaks to the warriors.

"We bring offerings as payment for entrance to the great city of our mother."

The leader of the warriors yells down, "Let us see these offerings, and we will decide whether they are great enough for entry." The Chief waves his hands, and three women drag furs of slain Ga-Taga before all the warriors inside the Msa-Oda. A woman hands the Chief a Ga-Taga antler that has been made into a large horn.

"Is this sufficient payment, guard of the city?"

The warriors look down at the furs and are pleased. The captain of the guard bows to the Chief, who blows into the horn, which echoes loudly against the stone walls. Many horns answer his call from inside the city, and the doors open. A line of warriors stands waiting to welcome their Enopay brothers and sisters back into the city. Young unmarried girls run in front of the Chief and toss cactus petals onto the ground. Anxious men run to their wives whom they have not seen in half a season, and embrace their families whom they have missed deeply. The celebration begins as they march to the great hut of Ny-a-Oda. Many Enopay pat Taeau on his shoulders as they walk to the hut, but they leave him behind. Taeau is so pleased with his newfound acceptance that he does not care about being left out of the celebration.

Taeau walks with Tib as they explore the city, staring at the sculpted architecture with curiosity. The pueblos are carved from the very stone of the

mountain, with paintings on the doors signifying to outsiders which family lives inside. Taeau and Tib climb up on one of the roofs and sit staring out into the night's horizon. He sees a cloud rising in the distance from the Ga-Taga herd. It is a magical night, and Taeau does not want it to end.

"Do you mind if I sit with you, Taeau?" The young man looks over his shoulder, startled to see Leotie dressed in her celebratory gowns.

"Yes, I mean no, if you would like," Taeau says with a confused look.

Taeau looks at Leotie's soft, deer-skin dress with its many finely painted patterns encrusted in beads and stones. Her hair has been tied into long, tight braids that hang in front of her shoulders. Her face has been painted with powder made from crushed stones of deep vibrant colors. On her eyelids a glowing dust reflects the starlight as she blinks at him. She limps to his side and slowly sits down, cautiously resting her injured ankle. Taeau has never seen her appear so much like a girl. They sit for a while in silence, glancing at each other only to start giggling. Tib gives Leotie a nasty look and turns his back on them both.

In a soft, gentle voice Leotie says, "Thank you for what you did today. I am grateful." Taeau looks at her, smiles, and looks back to the sky.

"I was scared for your life. I mean, it was nothing. Well, I mean, not that your life is nothing, but, you know, well, I mean, I did not even think about it." He feels like such a fool as the words leave his mouth, so he tries to change the subject. "Why are you not at the celebration?"

"I just wanted some air before I go. Do you like my dress, Taeau?" He looks at her again and is even more nervous as she shows him her dress in a playful motion.

"Nice, good look, ah, you, I mean, ya," and he laughs uneasily.

"Is there something wrong with your tongue, Taeau?" Leotie asks with a smile.

"No, there is not!" he says defensively.

"I did not mean to anger you. It's just, you seem nervous."

"Well, you would be nervous too . . . if someone who has gone out of her way to make you look like a fool comes to you dressed in fine clothing and looking beautiful with her face painted, speaking kind words."

Taeau's eyes open wide as he realizes what he just said, "I mean good looking . . . you know, for a girl."

Leotie smiles and laughs again. "Do you think I am beautiful, Taeau?"

Taeau's face goes pale, and he quickly looks away from her, not knowing what to say. Leotie puts her hand on his. Taeau looks down at her hand and then into her eyes. She blinks at him, showing him her sparkling eyelids. They both turn, gazing out into the night sky, smiling and listening to the wind blowing in the valley.

"Ahem." They quickly separate their hands as they both sit up and greet Alo, who is followed by Tib who is still giving Leotie nasty looks.

"It is time, Taeau. Leotie, you are missed in the hut."

"I was just keeping Taeau company. I will leave you both now." She looks at Taeau and takes out her knife. "Good luck and safe travels, Taeau." She cuts a lock of her braided hair and ties it with some string before giving it to him. "Something to keep you company on your journey." Taeau thanks her, wondering what she and Alo are both talking about. Leotie gets up with Taeau's help and leaves.

"I told you in time things would be right between you two," Alo says with a light voice.

Taeau never believed Alo, but his Gahano is wise. Taeau sees that now more than ever.

"Let us walk, Taeau, for we must now leave the city and travel down to the horses."

"Yes, Gahano."

They both start walking, and Alo tells Taeau stories of the city as they travel. He talks to Taeau about how the city was built and who lives in the pueblos that they pass. The three of them walk down the Path of Silent Steps enjoying the nice night air. The moon, unseen behind the blanket of the night, has begun its descent to the horizon, and a light morning cloud begins to fill the air.

"Where am I going, Gahano? Where are you sending me?" Alo looks at Taeau. "I am sending you on your vision quest. It is the last stage of your training. You will go to a place far away. And you must go alone, with no belongings, not even the clothes on your back. Tib has fought me hard, and I have agreed to let him go with you, more for his safety than yours. I have brought you here to say your farewell to Akima. I will personally take care of your horse while you are gone as if he is my own."

"Gahano, if I am to travel a great distance, how am I supposed to do it without Akima?"

"Do not worry about that now. Time is short." Standing at the edge of the fence that holds the horses, Akima walks over to Taeau and nips at his ear. Taeau pets his head, giving him a treat to eat.

"I am leaving for a while, friend, and I do not know when I will be back. Alo will take care of you." The horse looks at Alo, who bows to the animal. Akima brushes his head against Taeau's, and the stripe of color-changing fur that runs down his snout begins to glow. The horse stomps a hoof and licks Taeau before walking away. The mist of the early morning has grown thick, and it surrounds them as they face each other.

"You have grown well, Taeau, and tonight will be the last time you will call me 'Gahano.' When you return, you will be a man and ready to become a true member of the Enopay. The blood that runs through your veins is not of our people. It is old and from an ancient race long forgotten, but a brother you will be to me and to the rest of the Enopay when you return. You must leave on your quest immediately, so I must ask for you to strip away the clothes of your childhood."

Taeau does what Alo asks of him, removing his clothes as he shivers naked in the cool morning. Alo takes a small object from one of his satchels. Your former Gahano, Mia-Koda, has let me borrow this, as you have been under my teachings. It is the Moura Stone, a very powerful relic from a past age. Alo shows the stone to Taeau, but Taeau does not understand what he is looking at. It is a polished, round, light-colored stone connected to a rope made from silvery hair. Markings cover the stone, and there is a flat jewel of blue where Alo holds the rope.

"This is a gate opener. It will take you anywhere you need to go."

Alo takes out another pouch and grabs from it a handful of dirt. He sprinkles the dirt over the stone and whispers a chant. The stone's marking begin to glow as well as the jewel. He lets the stone go, holding onto the jewel. It dangles towards the ground, and Alo starts to swing the stone in large circles. The Moura Stone makes a loud high-pitched noise while cutting through the air. It creates a large circle of light as Alo swings it. Faster and faster, Alo swings the stone, and soon the open circle begins to close in on itself. Then, when the circle has closed, it goes silent, and a black void shines for a moment, fading away into a doorway. Taeau stands in shock as he sees a jungle on the other side of the door. He observes trees and plants, and can feel the heat coming from inside the gateway.

"This is where you must go. I will return for you when your journey is finished. Now go, Taeau, and become a man. Taeau, naked and confused, timidly walks through the door, and Tib follows him. It is midday when he steps onto the soft wet ground of the jungle. He turns to look back at Alo, but sees only jungle. He looks down at Tib, then back into the tropical forest. He recalls the dream he had just the night before in which he chased a vision of Ven in a place that looked similar to this, then he remembers his parents and the time he spent with Leotie.

He takes a deep breath and holds on tightly to the only thing he has brought with him, Leotie's lock of hair. He starts to walk into the jungle with no idea where he is or where he is going, but for the first time in his life he has a purpose. He looks down at Tib, who looks back up at him with his large eye. Taeau bends down and lifts Tib onto his shoulders. Taeau smiles before breaking out into a run and disappearing into the wild.

CHAPTER ELEVEN

Un-Nabus moves through the mist of a marshland surrounded by steep mountain cliffs, followed by his servant Gynok. The air is thick, and bubbles that escape from the mud release gases that turn the flames on Gynok's torch blue.

"Master, these lands sting my smeller."

"Why do you think these lands are called the Putrid Marshes, worm? What you smell is the slow rot of both plant and beast. With few winds and no run-off for the water, the stagnant stench of death fills the air. Few fish swim here, mostly snakes and bottom-feeding creatures like yourself call these marshes home. This is one of the last territories of the Oota-Daboon, an ancient warrior race created by the first Hhtuno lord. They are now shadows of their ancestors, scattered and divided. Many of the surviving Daboon are here, for few outsiders ever venture into these marshes. It is here where I will restore them to their old and rightful glory. This is why we have entered these marshes. Bother me again about another one of your discomforts, and I will feed you to a strangling snake who will digest you for a season."

"Yes, Master. Thank you, Master. What does one of the Daboon look like?" Gynok asks with a look of disgust as he thinks of being eaten by a slithering marsh constrictor.

"They are covered in long, thick hair, and a few of the strongest Daboon still have the poisonous quills on their backs. Their powerful arms have grown longer than their legs, and now most Daboon walk crouched on all fours. Over time, they have evolved a short rat-like tail, which stores fat and helps them survive long periods without food. They have flat rodent-like teeth and their claws, once sharp and lethal have become dull and curled for digging and traveling in the marshlands. But do not worry yourself about these things, my slave, because if you see one before I do, death will be close." Puddle looks around and stumbles as he tries to catch up with his master, Un-Nabus. "Gnyok, do you see that island of tall grass to the west?" Puddle looks ahead, shaking his head. "Continue there alone. I will meet you in the center. Do not turn around or flee, or merciless your punishment will be." Un-Nabus looks down at Gnyok's torch, and it goes out. Un-Nabus covers his head with his hood and transforms into the Hornbill. He flies high into the murky sky, disappearing into the fog. Puddle lowers his head and shivers as he trudges alone through the thick marshes without the protection of his master.

The grasses grow taller, hiding him as he walks. The sun is setting, for the dim light within the marshes grows darker. Puddle hears noises coming from inside the grassy island. He moves closer, slowly parting the vegetation as he walks. The noises grow louder and more intense. He sees the silhouettes of moving creatures and hides behind a dead tree stump. Slowly looking over the stump, Puddle sees large beasts feeding on a marsh lizard. The beasts' bodies are covered in mud, and their heads and arms are soaked with blood as they rip the carcass apart. One of the beasts stops eating and raises its head, sniffing the air. It begins to slowly creep away from the kill, moving closer to Puddle. Puddle hears a sloshing behind him and turns to see a shadow with two bloodthirsty eyes approaching.

"Ahhhh!, Master, help me, help!" Puddle yells as he tries to flee from the approaching shadow, but as he turns to escape, the other two creatures rush towards him. Puddle is frozen with fear as he shakes in the mud moving his head back and forth between the beasts. He quickly curls up in a ball, hiding under his tough leathery back. Puddle can hear the beasts communicating to each other in their growling language.

"Don't eat me, beasties. I mean you no harm. I have no meat on my bones. That lizard would taste better-"

"Slurp, foolish Muddler, slurp, such a soft and tender morsel you will be, slurp, I will enjoy feasting on you, little one, slurp."

A bellowing echoes from above the marshes, followed by a darkness that surrounds Puddle.

"Thank you, Master," Puddle murmurs as tears streak down his quivering face.

The beasts begin to roar and splash water towards the darkness. From the dark cloud that surrounds them, Un-Nabus appears. His voice is soft, but the ground shakes beneath him, "Sons of the Oota-Daboon, bow before me and rejoice, for your master has returned to you."

The largest of the three Daboon speaks, "I bow, slurp, to nothing." Then in his own language he growls, commanding the others to attack.

Un-Nabus raises his hands at the two Daboon, and the darkness covers their heads. They begin to scream, falling to the ground and tearing at their faces in terror. Puddle cries out and covers his ears as he hears their blood-curdling screams.

"Let you feel the true power of a Hhtuno lord, my children. Let great fear and pain seep into your souls as you hear your master's name for the first time. I am UN-NABUS, Lord of Hhtuno." The two beasts run off into the marshes, consumed with fear, bellowing in the night. Un-Nabus turns to the Daboon whom he has spared.

"This is a day of days, for your master has returned, and I will restore to you the power and strength of your race."

The Daboon slowly creeps backwards, looking for a way to retreat.

"Bow to me." Un-Nabus points his staff at the Daboon, and the darkness forces the beast to his knees. "I heard you speak the common tongue. How is this?"

"My father, slurp, taught me before I ripped out his throat. It is how I control my territory, slurp."

"You are a descendant of the great Daboon warrior Mar-Raa, and your blood is strong. I offer you this, my servant . . . swear yourself to me, and I will give you the power to unite all of the roaming clans. Once they have either joined you or fallen before your might, you will then bring them to me. No longer will the Daboon have to scavenge and live in filth. Join me, and together we will assemble the greatest army in all the world. Deny me, and only pain and suffering will you endure before your death."

The beast looks up at the man shrouded in darkness. "Slurp, I will join you dark one."

Un-Nabus smiles behind his hood as he walks to the side of the Daboon. He touches his staff to the beast's head. "You will be reborn tonight, and from this moment on you will be called Un-Ra." Un-Nabus takes a stone from his belt and drops it to the ground. "Your hand, Un-Ra, give it to me."

Un-Nabus raises a finger, and his nail grows into a claw that slices the Daboon's hand. "Now reach into the mud and grab the stone that I have dropped, and be reborn." Un-Nabus raises his hand and a mist seeps out of his dark mark, taking the form of the Book of Ixkin.

"Lower your head."

Un-Ra lowers his head as his new master commands. Un-Ra reaches into the mud and feels the cold stone in his grip. The pages of the Ixkin begin to shuffle, and then a page rips out from the book, shooting into the air before floating down to the crouching Daboon. The page begins to burn, sprinkling its ashes over the Daboon's back. Un-Nabus lowers his staff into the mud and walks around the Daboon, creating a line that circles the beast.

"Raahhh," Un-Ra roars, "pain, great pain!"

The Ixkin closes and dissolves into darkness as it seeps back into Un-Nabus's mark. Un-Nabus raises his arms into the air, and the marsh engulfs the Daboon in a cocoon of mud. Un-Ra struggles inside, trying to free himself as the cocoon suffocates him. Soon he stops resisting and falls to the ground, lifeless and still. The cocoon bubbles and swirls until it hardens around the beast. The surface of the cocoon begins to crack as it dries. Once the cocoon has dried and changed color, Un-Nabus lowers his staff and taps it against the cocoon.

"Rise, Lord Un-Ra, and show yourself to me."

Un-Nabus takes a step away from the mound of dried mud. The hardened cocoon begins to crack and shatter as Un-Ra slowly ascends from his mud-baked prison. His fur is dripping with a dark liquid, and his body swells. Un-Ra has grown and his shoulders have become broad. His quills have light-colored tips that drip liquid as they begin to harden. His re-made claws and teeth have become like blades, smooth and black, fierce and deadly. His eyes have evolved, growing wider and closer to his snout, and their color has turned from white to blood red. The beast raises his hands and touches a large stone helmet that he now wears. It is a jagged-edged helmet with burning symbols covering it.

"Lord Un-Ra, a powerful creature you have become. Now bow before me." Un-Ra bows without hesitation. "You will search out all of your kind, and they will join you, or they will die. You will take your army to the black shores where each Daboon will fill a sack with as much sand as it can carry. Once you have done this, you will march west toward the Whispering Canyons. You and your followers can kill and plunder all in your path. There you will wait for me at the Broken Stone. Never have you been to any of these places, but the helmet of your ancestors that has been remade will guide you. Do you understand?"

"Yes, my Lord, it will be done."

"Now go, and do not fail me." Un-Ra stands tall and roars loudly into the night, arching his back and brandishing his quills. Each quill echoes loudly and they strike each other as his back convulses. He then turns from his master and runs towards the other Daboon.

"Come, Gnyok. Our final journey together begins. We travel to the lowlands of Escamacu. It is there where we will claim the Len of Ituha. Once I posses that, your freedom I will grant." Puddle timidly uncurls from his protective ball and slowly follows his master as they leave the marshes.

Puddle and his master have sailed down the Catawba river, through the forest swamps and the land of the Kusso-Natchez on their quest to the

southern shores. Now in the early morning, he stands at the edge of the forest smelling the ocean on a light breeze that blows inland. Standing under what shade he can find, he licks his skin that has become irritated from the salty wind. Puddle knows his orders are to not stop until his feet touch sand, but he dares not leave the comfort of the forest.

"I wonder to myself why my slug of a servant has stopped and disobeyed my commands."

Puddle yelps in fear, curling into a ball at the sound of his master. He quickly uncurls and crawls to Un-Nabus's feet, begging, "Please, Master. I do not mean to disobey. It is the nasty sun and salty wind little Gnyok fears. It burns and dries my skin."

The darkness around Un-Nabus picks Puddle up by his back, moving him away from his master's feet.

"Better the burning of the sun than my dark grip digging into your slimy flesh." Un-Nabus watches with pleasure as his slave shakes at the thought of his master's punishment.

"Stand, Gnyok, stop your sniveling, and follow me to the water's edge." Puddle hesitantly follows his master towards the ocean. Crouching as he walks, Puddle tries to protect himself from the ocean winds. Once they reach the shore, Un-Nabus raises his hand, and Puddle watches as darkness spills from his master's dark mark and forms the book of Ixkin.

Puddle has never seen an ocean before and is confused by its vastness. He steps back, nervous as the waves crash against the sandy shores. He looks up and down the shoreline, seeing nothing but sand and water continuing to the horizon. The pages of the Ixkin flip, and Un-Nabus begins to read. "Yes, Yes, I see . . . it will be done to perfection." Un-Nabus looks down from behind the book. "Gnyok, have you ever seen an ocean sponge before?" Puddle looks up with a blank stare. "As I figured. Look here, worm, and do not forget what I say, or my dark fingers you will feel." Un-Nabus touches his staff to the shore, and the sand grows black. Puddle watches in wonderment as the sand begins to take shape, mimicking his masters words.

"Once you have dived along these ocean mountains, you will come to a place where light cannot touch. You will continue to dive, searching for a ledge on the mountain. There you will kill your companion. Once its blood stains the water, it will show itself to you. What you seek is a very rare blood sponge. When you see the sponge, you will wrap it in this water satchel. After you have done this, you must swim with all of your strength to the surface. Have you understood what I have spoken?"

"Yes, Master, but what companion?"

Un-Nabus reaches for his hood, pulling it over his head and transforming into the Hornbill. With his talons Un-Nabus grabs Puddle by his shoulders and soars out to the open ocean. Covering his eyes in fear, Puddle feels the claws of the bird open, and he screams as he falls towards the water. He waits for the pain of the crash, but it never comes. With his eyes still shut, Puddle can feel the ocean water splashing against his back. He opens his eyes to see that he is lying on the ocean, moving with the flow of the waves. Puddle flinches as he sees Un-Nabus standing on the water next to him. Un-Nabus opens the Book of Ixkin, and Puddle watches as pages begin to turn furiously. A page shoots out from within the book and floats in the wind. The page hovers for a moment, then in a burst of light it shoots towards Puddle, striking him on his stomach. His heart starts pounding, and his muscles start to spasm.

"Remember what I have told you. Take this water pouch and wait for the pain to start before you dive into the water." Puddle looks up at his master and says, "What pain-"

Puddle grips his throat as his skin splits open. The sides of his neck are on fire, and he starts choking.

"Dive, fool! Find the sponge."

Puddle dives into the ocean, and instantly he is relieved. Above the surface Un-Nabus takes out a shell from his belt and crushes it in his hand. Pieces fall, bubbling as they sink into the water. From the crushed shell swims a fish with large veiny sacs over its body. From its head hangs a long antenna that dangles between its black eyes. Its underbelly is lined with many flapping legs that propel the strange grub-like fish in the water.

Puddle frolics in the blue water as he tries to get a feel for the current. His body grows strong and his blood warms. He looks down into the abyss of the open ocean and sees streaks of glimmering light shining down from above. A swooshing sound behind him attracts his attention. He looks around and sees nothing but blue. He looks up and sees the distorted shadow of his master. Turning to swim away from the surface, he sees the small fish. It swims in front of him playfully. Puddle tries to catch the fish, but it moves too fast. Intrigued, Puddle swims after it into the deeper ocean.

The water becomes darker the farther down he swims, and Puddle loses the fish in the hazy water. He stops to look around and determine where he is. He looks up to find the surface, but it has long vanished. He looks down, and bubbles creep out of his mouth as he gasps at what he sees: a vast oceanic mountain range that plummets into the darkness of the ocean.

Puddle wonders how he is going to find anything in this maze of underwater rock. He thinks of what will happen if he comes to the surface

empty-handed. He thinks of the punishment that he will receive. Suddenly, a thought enters his mind, 'I will not go back. Master cannot find me here. I will live down here in the mountains, in the water, free and safe from him.' Filled with a rush of joy, he swims up and down in celebration. Then, Puddle slowly stops kicking in the water as he remembers what his master told him the day of his enslavement. The dark mark on his back begins to burn, and Puddle senses that his master is hearing his thoughts. Panic-stricken, he tries to remember where his master told him to find the sponge. He thinks back to the shore and the map of the ocean mountains his master showed him, but all he can remember is the fish. A light begins to glow behind him, and he turns to see what it is. An orb of light dangles in the water. The light mesmerizes Puddle, and he is filled with the feeling that he must touch it. His large eyes glow with light as he pursues it down the ocean mountain.

The further he swims, the colder the water becomes, cramping his muscles. He starts to hear a popping in his ears and pain in his head. Puddle swims into the side of the mountain and scrapes his forehead. The light goes out, and he wakes from his trance. As he regains his senses, the darkness begins to overwhelm him. Helplessly, he tries to feel for the mountain wall with his hands. Searching the wall, he begins to see the outline of his shadow. A light is growing behind him, and Puddle begins to shake in fear. He can feel the presence of something, something evil, something dangerous. He turns and screams as he sees an open mouth filled with hair-thin fangs, white lifeless eyes, and a dangling light. The fish is racing towards him ready to engulf his head in one bite. Frozen in fear, Puddle panics and stares at death that speeds towards him.

"Kick off the wall, you fool!" Puddle hears inside his head.

Puddle kicks off the wall just as the fish tries to consume him. He hears the fish ram into the side of the mountain. He looks back and sees the bio-light from the antenna now blurred by thick murky water, and pieces of fish that begin to fall like snow until the light dies out. Darkness reclaims the deep ocean for but a moment before a crimson glow grows, leading downwards. Puddle follows the trail of glowing water and his heart stops, "THE BLOOD SPONGE!" he shouts as bubbles fill the water.

This very small but vibrant sponge is now sucking in the blood from the dead fish. Its outer skin shines brighter as it absorbs more of the blood. Puddle moves closer to the sponge that clings to the rock of the mountain. He watches as blood from the fish is drained out of the water by the vampire-like sponge.

"Take out your water pouch and put the sponge inside it NOW!" Words from his master explode in his mind, propelling him into action. He grabs the sponge and wraps it in the water pouch. "Now swim to the surface, for the cold fingers of death are reaching for you."

Puddle feels the frigid ocean wrinkling his flesh. He starts to swim to the surface, his strength fading with every stroke. He moves fast, but his muscles are tightening and his lungs feel as if they are freezing. The water around him begins to fill with color, but his vision is becoming blurry. Puddle slows and his mind burns; he starts to choke and he touches his neck, feeling the gills around it shrinking. He tries to swim farther, but his arms fail him and he floats dead in the water. His eyes slowly shut as the cold waters take him.

The crackling of a fire and the comfort of its warmth stir Puddle. He weakly opens his eyes to see a fire burning by his side and grey wolf furs wrapped around his body. He sits up and looks around in confusion. It is dark, and his body is sore all over. He looks over to see a pile of shellfish by a log. The smell of the fish rumbles his stomach and waters his mouth. He sits on the log and picks up a very large clam. He opens his mouth to eat the shellfish.

"You did well today, Gnyok." Puddle drops the clam as he hears his master's voice. "The Blood Sponge is in good health, and our journey together is almost over. Now feast on your reward and rest, for we wake early."

Puddle wastes no time devouring his reward, and when his stomach is full, he falls back into a deep sleep. Un-Nabus disappears into the darkness, leaving his slave to his prize.

Un-Nabus opens the Ixkin, "You must follow the inlet into the everglades. There you will see many islands of trees and grass. You must find the island that is larger than the rest and covered in Brou trees. That is where the Mankah guards the Len of Ituha. Tomorrow will be the highest tide of the moon's cycle, and the glades will swell with ocean water. Release the Blood Sponge into the current that flows back to the ocean. There you must summon the Mankah and confront him. Unleash the Eel-Tu-Naw. This will distract him until they come. When they have arrived, go to the island and have your slave enter the cave. You cannot touch the Len until you have freed your servant. After you have the Len, you must go to the edge of the Whispering Canyons and reunite with your Daboon warriors." Closing the book, Un-Nabus raises his hand and the Ixkin transforms into darkness, seeping back into his dark mark. After the book is gone, Un-Nabus lifts his hood transforms into the Hornbill and finds a tree to rest in.

"Wake, Gnyok," Un-Nabus shouts, and he hits Puddle with his staff.

Puddle gets to his feet quickly. "Yes, Master," he says as he stumbles, trying to gather his things.

"We leave now."

They follow the shore to the bay searching for one of the many rivers that empties into it. Un-Nabus waves his staff, and the darkness that surrounds him takes the form of a small canoe. Once he and Puddle are inside the canoe, Un-Nabus points his staff inland, and the canoe begins its steady journey against the current. The canoe moves deeper into the everglades towards the tall marsh grasses and tree islands.

"There, Gnyok," Un-Nabus says, pointing, "is the island where the Len resides. Within that island the Mankah, guard of the Len, has slept for an age, protecting what we seek. He was once the citadel guard for the Hhtuno. But he betrayed the Hhtuno lord in a great battle, and today he will pay for his treachery. Once he is slain and the Len is mine, then I will grant you your freedom."

Puddle's eyes blink in excitement, for he has dreamed of this day. This could not be in a better place. The everglades are muddy and wet with plenty of cover and food. "Thank you, Master."

"Do not thank me yet. You have to survive long enough to be given your freedom." Puddle's smile disappears, and he starts chewing on his nails. The dark canoe stops on a shore adjacent from where the Mankah sleeps.

The boat disappears, leaving Un-Nabus and Puddle standing on the shore facing the island. Un-Nabus takes out the water pouch that holds the sponge.

"Gynok, take this and swim out to the deepest part of the river. Once you are in position lower the sponge into the water and squeeze it. Once you have squeezed the sponge, swim back to me or be consumed by what comes."

Puddle takes the sponge and swims into the river. The darkness that surrounds Un-Nabus swarms, circling his hand. He speaks into the darkness and as his lips move, the darkness around it grows and vibrates to his voice.

"Guard of Ituha, an ancient order whom you once called master summons you from your slumber. Wake and obey me, for I am the Atha-Ba, Lord of the Hhtuno and your true master. Show yourself, for I have come to reclaim what you possess but do not own."

Un-Nabus lowers his hand into the water and the darkness grows. With a deep thunderous crack the water dips, creating a wave that races towards the island. Hearing the crack, Puddle looks back to his master. He sees the wave moving closer and dives down to avoid being swept away by it.

Under the water he hears a deafening noise, so he covers his ears. When the wave passes, he opens his eyes and looks at his empty hands. He watches as the pouch quickly sinks in the water as if a large stone were inside. Puddle hastily swims after it, but loses it in the bottom of the grassy floor. Fear overwhelms Puddle as he searches for the sponge. "I will never find it, he will kill me, he will torture me, never will I get my freedom."

He starts to cry and pound his head in frustration. Then he remembers how he found the Blood Sponge the first time. "That's it." Puddle takes a fleshy part of his forearm and bites down into it. Blood seeps into the water in a dark red cloud. It floats down towards the river floor. Puddle follows the trail of blood until he comes to a rock lying inside the grasses. He sees the sponge gripping the rock and absorbing his blood. His breath is fading, so he quickly grabs the sponge and swims to the surface. He splashes to the top, gasping for breath. The water's surface has become very rough, and he can hear loud crashing noises behind him. He looks down at his hands and squeezes the sponge. At the first bit of pressure, a huge amount of blood is released into the water around him. So much blood is expunged that soon the water turns color. The more he squeezes, the more blood darkens the river and is swept downstream toward the ocean.

The sound of crashing trees and splashing water gets Puddle's attention. He turns to see chaos raging from within the island. Trees are being ripped from their roots and water is crashing in all directions, for some creature of great size and power stirs on the island. Puddle screams as he sees the Mankah emerge from the tree line. The Mankah looks like a common shell crab, but it is larger than any beast Puddle has ever seen. He does not move but rather squeezes the sponge harder with the shock of seeing such a creature. The Mankah has one gigantic claw that is half its total size. Puddle observes its six armor-covered legs and its soft, curled, wormlike body that it drags above the surface as it walks. Puddle looks up at the Mankah's two black eyes protruding high above its head. The body of the Mankah is covered in a thick, horny armor with large, thin, black hairs sticking out from the horns.

Puddle sees Un-Nabus standing on the shore of a smaller island, pointing his staff at the great beast. Un-Nabus and the beast appear to be communicating, but no sound can be heard. The giant crablike creature slams its legs into the water, brandishing its enormous claw. The beast lowers its two antennas into the water. Water begins to bubble towards Un-Nabus. Un-Nabus reaches for his robes and withdraws something that he shows to the Mankah. Un-Nabus crushes it in his hand, tossing the remains into the water. The ground starts to shake, and the water bubbles violently in front of his master. The crab moves deeper into the water towards Un-Nabus,

slamming and snapping its claw. The bubbling stops, and everything becomes still.

The Mankah takes a defensive position, waiting for an attack. Puddle sees the water sway back and forth in front of the Mankah. Then, from under the water's surface a giant lizard lunges out towards the crab. The giant beasts begin to battle. The crab hits the lizard with its claw and knocks it back into the water. A massive wave rushes at Puddle, and as he tries to avoid the tidal wave, he is swept closer towards the Mankah's island. The giant monitor slowly circles the Mankah hissing, showing its mouth dripping with poisonous saliva. It slams its long powerful tail into the water in the direction of its enemy. Puddle looks into the lifeless eyes of the reborn lizard and shivers. The eyes of the beast are blood-red, and from them dark liquid tears pour into the water. The skin of the monitor is covered in open sores that are filled with pus that drip with blood. The great claw of the crab snaps aggressively towards the lizard. The Mankah charges, trying to claw the lizard, but the monitor strikes the Mankah's claw with its tail and dives back into the water, reemerging behind the crab. Jumping on the Mankah's back, it bites and claws at the shell-like armor. Its attacks are in vain, for the armor is too thick and strong for the lizard to penetrate. The Mankah grabs the lizard with its smaller claw, throwing it to its back. Puddle turns, hearing splashing coming from down the river. Looking back and squinting his eyes, he sees something as it approaches. Puddle hears a loud roar of pain and looks back at the battle. The Mankah's claw has snapped off one of the lizard's legs and and is now tossing it into the air. As the leg flies over his head, blood rains down on Puddle. The leg hits the water and causes another large wave, and as Puddle dives under the water, he screams in terror at what he sees. Puddle frantically swims towards the island as if the water itself were on fire. The crab continues the attack, snapping its claw at the undead creature and grabbing the lizard by the neck. A loud snap echoes in the air, and the lizard's body goes limp.

Un-Nabus watches as his champion is killed. The Mankah turns to Un-Nabus and again lowers his antenna into the water.

"Is this the extent of your great powers, Lord of the Hhtuno? I have defeated countless foes many times greater than this fleshy vessel."

Un-Nabus speaks into his hand and lowers it into the water, creating another wave. "You are truly a great and mighty warrior, Mankah, a true champion of a forgotten age. Your armor is thick and your claws powerful. The stories of old do you no justice. You are far beyond my powers, but die today you will, and I shall have avenged your betrayal. Prepare for the emptiness of the afterlife guard of the Ituha." Un-Nabus bows to the Mankah.

The Mankah laughs, "You have no army, follower of the deceiver. I betrayed my creator so that the world would live not in darkness and slavery but in light. I have paid for my sins many times over. I live through the ages as a whisper who begs for a death that will never come. Now you speak to me of the ever-darkness that I so yearn for, how will-"

The Mankah flinches, stabbing one of its legs into the water. Un-Nabus smiles when he sees what dangles from it. A grey shark wiggles for a moment as the Mankah tosses it back into the water.

"COWARD!" the Mankah screams.

The Mankah stabs the water with all of its legs, trying to move back toward the island, but it is dragged deeper into the river. Puddle watches from the shore as countless fins pierce the water's surface, rushing towards the crab. Sharks in great number have followed the scent of blood and now come to feast. Three fins many times larger than the rest quickly swim towards the crab.

Un-Nabus raises his arms, putting on his hood and changing his form. He flies over the onslaught of countless teeth that rip and tear at the Mankah. The first of the great sharks leaps out from under the water, assaulting the crab. The Mankah slashes at it with its claw and cuts deep into the shark's flesh. As the shark splashes back into the water, a giant blood wave rushes towards the island. The crab is slowly dragged deeper and deeper into the water until its fleshy underbelly is exposed to the sharks that shoot out of the water, grabbing the Mankah's worm like body with their countless rows of sheraded teeth. Two giant sharks grab his massive claw and drag him under.

Puddle feels a deep sorrow as he watches the great creature die. Claws clamp down on his shoulders, and he feels the ground leave his feet. His master has taken him up into the air and now flies him toward the heart of the island. They circle overhead three times before diving down to the ground. Puddle splashes to the ground as his master releases him.

"Follow me, Gynok, and stay close."

They come to the cave of the Mankah. The opening of its shell is half sunken in the muddy floor of the everglades.

"You must do this alone, Gynok, and if you succeed you will be freed. You must journey into the heart of the shell, and there you will find the Len of Ituha. Grab only the Len and return to me. Now go!"

Puddle looks into the darkness of the shell and timidly walks through the opening of the Mankah's lair. Walking in the shell, Puddle can hear his movements echoing against the walls. He climbs the smooth circling walls as he ventures farther into the twisting tunnel. Puddle notices strange markings

carved onto the shell's walls. He stops at an inscribed figure that looks like his master. He rubs his fingers across the symbol and sees another one much smaller and hunched over. It is crawling in the direction of something covered in a small light. The sound of dripping water grabs his attention and he continues on. He comes to the final chamber, and there is a small opening in the ceiling that lets light shine in onto a small pedestal.

The pedestal is surrounded by water, and Puddle has to swim to get to it. As he swims in the shallow water, he sees gems and jewels shimmering on the bottom. Knowing nothing of greed or wealth, Puddle ignores the treasure and continues to the pedestal. He comes to the pedestal carved out of white stone and sees a black cloth laying on top of it. Puddle unwraps the object and lifts the cloth to expose the black Len of Ithua. The air in the chamber grows still. The light fades, and the treasure in the water sparkles and reflects against the shell's wall. Puddle grabs the Len, and the ground rumbles. The water turns black, and all the shimmering jewels have gone. Then the darkness begins to engulf the walls. Puddle looks around and sees the chamber sinking into the ground. He hears a crack and by the pedestal is sucked into the ground, and an eruption of mud and filth take its place. Puddle lunges for the exit, frantically swimming to the entrance of the shell. The walls are closing in around him, but he sees his master outside the cave.

Un-Nabus raises his hand, "Gynok, halt and throw me the Len." Puddle stops, "But I will be trapped."

"Puddle, listen to me. There is a powerful curse on the Len. Whoever takes it from the place where it rests cannot cross the opening of the cave with it in their hands, or they will die. If you leave the shell with the Len, you will be poisoned."

Puddle throws the Len, and it lands on the ground next to Un-Nabus. Once the Len leaves the entrance of the shell, the rumbling stops and everything goes quiet. Un-Nabus looks at Puddle and starts to laugh.

"You have done well, my little companion, and so I grant you your freedom. I release you and give you dominion over this cave. It will be yours and only yours until your death." Un-Nabus points his staff at Puddle, who feels a cool sensation on the back of his neck. Puddle touches his neck and feels that the mark of his master has vanished. He smiles in ecstasy as if a great weight has been lifted from him.

"Thank you, Master. Puddle is now free."

"Yes, my little friend, you are free to do as you please." Puddle starts to walk out of the cave, but a unseen force holds him back. He reaches out his hands and feels an invisible wall before him. He slams his fists against the force and screams, "Master! What is happening? Master!"

The cave begins to shake, and with tears pouring down his cheeks, Puddle watches his master disappear behind the shell as it stands upright, sinking into the everglades. Puddle climbs to the top of the conch shell and curls into a ball. The shell continues to sink until only a small point sticks out of the everglades. Sobbing loudly, Puddle shivers as he sits crouched in his shell prison.

Un-Nabus walks over to the shell and looks into the opening where light once shone into the cave. He sees Puddles, eye looking up at him, shaking in terror, "Please help poor Puddle. He was a good servant. Please don't leave me here, Master. Puddle does not want his freedom anymore."

"The night I rescued you from that lizard in the forest . . . do you remember that? You see, Puddle, I had been searching for my former master . . . and I found him cornered by a common lizard, curled in a ball pathetically begging for his life."

Puddle's eye opens even wider as he realizes for the first time who his master is. He rubs his scar and remembers back to the night his slave ran off into the woods.

"That's right. It is I whom you took as an infant from under a tree to be your slave. I, the small boy whom you starved and beat. It is I whose most precious possessions you took and crushed. It was I who ran crying, scared, and alone into the darkness of the forest. So, no, Master Ogden . . . I will not save you . . . but I will leave you now, forgotten and alone. You once saved me from the wild, then used me as bait to claim your cave from a beast beyond your power. I rescued you from certain doom and have used you tonight as bait myself. The circle of our union is complete. Goodbye, Little Master."

"Nooooo!" Un-Nabus hears as he walks away. He comes to the Len that is laying in the mud. He can feel its power, and the darkness that surrounds him pulses with the beating of his heart. He feels a pounding in his chest and a burning under his skin.

"Take it, my son. Pick it up and with it, claim the world as yours." He looks down at the small dark object. All of his thoughts and energy seem to be focused on this plain wood-carved flute. He looks at the Len and sees how the mud reacts under its power as if poisoned, consumed by a dark malice. The Len shakes as he holds his hand over it. "NOW!" he hears, and he grabs the Len. Instantly, he feels a power like he has never felt before. The darkness around him explodes, covering the island in a dark cloud. He hears a deep and dark laughter in his mind.

"Good, my son, good, feel the power inside you. It is time to claim your kingdom and begin again the reign of the Hhtuno. Go to the ancient tower beyond the Whispering Canyons and find your army of Oota-Daboon."

The Hornbill bellows loudly into the night. As the Len leaves the island, the mud and grass begin to sink back into the water. Puddle watches as the water rises in his new prison. He grabs at the opening, ripping out large chunks of shell creating a hole large enough for him to escape. He looks around to see the island sinking into the water. Puddle hears a splashing behind him and turns to see what it is. He sees a fin start to circle the shell. He cries out in fear as he sees other fins emerge from below the surface, circling around him. Crying, he stands on the tip of the shell and starts to jump, yelling at the circling sharks. On his last jump, the shell starts to sink, and the fins close in. Sobbing uncontrollably, Puddle curls into a ball as he feels the chill of the water surround him. He bounces on the surface like a floating log, helpless and exposed. The tip of a sharks' nose slowly rises from the water and Puddle vanishes under a quite splash and a thrash of a fin.

CHAPTER TWELVE

A full year has passed since Taeau left the Msa-Oda. The jungle has made him leaner, darker, and stronger than before. His face and hair have grown wild like the world around him. The diversity of life that thrives in this sun-filled world fuels his powers. Away from the distractions of society, his mind has become still. He sits without fear on the darkest nights, and as he meditates, dripping with the wetness of the jungle, visions come to him and the jungle speaks, telling him its secrets.

The night is cool and less humid than usual as Taeau warms himself by a slow burning fire. A river fish he caught earlier roasts above the flames. After he enjoys his meal, Taeau's eyes grow heavy. He fights off sleep and reaches for his drinking jug that is carved out of a large tree nut. He lies down and puts the nut to his lips, tasting the soft, cool water he has collected from jungle leaves. He takes a large sip and relishes in its refreshing relief.

"Cousin."

Taeau looks up from behind the nut to see something sitting on the other side of the fire. "Ven?"

He stares at the small glider that has appeared in his camp. "Am I asleep? I do not remember sleep taking me," Taeau says softly. He looks back at the vision of Ven. "This is not the first time you have come to me, cousin. Was it not you whom I dreamt about that night before I came to this place?" Taeau asks the apparition.

The small glider silently nods his head, and as he does, Taeau sees that the side of his face has an open wound.

"Why have you come? What is it you want from me? I know now I could not have saved you or your father even if I had tried. I was just a child . . . I was scared. Do you judge me for that, cousin? I am SORRY!" Taeau yells, throwing his jug. He turns to the fire and sees that Ven has vanished. Taeau lowers his head towards the ground, breathing heavily, "I am sorry friend, I miss you . . . I miss them all."

Everything goes dark and quiet as a strong wind blows, extinguishing the fire. Taeau turns and hears crying coming from the jungle. He sees Ven, but the glider is curled in a ball, shaking and sobbing loudly. Taeau crouches down and puts his hand on his cousin's back. He is surprised to feel the softness of Ven's fur.

"Why do you cry, cousin? I meant you no harm. I was only trying to make you understand." Without lifting his head, the glider points towards the dark jungle.

"What is it, cousin? What do you want me to do?" Taeau looks to the place where the young glider points and sees two white, lifeless eyes staring at him. Taeau jolts to his feet as a deep growl echoes within the velvet jungle. Taeau hears his cousin's crying grow louder.

The wind continues to blows against Taeau's face. "This beast has tormented us from the shadows for too long, cousin. I remember that night you came to me in the plains, and how this evil chased you from my side. I felt its cold, lifeless touch, and I too cried out in fear. DO YOU HEAR ME, BEAST?! I no longer fear the darkness, and it is time we are rid of you."

Taeau's necklace rises from his bare chest and burns with light, illuminating the jungle around him. The beast roars at the sight of the light and runs back into the darkness. Taeau pursues the beast, screaming curses and threats as he runs. He runs far, and again comes face to face with the white eyes. The eyes are engulfed by darkness, and the darkness is pinned against a rocky wall. Taeau looks up at the rock that climbs high into the sky. He has seen this rising rock before, but cannot remember where. A ray of moonlight pierces the canopy, illuminating his hunting spear that materializes stuck in the soft jungle floor. He takes the spear from the ground and crouches in a battle stance, pointing the spear at the darkness. "Tonight, beast, I shall slay you. Never return to haunt my cousin in this world or in the world beyond, or I swear that my wrath shall find you again."

Taeau yells the Enopay battle cry as he charges the beast, lunging the spear into its dark belly. The spear pierces the darkness, burning his hands until he releases it. Wind starts to swirl, then a light from above starts to burn Taeau's eyes. He raises his arm to shield his face and hears a deafening screeching from above. The noise is filled with such power that it brings him to his knees. His body feels as if a knife is carving into his flesh.

Taeau opens his eyes and he feels warm dew on his face. He blinks and looks up to see trees swaying above him. He is lying on his back with his arms and legs stretched out. Most of his clothes have been torn from his body, and his chest is wet. He sits up and looks at his body. Markings that resemble feathers have been carved on his arms, chest, and back. They throb, pulsing with pain as blood drips down his body. He looks around and sees that he is not in the camp he had made the night before. He stands up, limping from the pain of the body carvings he has suffered. There is an outline of his body drawn in the dead leaves and plants that cover the jungle floor. Where his arms should be, there are wings with scattered golden feathers. He smells smoke and turns to see a pile of smoldering objects.

"No!"

He runs to the burning pile to see what is left of his weapons and clothes. As he looks down, he notices that his spear has been broken and that the blade he had made from chiseled rock is shattered. The lock of hair Leotie gave to him is burning in the pile.

"Who did this? Show yourself!" Taeau yells into the jungle.

A rustling at his side brings Taeau to a crouch, and Tib walks out from the cover of the jungle.

"Did you do this, you spiteful runt? Did you destroy my things? Why? Answer me!" Tib looks up at Taeau and shakes his head in defiance. "No, it was not you." Tib nods his head. "Then who was it? Do you know who did this?" Tib points to the sky, turns, and walks back into the jungle.

"Where are you going? Answer me," Taeau demands, following the small Wicker through the bush and into a clearing. "Tib, how do you know of this place? I have been here before?"

Taeau recalls last night's dream and the chasing of the beast. He remembers the dream he had the night he left the Msa-Oda, and how he chased his "cousin" into a dense forest. He brushes a large plant away from his face and sees the rock wall that climbs towards the sky and disappears into a thick, low cloud. Taeau stands in silence as he stares up at the cliff.

"Am I awake, Tib? Is this all real, or am I still back by the fire, sleeping?"

Tib walks up to Taeau and kicks him in his shin. "Ouch," Taeau yelps, as Tib points up towards the top of the precipice. He hugs Taeau's leg, and the young man kneels down.

"Forgive my words, friend, for I did not mean them. You have always been good to me, and I thank you."

Tears fill Tib's eye, and his markings go dark as he shakes his head at Taeau. Taeau pats him on the head and walks to the rock. He gently grazes it with his hand, feeling the moisture that beads down its stone face. He finds his footing on the rock and reaches upwards, grasping a nook in the rising cliff.

He skillfully climbs the side of the rock, for his mind is clear and his body fit. The sun rises behind him, drying the stone and choking moisture from the jungle below. The wetness rises and fills the cloud above him. The rock cuts into his hands and feet, but the pain only drives him forward. The wind whistles across the wall, and he stops to listen. He looks off into the horizon and watches the rising sun. It is as if he can sense the world and all its creatures, a world that embraces him as a son, pushing him further on his quest.

Taeau reaches the cloud that hugs the rock and fades into its whiteness as he continues his climb. He can no longer see the jungle below him, and a chill races up his spine. The change in temperature cramps his muscles and slows his climb.

Taeau looks out into the cloud and sees his mother. She is healthy-a vision of beauty and love. Taeau smiles and a tear falls from his cheek. Then his father walks behind her, holding her hand. He is thin, starved, and weak. In his eyes there is only sorrow and anger. The ghostly figure reaches towards Taeau as a whip cracks against his father's back, bringing him to his knees. Taeau looses his grip and slides down the mountainside. He stops himself and peers back into the cloud. The visions have vanished, and Taeau breaths deeply, disturbed by what he has seen.

He looks up and squints at the light beyond the cloud, and he draws upon all his strength to reach it. His hand is the first to feel the warmth of the sun again. He leaves the cloud, and he can now see the precipice of the formation he has climbed. As the sun warms him, his heart pounds as he approaches the top. His bloody fingers grip the mountain, and he pulls himself up over the edge. He climbs over the ledge and lies with his face touching the flat sun-baked rock.

He touches his face to the stone. "Thank you for allowing me to climb your side, great and ancient stone. You are now my brother, bonded to me by blood."

He gets to his feet and looks back towards the sun. It is bright, but Taeau stands proud as he looks into the celestial fire with his arms raised.

"My name is Taeau, Great Father. I am the child of Meno farmers; the nephew of the great Salali Black Claw; the student of Alo, Shaman of the Enopay, and I have walked in the footsteps of the great Mia-Koda." He closes his eyes and continues his speech, "You have watched me all my life, looked down upon me without judgment. Now I have climbed this rock and stand before you without shame. Show me your wisdom and grant me my vision!"

A deafening screech shakes him on the summit of the rock. He covers his ears from the piercing noise. When the screeching stops, the ground rumbles beneath him. Taeau slowly turns to face his vision. His eyes dilate, and droplets of sweat drip into his open mouth as he stares at the magnificent creatures lining the top of the formation. They are beasts with feathers of the deepest brown and red that Taeau has ever seen. Twice the size of the largest Enopay or Meno warrior, the bird-like creatures stand upright, wrapping their immense wings around their bodies and exposing only their heads and feet. The creatures' feet are like those of a desert raven, with massive black talons, and their long hands have slender fingers and curling claws. The creatures' heads are covered with a mane of vibrant feathers that shimmer with color as they move. All but one of the creatures is perched at the edge of the circling formation. Standing taller and grander than the rest Taeau believes this creature must be their leader. The beast's short curved beak stays shut, but Taeau hears a stern voice within his mind.

"Do you know what I am, child of the Delar?" Taeau has never seen such a creature, nor could he ever imagine one like it existed.

"I am a Wa-Hone and we are the masters of this land. We have waited for your arrival for generations." The Wa-Hone slowly circles Taeau. "All of your life you have run from your past, consumed with guilt and confusion. You have always wondered who you are, and have known you never truly belonged. One cannot achieve his vision if he does not know who he is. You are the last of a great race of man. The blood of the Delar runs through your veins."

"How do you know this?" asks Taeau

"You wear the necklace of the Delar around your neck." Taeau takes his necklace in his hand. The Wa-Hone walks up to him and gazes down at the necklace.

"Now that you know who your ancestors were, are you ready for your vision?"

Taeau shakes his head in response to the question. The Wa-Hone's wing glides over Taeau's arm, and a brace grips his wrist. It is made from animal skins with a blue stone surrounded by ornate Wa-Hone wings carved from precious metals he has never seen before. Taeau feels the talons close around his wrist. The weight of the brace pulls him to the ground. Taeau tries to move his arm, but he cannot. Then, the stone on the brace begins to shine. Bright blue flames shoot out from the stone and climb up his arm. A burning greater than any Taeau has ever felt consume his body. The flames grow and engulf him as he lies on the ground screaming in pain. Moving in and out of consciousness, Taeau struggles to survive, for the sound of the raging flames are all he can hear. Ahead of him he sees a figure slowly form

through the flames. Taeau looks upon the phantom and cries out. "Black Claw . . . help me . . . uncle. The pain is too great. I cannot bear it," Taeau yells as he squirms from the burning.

Black Claw appears at Taeau's side. The vision places his great claws on Taeau's shoulders, which start to cool, as the flames avoid Black Claw's hand.

"Fight back, child. There is strength in you yet, strength greater than you know. Feel no pity for my son or me. We are at peace now and are proud of you. You must release yourself from the bonds of guilt and forgive yourself, for we do. There is much you must do, nephew. The survival of our families depends on you, NOW RISE."

Taeau looks down at the brace and fights the flames. He closes his eyes and embraces the pain, letting it seep into his flesh through the markings that were carved during the night. He gets up from his knees and raises his wrist from the ground. The flames die, and he begins to hear voices all around him. He stands tall and lifts his arms into the air. He opens his eyes and sees the Wa-Hone pointing to the edge of the cliff, where a golden Wa-Hone stands proud and stares out toward the sun. He walks towards the golden vision. He pauses before it and reaches out his arm towards the creature made of light. The blue flames rising from his skin vanish inside the golden light of the creature. He knows what he must do, and he takes a step forward, letting the light of the Wa-Hone surround him. Taeau feels the energy of the Wa-Hone inside him and he looks out over the ridge of the rock. Taeau raises his arms, and the creature's wings follow his movements. Taeau grabs the edge of the cliff and stretches his head out over the precipice. He opens his mouth, releasing the power inside him, and exhales a deafening screech out over the jungle. He calls to the Wa-Hone, and it is answered. He hears the screams of others echoing in the wind. His necklace and brace shine as the golden vision explodes, fading into the air. He closes his mouth and stumbles back in exhaustion. He hears the flapping of wings all around him and the sound of claws scraping against rock. He stands still, rubbing his eyes as his sight returns. Taeau sees the many Wa-Hone lined up around the edge of the ridge. These proud creatures stare at Taeau silently with resolute approval.

"You have called upon us in our own tongue, son of the Delar, and we have answered. You have proven your strength and courage to us. I have as reward a great gift for you. I know the true Delar name given to you by your birth mother. Would you like to hear it?" Taeau says nothing.

"Akelou is the name that your mother gave you." But the voice that Taeau hears is not that of a Wa-Hone but a voice he has not heard in many seasons. Out from behind the Wa-Hone walks Mia-Koda, with Tib following close by.

"Mia-Koda!" Taeau yells as he runs to her embrace.

"I said to you before I left, 'not again will I see you until you are a man.' I have kept my word and am very proud of you." Taeau looks down and sees Tib hugging his leg.

"How did you know my real name?"

"Awa the Brown looked deep into your mind and heard your mother's voice speak your name. Now give me your wrist and let me see the brace of your ancestors."

Taeau shows Mia-Koda his new treasure, and she sees that the blue stone has changed to gold.

"Great leader of the Wa-Hone, we leave you now, but soon we will be together again." The Wa-Hone bows to Mia-Koda and raises his great wings, taking flight. All of the other Wa-Hone do the same, leaving the young man and his mentor standing alone together on the rock.

Taeau picks up a feather left by Awa the Brown and grips it tightly. His face tightens as he begins to understand the events that just took place. "They were not my birth parents. Meadow is not my true mother . . . Dirty Hands not my father. What does this mean, Mia-Koda? Who are my parents?"

"Nothing has changed, Taeau. The love and bond you share with your foster parents is no less strong. Your parents they still are, and as for your birth parents, all I know is that they are dead and your mother was the last true blood of the Delar. Now the Enopay are waiting at the Msa-Oda for their newest member. But before we go, which name shall you now be called? The one given to you at birth, or the one given by your father the day you came into his family?"

"'Akelou' is my rightful name. 'Taeau,' I will leave behind with my youth on this rock."

"So be it, Akelou. Let us go home, for many are waiting for you."

Mia-Koda reaches into her robes and takes out the Moura Stone. She grabs dirt from a pouch and sprinkles it over the stone. She softly speaks to the relic, dropping it's stone from her hand and beginning to swing it in circles. A thin line of light pierces the air as it spins. The light begins to collapse inward until a doorway is created. The circle of light flashes, and a valley can be seen within the door. Akelou walks through the doorway and smells the cool dusty air. He arrives back one year to the night from when he left. He looks up at the city that is lit by many torches, and he feels welcome.

"The Enopay are celebrating another successful hunt. You have returned on a clear and joyous night." Mia Koda points into the distance, "Your former Gahano approaches."

Akelou sees the outlines of Alo and his horse Akima approaching closer. Stomping the ground and whinnying loudly, Akima can sense his master. His markings begin to flutter with excitement.

"Go to him, Akima." says Alo as he releases the horse.

Akima races to Akelou and licks his face, nipping at his ears when they meet.

"Good boy, I have missed you . . . I have missed your smell," says Akelou with tears in his eyes.

Akima bows his head and knee, requesting Akelou to mount him. Akelou mounts his friend, patting his neck. As Akelou pets his dear friend, he looks down at Alo.

"Thank you, Alo, for watching over Akima. I am grateful."

"There is no need for thanks, Taeau." Alo grabs Akelou by his calf and looks up at him. "You left me as a child and have come back a man."

"My name is no longer 'Taeau.' I left that name in the jungle. I am Akelou now," he says proudly.

Alo bows to Akelou, "I think it is time for you to join the Enopay."

Mounting their horses, Alo and Mia-Koda ride with Akelou back to the Msa-Oda. They travel up the Trail of Silent Steps and come to the gate of the city. A watchman yells out from atop the gate. "Who do you bring into our city, Alo?"

"I bring Abokswigin and the Wicker Tib from the Black Forest. As for the other you speak of, he is now one of us." The guard looks down and sees Akelou on his horse.

"Taeau has returned, open the gate," shouts the watchman.

As they come to the great hut, Alo stops Akelou.

"Now that you are a true Enopay, you may enter the Pueblo Oda. This is our most sacred place, and you must respect and understand what you enter." Alo points to the roughly dug holes on the ground.

"Crawl through this hole to enter the hut of our mother moon. You must pass through her womb and be reborn inside. Alo and Mia-Koda crawl into other holes that have been dug out. Akelou and Tib stand outside staring at each other.

"I am nervous to see everyone one again, Tib. I left on a great day, and I hope they have not forgotten me . . . especially her." Tib smiles up at Akelou and pats his leg before walking away.

Akelou takes a deep breath and crawls into the hole. The tunnel is small, and he struggles to pass through it. In the tunnel everything is dark, and the celebration inside is muffled. Seeing the end of the tunnel, Akelou crawls toward the covered opening. He falls head first into the hut and into a puddle of wet clay. He gets up and wipes off some of the mud. The hut is heated by a large pile of red hot stones in the center of the floor, and the only opening is a small moon hole in the ceiling. Rows of Enopay are sitting in a circle on the floor of the hut as well as line the walls of the hut. Akelou, not wanting to show his nervousness, walks proudly into the center of the room. Alo raises his hand as he stands next to the Chief. "It has been a full season since the child Taeau left us in search of his vision. He was alone in the wild and without help. Now, having found his vision, he enters this hut as a true Enopay."

The Chief stands, "How do we know that the outsider has found a vision worthy of the Enopay people?"

Akelou looks around, seeing the people nodding their heads in agreement, and understands what he must do. He raises his arms, letting everyone see the lines carved into his skin. His necklace burns against his chest, and his heart pounds. The Enopay gasp as golden flames rise from Akelou' s markings and take shape around him. The golden wings and feathers illuminate the hut. Some of the women scream in fear and run to their mates. The Chief watches as the silhouette of a Wa-Hone forms around Akelou's face. Akelou opens his mouth and screeches the call of the Wa-Hone. The screeching shakes the hut, bellowing out the moon hole and echoing across the valley. Akelou falls to his knees gasping for breath as the light fades. The Enopay are amazed and look to the Chief.

The Chief rises from his seat, "Your Enopay name from this day forth will be Screaming Eagle."

The hut explodes into yells. All of the Enopay welcome him into the tribe. Akelou sits down between Alo and Mia-Koda, watching the men and women dance around the glowing rocks. He eats Ga-Taga meat and drinks wheat beer. Many of the Enopay come over to Akelou to talk to him about his journeys and tell him about what has happened in his absence. Akelou basks in the acceptance of his people. He sits with a smile on his face and great happiness in his heart.

"Are you only going to sit, drink, and talk all night with the lonely men, Screaming Eagle?"

Akelou looks up to see a face he has thought of many times since he has been gone. She is wearing her ceremonial dress, the one she wore the night he left for the jungle. "Good to see you again, Leotie," he says, wiping Ga-Taga meat from his face.

She grabs his hand, "Will you dance with me?" she asks as she drags him down to the dance floor.

While she tugs him along, he begins to panic with the realization he has never danced before. Akelou nervously watches the others, while Leotie leads him to the hot stones. Most of the Enopay are dressed in ceremonial costumes as they dance around the stones. Beating drums and the women's singing lead the dancers in a primal, chaotic rhythm. As the pair starts to dance, the heat and scent of those around him ease his mind, and his body takes control. He stays close to Leotie, and they dance as hard as anyone losing themselves to the night, intoxicated by the celebration.

The night gives way to morning, and many of the Enopay have left to sleep off their full bellies and tired legs. Akelou and Leotie sit very close to one another, whispering quietly into each other's ears. Enopay lie scattered on the floor, sleeping from too much celebrating. Something catches Akelou' s attention as he looks up through the opening in the ceiling. He is tired and a little drunk, but his vision is true. Leotie puts her head in his lap, and Akelou runs his fingers through her hair and she starts to fall asleep.

"What are you looking at?"

"I don't know. I thought I saw something up above the hut."

"It is probably a bird, silly, maybe a raptor searching for desert snakes and mice." His eyes grow heavy as he dips in and out of sleep.

"Alo!" yells Mia-Koda, pointing at the opening in the ceiling. Akelou wakes and sees a very large bird staring into the hut from above.

"It is a crane from the swamps of Noshota, a messenger of the Pokwa," says Mia-Koda.

"The long-legs that live to the south?" asks the chief. Mia-Koda raises her hand, and the bird flies down toward her. Everyone gets to their feet and stares at the bird. It is a grey bird with a long neck, a narrow pointed beak, and legs that look like fragile twigs. The bird's underbelly is the purest of white, while dark feathers circle its eyes and back. Around its neck hangs a scroll wrapped in some kind of leaf.

"It is a message from Theopa, King of the Pokwa. Someone bring water," Mia-Koda says as she walks down to the floor of the hut. She stands under the moonlight that shines in from the ceiling above. She opens the scroll. "There is no writing on the scroll, Abokswigin," says the Chief.

"The script has been written with a reed dipped in the swamp mud where night mushrooms grow. Only under water that reflects moonlight will the writing become visible. The writing will not last long, for the mud will slowly wash away, hiding its message," says Mia-Koda as she pours water over the scroll.

Chief of the Enopay, old friend of the Pokwa,

A beast from an ancient time came to our swamps under the banner of the false King Columbus. He demanded our loyalty and dominion over our lands. When I refused, he slipped into my house under the cover of night and kidnapped my daughter.

He has taken her to the tower of Ogdah at the edge of the Whispering Canyons, before the Great Lake. My Pokwa warriors cannot pursue her kidnappers to these lands.

I, Theopa, leader of the Pokwa, plead for your help in her rescue. We will need you most skilled warriors if we are to reclaim my daughter. I await your reply with great hope and humility."

"We must go to their aid," says Alo, looking up at his chief.

"Why should I risk the lives of our men for some slippery long-leg in the distant swamps?"

"He is your ally, and the Enopay need to keep what few friends they have close," says Mia-Koda.

"Do they now, Abokswigin? The long-legs and the Enopay have not had contact since the days before my father. We owe them nothing, and I cannot afford to sacrifice any of my men."

"What if there were a brave few who would volunteer to go to their aid?"

The Chief looks out at the remaining men still in the hut.

"I will spare only two of my ranks, but none of the greater-skilled warriors are permitted," the Chief says as a large warrior who has stepped forward now backs down.

"Who of you will go to the long-legs' aid? " Mia-Koda loudly asks. None of the Enopay answer her request.

"I will, I will go to the aid of these Pokwa," says a voice in the back.

"Who said that? Show yourself."

Akelou steps forward, lowering to one knee before the Chief.

"Ha, granted," says the Chief. "If you are in such a rush to leave us the night you return, I will not stop you."

"Is there no other man brave enough to ride with Screaming Eagle?" asks Alo. Leotie walks up behind Akelou, "I will join Screaming Eagle on his quest."

The Chief shakes his head and looks down harshly at the volunteers. "Let the woman go. Let these two who do not have Enopay blood journey to the aid of the mud dwellers. The decision is final. The hunting celebration is over. Now leave, all of you," orders the Chief.

Mia-Koda, walking with the crane on her shoulder, comes to Akelou's side. "Go, both of you. Gather what things you need, and meet Alo and me by the horses." Leotie bows, turns, and leaves the hut first.

"Ready for this are you, Screaming Eagle?" asks Alo. Akelou stares him down and stands proud. "Good to hear it," Alo says proudly.

They collect their horses and Tib before traveling down the Trail of Silent Steps. Leotie meets them, dressed in the same clothes she wore the day she entered Akelou's camp in the Black Forest. Her hair is tied back, and she carries her bow as she walks with her horse.

"We leave for the swamps, and there is no turning back. I hope none of you mind a little mud," Mia-Koda says with a smirk as she takes out the Moura Stone. She scrapes the mud from the scrolls and rubs it on the stone. She releases the relic, dangling it close to the ground. She starts to swing the stone, creating a doorway to the swamps. Mia-Koda leads her horse and Tib through the door first. Leotie follows with her horse, but before Akelou can walk through the door, Alo grabs him.

"She is special in more ways than you know. Take the greatest care of her, for she will do the same for you." Alo squeezes Akelou's arm tightly before turning and walking back to the Msa-Oda.

Akelou takes a last look at the city as the sun begins to rise above it, waking the world around him and engulfing the clouds in burning flame, before he turns and walks through the doorway.

CHAPTER THIRTEEN

"What is that smell, Abokswigin?" Leotie asks as she covers her nose in disgust.

"That is the delicate swamp mushroom, child. They release a potent-smelling pollen when disturbed."

Mia-Koda raises her staff, and its tip begins to shine. The air shimmers, reflecting the light from Mia-Koda's staff. Akelou waves his hand through the glittering particles and watches as the pollen swirls around his fingers. Mia-Koda lowers her staff, and the pollen slowly fades.

"The Moura stone brought us here because the ink used in the scroll is made from this mud. We are in the domain of the Pokwa, and it won't be long until we are noticed. The Pokwa are a proud and powerful race who will hold you to your words, so watch what you say. You must all be careful around their younglings, for their vibrant colored skin secretes some of the strongest toxin I have encountered."

Mia-Koda swings her staff suddenly, and brings it to a stop in front of Akelou's face. Akelou steps back defensively, staring at Mia-Koda. She turns her staff to show him a dart lodged in the wood. "We are not alone. This is a poison dart used by the Pokwa guard. The color and groove patterns on its surface will tell you its maker." Mia-Koda looks around, "Show yourself . . . we come at the request of Theopa, your king." She lifts her staff towards the trees, "They will be hiding high on the trunks."

Akelou looks around him but sees only foliage. Staring at the trees, he takes a step closer and makes out two large eyes staring down at him. He sees the creature with its long legs gripping the tree and a dart blower pressed to its lips. The Pokwa, realizing it has been spotted, leaps from the treetop. It lands not far from them with a splash. The horses become restless and start kicking around in the muddy water. The Pokwa puts its dart blower away and grabs a weapon from its back. It is a staff with a large stone tied to it with Pokwa rope. His skin is a dark muddy color with large stripes, and he

wears body armor made from the bark of trees. On his face there are three thin markings carved into his skin.

Leotie has taken a defensive position behind Mia-Koda with her bow drawn. Tib stands on Leotie's horse with his fists clenched, ready for a fight.

"You can tell the other Pokwa guards they can lower their dart blowers . . . we come to aid the Pokwa, not harm you."

The Pokwa croaks and stomps its feet at Mia-Koda.

"I was summoned from a scroll by King Theopa. We came as soon as we were able."

The Pokwa swings its weapon and inflates its large throat, making a vibrating sound that disturbs the water around it. Akelou hears other Pokwa leaping from the trees overhead. They land in blurs, showering Akelou and his companions in muddy water. The horses become frantic and throw Tib from their back. He lands on the ground and sinks into the mud. Struggling to free himself, he screams, flailing his arms and legs to stay above the water. The Pokwa guards surrounds them, brandishing their weapons and communicating to each other in their language.

"Let them pass, Doa, she is friend to the Pokwa-she was a friend to my father." The circle opens, and a very large, battle-worn Pokwa walks through. His armor is greater and finer than the others. His helmet is covered with large teeth, and a strange symbol is carved on it, similar to Akelou's necklace.

When this large Pokwa mentions the death of his father, all the Pokwa fill their throats with air and bellow.

"You must be Oboe, son of Obe. I knew your taken father well. He was a great warrior and leader of the Pokwa. I hope your family is healthy and your mate strong," Mia-Koda says as she bows to the Pokwa. "We have traveled with speed by means I will not explain. I have read the scrolls written by your king. We have come to the aid of the Pokwa and seek to hold a council with the court. This is Leotie, a fierce warrior and skilled tracker." Leotie lowers her bow and bows to the Pokwa. "This is Akelou, adopted son of the Meno farmer Garvais and nephew to Black Claw, who was known to the Pokwa."

Oboe looks at Akelou, "I mourned the loss of the Menoli warriors killed by the cursed beast that now plagues us. I led a small war party to aid the fallen city, but we arrived too late. Come, Mia-Koda . . . we leave for the city. You will be safe while you are under the protection of our guard."

Oboe leads them deep into the swamp, and as they travel, Akelou notices that the Pokwa walk awkwardly in the shallows but move with great agility in the deep mud and in the trees. Leotie and Akelou struggle to wade through the swamps, tirelessly defending themselves from the many biting and pestering insects. The Pokwa wait for the hordes of insects and engulf large quantities of them by jumping through the swarms with their gaping mouths.

"How is Theopa dealing with the kidnapping of his daughter?" Mia-Koda asks Oboe.

"Like any parent, gulp, whose son or daughter has been kidnapped. He is filled with rage, and no Pokwa sleeps soundly, gulp, until his taken daughter is returned. The guard is tense, and the armory is busy carving darts and shaping weapons." He holds out his large hands, "Wait here as I talk to the inner guard, gulp, who will tell others of our coming."

Oboe crouches down and leaps high onto a nearby tree.

"What do they mean by 'taken' daughter Mia-Koda?" Leotie asks.

"Well, their young are sent away to survive alone in the swamps after they hatch. The Pokwa eggs are fertilized randomly by males who have earned breeding rights. When the talepoles return from the open swamps, they are adopted into families. After they are adopted, the young Pokwa are treated as if the same blood runs through their veins. It is why the bond between the generations is so strong."

Akelou thinks to himself how wonderful a system this is. He wishes he had lived here as a child where he would not have been ridiculed for being different. Oboe lands beside Mia-Koda, splashing Akelou and Leotie and stirring the horses, which toss Tib from their back. He splashes mud and shakes his fists at the Pokwa. "Come . . . we are close now. The king will be waiting for us," says Oboe.

As they come closer to the city, they begin to see the half submerged mud huts that the Pokwa live in. Eyes pop out of small openings as they walk to the muddy home of the king. Younglings jump in and out of the water wrestling with each other. Their bright skin makes them easy to see against the dull colors of the swamp. The thinner and taller Pokwa females chase after their young. On their arms and wrists they wear jewelry made from bone and local stones. These bracelets and necklaces define their marital and social status within the city.

A crowd begins to gather around the visitors as they walk. Akelou can feel their stares of distrust, and he is reminded of when he first came to the Enopay. The males and a few female Pokwa rise from their huts with weapons in hand, responding to the commotion outside. Akelou and his companions approach the entrance to the Choa, a mountain made of dried mud, stones, trees, and grasses, home of the Pokwa king and his court. In the

center of the mountain is a unnatural boulder with a flat, chiseled face. Akelou wonders where and how such a massive rock came to be in a swamp like this . High on the boulder is a carved opening that leads into the king's court. A terrace protrudes over the swamp below, and Akelou watches as a figure disappears from it.

Mia-Koda turns and speaks, "Tib, stay here with the horses. We will not be long." He quickly agrees and throws her a scowling look while standing on Akima, still covered in mud from his falls.

Walking through the guarded entrance, they come to the breeding hall where they follow a narrow path between the breeding pools. The Pokwa females attending to the pools leap onto the edges of the path as they see the strangers. They aggressively guard the pools and appear ready to strike at any moment. Their eyes are filled with the gaze of a mother defending her young, and Akelou understands he must be careful.

Once they are out of the breeding hall, Oboe leads them to a circular stairway made from tree roots, and rock. Both Akelou and Leotie struggle to climb the steps. "You could not use the Maura Stone to bring us to the top of these stairs could you Abokswigin?" asks Leotie with a tone.

"And what do you think the Pokwa guard would do to three strangers that appear out of nowhere, only footsteps away from their king's door?"

Once up the stairs, they come to a hallway that leads to a single, heavily guarded door that is finely chiseled and engraved with Pokwa symbols.

Mia-Koda explains, "That is the entrance to the hall where Theopa and his court sit. The king is powerful and well respected by the Pokwa, but the Pokwa court is equal to him. They share power, forming a balance of power equally governing the Pokwa. Not all Pokwa can speak in the common tongue, but the king does, hard as it may be to understand him. Follow my lead, and make no sudden movements or outbursts."

Mia-Koda approaches the guard as she indicates that Leotie and Akelou should leave their weapons behind. The guards lower their spears only after Akelou's and Leotie's weapons are on the ground. The hall is carved from the great Choa stone. A few crude, chiseled columns connect the mud-covered floor to the ceiling. The king sits on a throne made from an uprooted tree, and below him is a round table carved from the Choa stone itself. The nine Pokwa members of the court, who are of different ages, colors, and sexes, sit at this table. The eldest members of the Pokwa court sits closest to the king. Three of the nine are female, two of whom look to be of a high social class, for they wear jewelry covering their arms and wrists.

The third Pokwa female could almost be mistaken for a male warrior if not for the feminine decoration on her arms. A handprint made from their own blood appears on the stone in front of their place at the table. Mia-Koda walks to the stone and bows to the court and to its king. Akelou and Leotie follow.

"We come before you, Theopa, answering your scroll." The only response Mia-Koda receives from the court and its king is a defiant silence. The king rises from his throne and speaks.

"This is the answer the chief of the Enopay gives me. I ask for aid in a time of great need, and he sends, gulp, only two of his people. He sends the Pokwa two children and an old woman. This is how the Enopay, gulp, disrespect the Pokwa in a time of great crisis." The court fills the hall with croaking and the stomping of feet.

Mia-Koda calmly raises her hands and speaks, "The Enopay chief has allowed two great warriors to come to your aid wise King. Leotie of the Enopay is their greatest tracker. She is a fierce and proven warrior. She will be valuable in finding and rescuing your daughter."

Leotie looks up to the king, "I will not stop until your daughter is returned. This I pledge with my life on the honor of my people."

The king looks at her, unimpressed. "Gulp, what of this other child you bring before me?" The court turns to look at Akelou.

"This, Theopa, is no child, for he is the last of an ancient race to which all Pokwa owe their allegiance. He was raised by Meno parents, and is the nephew of the murdered Salali, Black Claw, who was well known to the Pokwa." The mention of Black Claw's name seems to have an impact on all of the Pokwa in the room. "His name is Akelou, and he is the last of his race."

"What do I, gulp, care of his bloodline? My daughter has been stolen from me, and my people grow uneasy without the presence of their princess. I need warrior men, not a boy with a forgotten ancestry."

Mia-Koda walks up to the king and points back at Akelou, "He is a Delar, and he wears the necklace of his people."

At the mention of the Delar a great commotion rises among the Pokwa.

"Gulp, you lie. The line of the Delar was destroyed."

"It was never destroyed, Theopa. Only hidden from the world. He is a true Delar."

Akelou stands and shows his necklace to the Pokwa with great pride. He looks at Leotie, and she gives him a cold stare.

"Is this true, son? Are you a child of the Delar?" Akelou looks up to the king.

"Yes, King. I am." He raises his wrist, showing everyone in the hall his brace.

"Then my daughter is saved." The king lifts his hands in the air, and all the Pokwa rejoice in a loud, croaking, foot-stomping celebration.

The king steps down from his throne and moves through the celebrating Pokwa. Theopa puts his long, gripping hands on Akelou's shoulder and escorts him into his private chambers.

"Come, son of the Delar." He points to Leotie and Mia-Koda, "See to all of their needs and wants Oboe. Prepare a small scouting party to lead our allies from our borders." Oboe bows to his king and leaves the hall, followed by Mia-Koda and Leotie.

Theopa takes Akelou to his chambers through a door behind his throne. The room is open, wet, and filled with the skins and teeth of the grey crocodiles, the oldest and deadliest enemy of the Pokwa.

"Sit, Akelou, and take counsel with me."

Akelou notices a change in the king's voice from stern and solemn to wavering and unsure. Akelou sits on a stump near the bed of the king, which is made from the soft red clay of the Noshota swamps.

"Mia-Koda came to me some time ago, telling me of a strange child that had come to her in the night. She told me what that might mean, and she told me of the signs and visions. She advised me that the winds of change have begun to blow and that they will only become stronger with time. I did, gulp, not heed her warnings, and now I am paying with a father's, gulp, anguish. Mia-Koda believes in you, and so must I . . . do you know why the Pokwa so revere the Delar?"

"No, I do not know much of my kin or their stories."

"A very long time ago, gulp, the Pokwa were just small, simple creatures surviving in the swamps and wetlands of the world. They were preyed upon by many beasts, most of all the grey crocodile, which still to this very day the Pokwa fear most. It is told that in the ancient times, a child of the Delar who loved all creatures, from the deadliest cats to the smallest leaf crawlers, took a Pokwa into his hand and with his great power he changed us. Gulp. The Pokwa grew with him and they become like brothers. The great

Delar taught us the powers of speech and the skills of combat. Once the first Pokwa came of age, the Delar left. The Delar, not wanting the Pokwa to be alone in the swamps, remade another of the Pokwa's kind. It was on that very day that the first Pokwa swore an allegiance for all his sons and daughters. Our first king swore with his blood that his children would be loyal to the Delar until the end of time. Many generations later, the same Delar came back to the Pokwa and asked them to honor our first father's oath. The darkness had come and the wars had started. The Pokwa, gulp, soon learned the cruelty of war and the treachery of evil. The deceiver came masked as an ally and a brother of the Delar, and he turned Pokwa against Pokwa. It was the darkest hour of our people. The Pokwa became divided and many perished. Those who let the whispers of evil cloud their minds changed, no longer resembling their kin. When the wars ended, we drove these new creatures away, slaying all we could. We hear about the changed ones rarely, gulp, for they live underground in the filthiest of mud, away from the light, left to rot with their wickedness. It is said that they have the power to speak into the minds of their enemies and bend them to their will. Legend says they learned this skill from the great deceiver himself. Time went on, and the Delar slowly disappeared from this world. We Pokwa became more and more alone. We now have only our stories and a few precious gifts left to us by the great fathers. But now a new darkness has creped back into our lives. We can feel it in the swamps around us-the plants whisper ancient fears to our females and younglings who can still hear their voices." Theopa turns his back to Akelou and opens a wooden chest beside his bed. Reaching into it, he takes out an object wrapped in cloth. "You must, gulp, rescue my daughter, for she is the future of the Pokwa . . . she is the key to our survival." He turns to Akelou and places the wrapped item on the young man's lap. "This is the Nol. In the tongue of the Delar, it means 'blade of wind.' This axe was made by the forgotten craftsmanship of your people. The Pokwa king who saved us from the Dark Age wielded it. The Nol is our most sacred possession, and there is great power within it. Gulp, I return it now to you. May it help you on your journey."

Akelou unwraps the weapon and looks at the Nol. It is a one-sided axe made from an iridescent ore that glistens in the light. The handle is made from hardened forest wood, with the carved symbol of the Delar through the handle. He feels a strange connection with the axe as he swings it through the air.

"There is a Delar enchantment on this axe, gulp, when thrown it will always return to its wielder's hand. May it, gulp, slay any enemy that stands between you and my daughter."

Theopa points to a far wall in the room and steps aside. Akelou stands up and tosses the axe, lodging it into the mud wall. "Now you must call it back to you, and in time you will have no need for the words."

Akelou reaches out his hand and calls his weapon, "NOL!" The axe flies back from the wall into his grip. Akelou is impressed, and as he wipes the axe clean, it makes a hypnotic ring that resonates in the king's chamber.

Akelou bows before the king, "I will not fail you."

"I believe you, young son of the Delar. Now go and take what you need and be on your way. I fear that war will follow your footsteps, gulp, no matter what the outcome of your quest. The wicked king that rules the great tower will not take lightly the insult of my daughter's, gulp, rescue. A war far worse than the one forged against the Menoli city will soon be at our door. We must start preparing for it." The king sits on his bed and sighs with the breath of a burdened leader. "Be safe, Akelou. May valor and strength find you and your companions."

Akelou understands that the time has come to leave, and he departs the king's chambers. As he leaves, he finds the hall empty. Exiting the hall, he walks to the winding stairs. As he admires the axe the king has given him, he hears the sound of sloshing mud. He raises his axe and stares down the stairs.

"Show yourself," he calls out.

He hears a soft, unsteady, childlike voice, "Do, do not harm me, short-leg. I only very much wanted to see, with my own eyes, whether the rumors are true."

"What rumors would those be, hidden one?" Akelou asks as he searches to find the voice.

"That a great Delar has come to our swamp."

"Show yourself, and I will give you an answer." Akelou looks up and sees an outline of a camouflaged youngling clinging to the muddy wall. Once the youngling sees that Akelou has spotted him on the ceiling, his colors become vibrant.

"Come down here, child, and tell me your name."

The young Pokwa jumps from the wall and lands at Akelou's feet. His skin is the color of leaves in mid-autumn, and he has very little of his tail left. "My name is Toe, son of Oboe," he says timidly.

"I know your father. He is the Captain of the Pokwa, is he not?"

"HE IS! Gulp, and he apologizes for his son sneaking into a place he should not be. Toe comes here even after being told just moments ago not to by his parents." Oboe walks up from the stairs, staring down at Toe. Toe becomes very still, his colors darken rapidly, and his eyes open wide. "Now that you have seen the Delar, I suggest you go back home, tell your mother what you have done, and await my return."

"Don't make me tell mother. Can't I just wait for you to come home-"

"You will do as you are told!" Oboe yells.

Toe jumps onto the wall, scurrying past his father and out of sight.

"I swear, that youngling fears his mother more than he fears me. Gulp, I hope that you will take no offense at my son's curiosity."

"None at all. A handful he must be."

"He is that. I took him after my first son was killed by a cursed grey crocodile. My wife took his death hard, and I fear she overprotects this one. Well, son of the Delar, gulp, I am to take you to your friends. They have already gathered the necessary supplies for your journey."

"Thank you, Oboe."

As Akelou accompanies Oboe through the city, the Pokwa seem excited, gathering in groups and gossiping loudly.

"Word has spread of your lineage, Akelou. You bring hope to these Pokwa, but I do not share in their joy. We have come to a crossroads. If you succeed, then there will be war and many Pokwa will die. If you fail, the city will loose its future queen and our future will be dark. Either way young, gulp, Delar, our world will change and never be as it was. I fear for my family, I fear for my kin, and I fear for my king." Oboe turns and looks back to the Choa and sighs.

When they reach the others at the edge of the city, Akelou looks up at Tib who is riding Broomay. Leotie is ahead of the others, holding her horse's reins, her back turned, and Mia-Koda is talking to a member of the court as she holds a large sack over her shoulders.

"Ahh, Akelou, I see you have finished your talk with the king. Thank you for bringing him, Oboe. We leave right away. Is the escort party ready?"

"Yes, we will meet them further in the swamps, for they are securing our passage north."

"Very well, Akelou, take this sack of supplies and mount them on Akima."

Akelou does as she asks, throwing the sack on his horse and catching a cold glance from Leotie. Mia-Koda bows to the one to whom she was talking, and they part ways.

"It is only a two-day journey to the northern rim of the swamps," says Oboe as he turns and begins their journey. As they travel, other Pokwa emerge to talk to Oboe. Akelou watches as some of the Pokwa silently glide down from the canopy above. They remind him of the Salali, but instead of gliding with their arms and legs, these Pokwa use their hands that are covered with flaps of loose skin.

Mia-Koda and Leotie walk ahead of Akelou and Tib. Akelou has noticed that since they have left the Pokwa city, Leotie has not spoken a word nor made any eye contact. Aware that he is being observed from behind and almost certainly from above, he does not press the issue. The day begins to fade, and Mia-Koda tells Leotie to scout ahead for a place to make camp. Mia-Koda stops and waits for Akelou to come to her side.

"How are you, Akelou?" she says with a look on her face of one who knows the answers to her questions.

"I am fine in spite of not knowing the road we travel or understanding why Leotie has yet to speak to me since the gathering at the hall."

"Hmmm . . . noticed that too, I have, though I am not surprised."

"Can you tell me why Leotie is acting with such foolishness?"

"Foolishness, huh? And what do you know of foolishness, you are the same person who spoke only a handful of words to me during all that time we spent together in the forest. Now I understood there was a reason for your silence. I knew you were dealing with the pain and confusion of your loss. You, Akelou, are not the only one with a troubled past. It is quite naive to pass such judgment on others' foolishness without knowing much about them, just as it was foolish the way many of the Enopay treated you when you first came to their tribe."

"Well, then tell me about her past, so I can understand better." Mia-Koda takes a deep breath and looks deep into Akelou's eyes.

"Do you know anything of the Eastern world beyond the shores, Akelou?" Mia-Koda can tell by the inquiring look on his face that he has never heard of this place. "There is a world to the east across the treacherous sea, that no vessel in our land I know of can cross. It is a land filled with different people than you and I. Their skin is pale and their bodies strong. In this land there is a king, and he sits tall on a throne made of a stone whose beauty has no equal. He is a good king who is married to a very clever queen.

Their marriage was arranged to secure loyalty and peace in the empire. The king soon had three offspring with the queen, all of them male.

"After the third child, the queen became cold and meddlesome in the king's affairs. She would often leave the King and take their youngest son to visit her family. Her trips lasted longer each time she left. It was during one of these absences that the King fell deeply in love with one of the servant women in the castle. They had an affair, and this new love filled his soul with joy. They conceived a child in secret. It was a girl, and the King was very pleased. When the queen returned, she found the king and his lover together in bed with the child between them. She became furious with the king and threatened that if he did not banish his lover and their child, then the queen's family would go to war for this dishonor. Not wanting to break the peace, he did as the queen commanded. He threw the servant woman and her child to the harsh streets of the city. The king's lover, broken and humiliated, did not survive long. She died of plague, leaving her daughter alone to fend for herself.

"The young girl endured many hardships, but managed to survive as an orphan in the streets. Starving and alone, she found her way to the docks and stowed away on a merchant vessel. The ship was lost at sea during a terrible storm, and no one but the young girl survived. When the Enopay found her, washed up on a beach, she was barely alive. They adopted her into their tribe, where she overcome many prejudices that you are well familiar with."

"So, Leotie is the bastard daughter of a great king of a foreign land. But why is she mad at me?"

"You must open your mind, Akelou. To her, the Delar must be some form of royalty. She knows the cruelty of such people and has many demons in her past that she has yet to fully overcome."

"So she thinks I could hurt her, like her father?"

"I believe she will not let herself be hurt or discarded by anyone ever again. Her life has made her a tough and untrusting soul. Until you, I have never known her to be close to anyone. She is quite old to not have a mate and a family in the eyes of the Enopay."

Mia-Koda rests a hand on Akelou's shoulder and moves ahead, leaving him to ponder her words. Akelou looks at Leotie and understands how she felt as an outsider, for he has been one his entire life.

"We camp here for the night," yells Oboe.

While the Pokwa secure the area, Tib piles firewood in the center of camp. Mia-Koda takes some dust from inside her robes and tosses it over the wood, igniting it in flames. The mood around the fire is quiet while they make their beds and eat. Akelou swears he saw Oboe grab a snake-like creature from a nearby tree and eat it while it was still wiggling.

"Where will you and your fellow Pokwa sleep, Oboe?" asks Leotie.

"We Pokwa, gulp, sleep in the trees, Leotie. It is not only safer but cooler in the heat of the summer months. Before our awakening, we Pokwa mostly dwelled in the trees and tall plants. Do not worry about your safety tonight, my friend, gulp. Enjoy your sleep. We will lead you to the northern border by mid-day tomorrow. I imagine a good night's rest will be harder to come by after you leave our swamp." Oboe looks up and points at Mia-Koda. "Mia-Koda, a bit of your counsel and a smoke before I retire?"

"Yes, Oboe, I would enjoy that."

Noticing that he and Leotie are alone, Akelou decides the time is right to talk to her. He goes over and sits next to Leotie and gazes into the fire.

"The trip has gone well so far, do you not think?" Leotie sits silently, staring at the fire and chewing on dried Ga-Taga meat. Thinking it best not to mention what he knows about her past, Akelou plays dumb.

"Have I done something to wrong you, Leotie? I feel a coldness between us."   "Is that a fact, O great son of the Delar? Well, I have news for you. I do not owe you any explanation, your majesty. Did you ever plan on telling me you are some kind of royalty or something? Or was it that you were trying to find a new tribe to rule over?" Akelou opens his mouth to get a word out, but he is not fast enough. "I wonder if your castle with its lords and great wealth misses you. I know how royalty treat those whom they think are beneath them. You pretend to care, but you just use others for what you need, then throw them out on the street. Well, no thanks, great prince. You won't do that to me," she barks as she gets up.

Failing to get a word in, he looks down at Tib who gets up and kicks dirt at him before walking over to sit by Leotie's side. Akelou stares at Leotie's back, waiting for her to cool down. He takes out his knife and cuts a lock from his hair. He ties the middle and burns an end in the fire.

He walks over to Leotie and looks down at her, "The night I left the Msa-Oda, you gave me a lock from your hair. I kept it close to me every night in the jungle until it was taken from me and burned." He reaches out to give her his lock. "I give you this in return. Tomorrow will come, and if you want to return home, Mia-Koda will take you. I have to see this through, for I cannot turn back. I do not have your skills with a bow or talent for tracking. I need you, Leotie, for I see nothing but failure without you." He hands her the lock and looks into her eyes as tears streak down her face.

Akelou takes a deep breath, "I do not know who my real parents are. I only learned about my Delar blood the night I returned to the Enopay. I was raised by poor Meno farmers. They never told me I was not their true son, but I always knew. I saw my uncle and cousin murdered by the same monster that kidnapped Theopa's daughter. The night they were murdered, Mia-Koda came and took me from my foster parents to live in the wild. I have not seen them since." Akelou sits down and nudges himself close to Leotie. "Mia-Koda has told me about some of your past." Leotie looks away, crying even harder. "I know what it feels like not knowing your parents or having a family or people of your own-"

"You know nothing of what I went through!" she shouts. "What it was like living on the streets in that cursed city. Even when I came to the Enopay, it was not much better. Things happen to young girls when they are alone, things that change them, so don't tell me you understand." Leotie stands up and walks away, holding herself tightly and shivering in the murky swamp.

Akelou comes to her again and puts his hand on her shoulder. "I wish I could see the moon. It always makes me feel better. It is the one thing that never left me. Even when I could not see it, I knew it was there," says Akelou. Leotie turns and dives into Akelou's arms, "I never want to have this talk again," Leotie says.

Akelou wakes in the morning to cool dew covering his face. He sits up and looks next to him, seeing Leotie's empty bed.

"I let you sleep. Everyone is getting ready. You'd better get dressed quickly if you want to eat before we move out," Leotie says as she smiles at Akelou.

Akelou feels the eyes of the others as he joins them by the fire. He drinks hot Pokwa tea, and it brings warmth to his blood. They break down the camp and start the journey north. As they travel, more and more Pokwa continue to jump into and out of the trees of the swamp. The Pokwa seem to be more on edge the further north they go. Soon the soggy swamp floor gives way to cool dirt. Akelou can tell that the farther they travel from the lush swamps, the more the skin of the Pokwa looks dry and irritated.

"This is where we leave you. Gulp, be careful, for you will travel through dangerous and wild land. Farewell, and may good fortune return with you," Oboe says to Akelou and his companions. Before he disappears into the swamps, he grabs Akelou by his arm.

"I promised my son, Toe, that I would give this to you." Oboe hands Akelou a long, tightly wrapped swamp pad. Akelou opens the wrapped leaf and picks out an arrow.

"The arrow was made by my wife, and its tip is covered with the wetness of my son's back. Although the potency of his poison is not what it used to be, it can still be fatal if the arrow strikes true. May it be of some use to you on your quest. Good luck, my friend."

Oboe smacks Akelou on the back and leaps into the darkness of the swamp. Mia-Koda walks up to Akelou, pulling Broomay behind her and hands him a map and a pouch from her belt.

"Follow this map to reach the tower. Keep a sharp eye open for creatures and enemies in the forest. You must be alert and ready for anything.

"Once you get to the tower, you must climb down to a hidden tunnel. There you will enter the tower from below and find your way up into the dungeons. Waste no time. Find the princess and use the Moura stone to leave. This pouch has mud from the outskirts of the Pokwa city. You must cover the stone with the mud, then speak the incantation of Moura: "e-maour-iam." I will be waiting for you."

"Why are you not coming with us?" Leotie asks.

"I have much to do and many others to take counsel with."

She takes out another pouch and sprinkles dirt over the stone. She whispers the incantation, spinning the stone in the air. Once the door is created, she pushes Broomay through.

"Take the end, Akelou. Once I am through the door, yank on the stone." She turns and walks though the door, handing Akelou the stone.

They wave goodbye as Akelou pulls on the stone, which closes the door. Leotie and Akelou look at each other and then down at Tib. They turn toward the forest and begin their journey. Leotie takes the lead, and as she does, Akelou sees the lock of hair he gave her is tied to the end of one of her blades.

CHAPTER FOURTEEN

For nine days Akelou and his companions have been traveling west. After a successful hunt earlier in the day, they have made camp and now sleep with their bellies full of deer meat. Akelou wakes and walks to the edge of camp to relieve himself. Standing by a tree, he hears a rustling in the forest. Akima starts to kick his legs and whinnies at the darkness. Akelou rubs his tired eyes and looks behind his horse where he sees two moon-shaped orbs staring at Akima.

"The horses!" Akelou yells.

Akelou grabs his axe from Akima's saddle and faces down the intruder.

"Feather Runners!" Akelou yells, and he swings his axe at the beast. The Runner flashes its talons and crouches as it prepares to lunge at Akima's throat. The Runner jumps, claws, and opens its mouth for the kill, but Akelou releases his axe, striking the Runner in the abdomen. The Runner falls to its side kicking its legs and screeching in pain. Akima pounces on the beast and finishes it off beneath his powerful hooves. Akelou pets his neck, calming the animal and moving him away from the slain Runner.

"It's alright, boy. You are safe now."

"Akelou!" Leotie yells.

Akelou looks back as two Feather Runners circle Leotie and Tib. Leotie has no weapons, and Tib is screaming at the Runners, trying to ward them off. Akelou takes a step towards them, but before he can help his friends, a Runner slashes Leotie across her back. She falls to the ground, unconscious in a pool of blood.

"Nooo!" Akelou yells as he throws his axe at the Runner closest to him. The weapon flashes in the dark, striking the beast's neck and nearly severing its head, before returning to Akelou's hand. The remaining Runner roars at Akelou and flashes its razor sharp beak as it puts its foot on Leotie. It lowers its head, digging its talons into her flesh. Akelou raises his axe, but then hesitates, startled by something moving within the darkness. Akelou can

see a shadow soaring down from the trees: a Salali lands on the Runner's back, driving its claws into the beast's eyes. The Salali grips the Feather Runner and bites its neck. Trying to escape the Salali's grip, the beast bucks to throw the glider from its back. The glider lifts the Runner's head, exposing his neck and upper body. Akelou raises his axe and tosses it in the direction of the Runner. Akelou catches a glimpse of the Runner and sees a large scar across its one eye. As Akelou blinks, the Runner is knocked down from the blow of the axe. Akelou runs to Leotie's side to make sure she is still alive.

"Thank you for helping us. I am in your debt," Akelou says to the stranger. The Salali walks over to Akelou and looks down at Leotie, "She is badly injured. We must get to safety before other beasts smell the blood. My family's hut is close and in the safety of the trees. We must move quickly."

Akelou looks at the Salali's two black thumb claws that are dripping with blood. "What is your name, friend?"

"My name is Argle. We must not linger. Follow me."

Akelou picks up Leotie and puts her on her horse. Her breathing is growing softer, and blood drips from her fingers. Akelou grabs the reins of both Akima's and Leotie's horses and follows Argle. Tib rides with Leotie, patting her hair and rubing her back. Argle leads them to a clearing filled with tree stumps, in the center of which is a massive tree with thick outreaching branches and a dense canopy. Inside the canopy Akelou can see a crudely constructed hut.

"I will take her inside, but you must leave your horses below," says Argle.

Akelou hands Leotie to Argle, who climbs up the tree with her on his back and tosses down a rope ladder for Akelou to climb.

"Tib, stay here with the horse and call out if there is any danger." Tib nods his head in agreement.

As Akelou climbs the ladder, he hears arguing coming from inside the hut. He hears Salali speech and a female voice.

"Argle, you bring strangers into our home...your father will be furious-"

"He is not my father, and these strangers are in need of our help. They were ambushed by a pack of Runners that I was tracking." Argle's ears perk up as Akelou climbs into the room. "My mother will help mend her wounds." Akelou goes to Leotie and takes off her blood-stained clothes.

"She is burning up. Do you have any tree wasp honey?" Akelou asks as he feels Leotie's forehead.

"We do, I will bring it and some rags to help with the bleeding," says the female Salali.

Still looking down at Leotie, Akelou speaks to Argle, "I should be able to help her, but I need to know if we are welcome here?"

"There will be no trouble for you here."

The crashing and breaking of a bowl grabs Akelou's and Argle's attention. They look up to see the female Salali staring at Akelou. At the sight of the Salali's face Akelou's breath goes cold.

"Taeau, is it really you?" the Salali asks as tears streak down her face.

Akelou stands up nervously, "Yes, Mrs. Claw." Akelou can barely get the words out of his mouth before she jumps towards him, crushing him under a hug.

"I have wondered what happened to you, child. You have grown well, Taeau, tall and strong...I only wish Ven..." She stops speaking and continues to sob.

"Ok, well, first let us see to these wounds."

The three of them kneel by Leotie's side. Argle gives his mother and Akelou a confused look as his mother speaks. "Do you know any medicine, Taeau? Can you help her?"

"I can close these wounds well enough, but the fever is what we must fear." Akelou signals for the others to move back. He takes out his necklace, gripping it in one hand and laying the other on Leotie's back. He closes his eyes and starts to sway back and forth, mouthing a chant Alo taught him. His necklace shines so brightly Argle and his mother turn their heads. The blood pouring from Leotie's wounds stops and begins to dry. Akelou opens his eyes, and his necklace goes dull. "Mrs. Claw, we need to rub the honey over these wounds it will help keep them clean." They rub the honey over Leotie's back and cover her tightly with blankets.

"If she makes it through the night, she should survive. She will have to fight the fever alone, for there is nothing more I can do," says Akelou.

Mrs. Claw's and Argle's ears twitch, and they look at each other. The horses stir down below. "That is Broken Wrist coming back from looking for you, Argle. He will be angry. Taeau-"

"My name is Akelou now, Mrs. Claw."

"Good, then you can call me Half Moon. Calling me Mrs. Claw will not help with Broken Wrist's mood. Now stand back and let me deal with him." Argle steps back towards Akelou as a lean, mean-looking older man comes up the ladder with a spear in his hand.

"Half Moon, what is going on?" he yells. Half Moon goes to Broken Wrist trying to calm him down. "Whose horses are those, and why is there blood covering the ladder? He looks around the room and sees Akelou and Leotie. He points his spear at Akelou. "Who are you, what is your business in my home-"

"Your home!" Argle interrupts, pointing at Broken Wrist.

As he stares at Argle, Broken Wrist's face grows red. "You move over there by that wall," he says to Akelou.

Akelou does as he says. Broken Wrist walks to Leotie and looks at her wounds. "These are wounds made by a Runner's claw. Was it you who killed the three Feather Runners to the east?"

"Yes., We were ambushed, and in the attack she was wounded by a Runner's talons. She would not have survived if not for Argle's help."

"You went after the Runner pack again, after I warned you not to. You directly disobeyed me. I do not care that you are not my son. You will mind me in my home."

"That's right, yell at me after I have saved their lives."

"I am glad you were able to help, but I will not be disrespected by you again. Do you hear me, Argle? You have not yet come of age."

"Broken Wrist, that is enough. This is my nephew, Akelou, Argle's half cousin. He is the son of Dirty Hands, the Meno farmer who was Black Claw's brother." Both Argle and Broken Wrist stare at Akelou. Then Broken Wrist lowers his spear, "Is that true, son?"

"Yes, my name is Akelou, and my companions and I left the Noshota swamps nine days ago for the Whispering Canyons."

"What purpose do you have there?"

"The Pokwa princess was kidnapped by Ush-Ka and his men. The Pokwa king entrusted us to rescue his daughter." Half Moon gasps, stumbling back at the mention of Ush-Ka's name.

"Ush-Ka, the dog that murdered my father and brother!" Argle yells.

"Enough of this...Argle, see to finding Akelou a bed. We will finish this in the morning," Broken Wrist says as he helps Half Moon up from the floor.

Akelou looks at Argle, "I can sleep here next to Leotie. I will gather my things from the horses below."

"I will help you," says Argle.

Broken Wrist and Half Moon climb through an opening that leads into another level of the hut. Argle and Akelou climb down to the horses. Argle jumps and glides to a nearby tree, disappearing into the darkness.

"You alright, Tib?" Tib shakes his head and points up to where Leotie lies. "I do not know, but she is strong and a survivor. I am going to sleep beside her. Can you camp down here and watch over the horses?" Tib pets Leotie's horse as he nods his head. Akelou grabs his furs from Akima's saddle and picks up some grain for his horse. "Keep a watchful eye tonight, friend, for there are many beasts roaming these woods." He pets his horse and climbs back into the hut.

As Akelou climbs up the ladder, Argle floats in from the darkness, grabbing the tree. "So are you really my cousin?"

"Yes, Black Claw your father, was my father's adopted brother."

"Did you know my father and brother well?" Akelou stops climbing and looks at Argle, "Yes I knew them both well...Ven, your brother, was my best friend."

"I do not remember much about them. I was only a Pemi when they were killed. Mother says I have my father's claws."

"She is right. Your father was a great Salali. He would be proud of what you did for us tonight." Argle smiles before they climb up into the hut.

"I sleep in the hammock over there," Argle says, pointing to his bed. You can take my sister's hammock if you like. She left us last spring for the city to find a mate."

"The city still exists?"

"Yes, but Broken Wrist says it is controlled by barbarians. Mother says the city is not safe for me because I am Black Claw's son. My father killed many Nossa in the massacre at the city. The Nossa would capture and enslave me only to send me to Columbus's mines. Broken Wrist says that there are few males left in the city, that most have been made slaves and taken away. Well, good night, I will see you in the morning" Argle says as he climbs into his hammock.

Akelou lies down next to Leotie and thinks of his foster parents and whether they are still alive. He falls asleep to the image of his father and of the last night he spent with his mother, asleep in her lap.

The next day, as Leotie's shivers and Argle and Broken Wrist argue, Half Moon and Akelou talk about their lives since they fled the city. Akelou tells her about his adventures, and she tells him how she worries about her

children. Half Moon is not the Salali Akelou remembered. She used to be confident and sure of herself. Black Claw himself feared her stare and took counsel with her. Now she speaks only of uncertainty and worry.

"Broken Wrist lost his mate in the siege. They never had any children. He was Black Claw's most trusted friend. I do not know how we would have survived without him. The two of them will soon kill each other if Argle stays any longer. He needs to find his own place in this world. The time has come for me to say goodbye." She puts her hand on Akelou's, "I must ask you a favor, Akelou. Take Argle with you on your journey."

Akelou does not know what to say. "Our road is dangerous. One of my companions may die on your floor. I cannot promise he will be safe."

"It was not by chance that my son came to your aid. His destiny and yours are one and the same. I see that now, and I have to trust that everything has happened for a reason."

"I can't believe you are asking me this. I watched Ven and Black Claw die. I can't be responsible for the life of another of your family."

"There is nothing we can do about that now," she says coldly. "Life is hard and death is unfair. I did not want to lose my oldest son, but I did. And I do not want to say goodbye to my youngest son, but I must. Argle's best chance to come of age is away from here, and you are my last hope. Please, Akelou, think about it."

Half Moon leaves Akelou alone with Leotie, and he wipes some sweat from her forehead. Frustrated, he climbs down the rope ladder. Tib has made a small camp and is cooking a forest rat he trapped.

"How was your night, Tib?" Tib just shrugs his shoulders. "How about you, boy? How are you?" he asks Akima. "I need to clear my thoughts. I will be back by dark. We leave tomorrow, with or without Leotie." Tib stares up at Akelou with a look in his eye. "Do not look at me with such judgment. The Pokwa are depending on us. I will open a door back to the Msa-Oda and leave her in their care if she is not well enough to continue."

He walks into the forest and wanders, lost in thought. The daylight soon loses its eternal battle with the night when Akelou suddenly realizes where he is. He clears some bushes and stands in their camp from the night before. He looks at the cold coals of the fire and sees tracks left by the scavenging creatures that have taken the bodies of the Runners off into the bush. Akelou walks to the spot where Leotie was injured and sees the bloodstains on the dirt. Guilt weighs heavy on his shoulders, and he thinks of the consequences if she were to die. Akelou begins to understand that he needs more help. With Leotie hurt or unable to continue, his group will suffer and his quest might be doomed.

He sits down in front of what is left of the fire. Akelou rubs his necklace as he thinks about Half Moon's request. A breeze starts to blow, picking up some forest dirt. Akelou stares at the swirling dirt, and it begins to take shape. Two eyes stare at him, then a body forms around them.

"Black Claw?" he whispers.

The apparition smiles before it is whisked away by a light breeze. Akelou hears the trees rustle, then Argle lands where the vision of his dead father revealed itself.

"What are you doing here? Why have you left the hut? Leotie is asking for you. Her fever has broken. We should return and get you ready to return to your quest."

Akelou looks at Argle and takes a deep breath, knowing now what he must do. He says to Argle, "Leotie will not be able to track, hunt, and help us on our quest until she has healed. Our quest is at the verge of failure, and we need help. I need you, Argle. The Pokwa need you. Will you help us?"

Argle puffs out his chest and tries to hide his excitement. "Y-Yes, I would be honored to help you, cousin. I will not shame you, and I will not shame my family even if it costs me my life."

"I believe you. Now lead the way back to your hut, for there is much to do."

Anxiety grips Akelou as he slowly walks back to Argle's home. Argle's joy fades as he realizes he has never left his mother's side for more than a few days. Argle knows she will be sad, and he dreads looking at her face when he says goodbye. Once they reach the hut, they quietly climb through the floor and see Leotie sitting up, with Half Moon by her side.

"Gave up on me, did you?" she says as Akelou enters the hut.

"Sorry I was not here when your fever broke, but I gathered some stems of the Siow plant to help with your healing."

Leotie turns over, exposing her wounds. Akelou chews on the green plants and covers her wounds with the healing paste. Leotie moans as the paste seeps into her lesions soothing her pain. Half Moon looks into Akelou's eyes and knows he has made his decision. She looks up at her son, and a tear falls onto the wooden floor. She gets up, and without a word she climbs into her and Broken Wrist's room. Argle watches her leave and tries to build up the courage to say something, but he cannot. Akelou lies next to Leotie and falls asleep.

The next morning, Leotie wakes early. She gets up and limps around the hut with her blankets wrapped tightly around her shoulders. Half Moon is already up and gives her some food to help with her strength.

"I patched and washed your clothes as best as I could, dear. The bloodstains were deep."

"Thank you. I am indebted to your family for all you have done."

Half Moon helps her dress. "You owe us nothing. Just take good care of my son."

Leotie looks at Half Moon, surprised. "Your son?"

"Yes, I believe that Akelou has asked him to accompany you on your quest."

"If this is true, I will protect him with my life as you have helped save mine."

"I thank you for those words. You bring comfort to my heavy heart."

Half Moon makes Leotie some honey tea before returning to her room. Akelou wakes and sees that the sun will soon rise. He notices Leotie and decides it is time to ask her about the journey.

"Leotie, can you ride?" She nods her head and kisses Akelou on the cheek before climbing down the ladder. Akelou climbs into Half Moon's room. "I will keep him safe, but I cannot promise you will see him again."

Half Moon hugs Akelou, "I will bring him to you." Akelou agrees and leaves the hut. Down on the ground, he see that Argle is talking to Tib.

"Argle, your mother waits for you." Argle looks at Akelou and slowly climbs to his mother. When he gets into the hut she is waiting for him.

"Come here, son. There is something I have to show you. I knew this day would come." She unwraps a dusty blanket. "These were your father's. I removed them from his body as we fled the city." Half Moon unwraps Black Claw's helmet and false claws. "Take these and leave with your cousin...find your way in this world and do not look back." Tears trickle down her cheeks. Argle hugs his mother, but she does not have the strength to look at him.

"I will always love you, mother."

"I know, son...now go...I will be fine." Argle turns and walks out of the room, leaving Half Moon crying on the floor. He sees Broken Wrist standing in the middle of the hut with a spear. Broken Wrist walks up to him.

"I was not the father you wanted, and I loved the father you lost like a brother. I will protect her as long as I draw breath." He breaks the spear across his leg. "This was the spear that took your father's life. I have kept it all this time, not knowing what to do with it." He hands Argle the bloodstained spear tip. "This is the only thing I have to give you from your father." Broken Wrist steps aside, letting Argle pass.

"I have always taken out my anger at not having a father on you. I am sorry for that, and I know you would have been a good father if you were given a chance," Argle says as he passes Broken Wrist.

"I do have a son, Argle, and I am proud of who he has become." Argle walks to the ladder and disappears, leaving Broken Wrist standing alone and holding the end of a broken spear.

On the ground, Akelou helps Leotie mount her horse. "We will travel slowly as you gather your strength." Akelou turns at the sound of scratching against a tree. He looks at Argle in his father's armor.

"We travel west and do not stop until dark. You can scout our path from the trees." Argle agrees and jumps into the canopy of the forest. Akelou moves the horses, and Tib rides with Leotie, massaging her back. He looks back at the hut and sees Half Moon looking out at him. He raises his hand to her and sees Broken Wrist embrace her from behind.

With every sunrise, Leotie's health improves, and Argle proves to be a valuable scout. The Forest has begun to change as they approach its western borders. The trees and plant life are thinner and more spread out.

"The map says we should be leaving the forest tomorrow and arriving at the base of the Whispering Canyons. It says we must follow this path or be lost in the maze of carved rock," Akelou reads to the others.

Argle gets up from the ground where he has been eating the last of his forest nuts, "I will get to the base of the canyons first and scout our position. We should re-supply our water and food for the canyons."

"I agree. Tib, in the early morning, take Akima and fill our water bladders by the stream we passed earlier. We will leave the horses behind in the forest. They will not survive the trip through the canyons."

The four companions lie down to rest. Akelou falls into a deep sleep. He sees a strange race of men, a long-toothed dog, and eyes staring at him in the darkness. He tries to look deeper into the darkness, but it grows blacker, and then a deep echo shakes him and a blazing light wakes him.

Akelou gets to his feet, looking around and seeing that Tib and Argle are already gone. He starts to break down camp when Leotie wakes.

"How do you feel today, Leotie?"

"Well enough," she says as she stretches her arms. They pack up the camp and share some honey tea that Half Moon gave them. Tib comes back into camp with the replenished water bladders. The companions mount the horses and ride west. The wind blows harder and harder, slowing their travel. The forest is opening up, and the ground has become dry and arid, with stones that clank against the horses' hooves.

Ahead of them, an earthly light grows, and the forest disappears. Leotie points upward, and Akelou looks up to see Argle floating towards them from a distant tree.

"I have seen the canyons and found the path you showed us. Follow me." They follow Argle and come to the eastern edge of the canyons. They look out at the canyons and are overwhelmed with its beauty. Akelou stands on the cliff and looks to the northwest while holding his necklace

"What can you see, Akelou?" Leotie asks.

"I can see the outline of the tower and a rising mist beyond it, a three, to four-day journey."

Akelou takes out a pouch, grabbing some dirt from the rocky cliff.

"If we succeed in our quest, I will open a door back here. Once we are safe, we will get the horses and travel back to the Noshota swamps." He grabs Akima, putting the horse's head against his.

"Take care of Leotie's horse, my friend, but do not wander too far, for we will return." Akima snips at his master's ears as Akelou removes his reins. Akima turns with Leotie's horse, and together they run into the forest. Akelou takes out the map and leads them into the canyons.

CHAPTER FIFTEEN

After traveling in the canyons for three days, Akelou and his companions are sleep-deprived and sunburned. They have fought a continuous howling wind that whistles against the sun-baked rock, the wind is filled with small grains of sand that pelt the skin and cling to fur. There is little shelter in this arid landscape to shield them from the elements. The canyon crosswinds make starting a fire difficult, so the four travelers sleep together at night, huddled and shivering in the cold.

The sun has set as they settle into a small cove in the rocky walls to rest. They take out what rations they have and eat in silence. Leotie is in charge of their water supply that has become dangerously low. The wind sucks the moisture from the air, blistering their skin and cracking their parched lips. Akelou is exhausted, and he tries to shut his eyes to sleep, but he can only hear the howling of the canyons. The world goes dark, and soon the sound of the wind becomes distant. A stabbing in his ribs wakes him. He opens his eyes and hears Leotie's voice.

"Akelou, the wind has stopped. Listen," she says, licking dust from her lips. Akelou lifts his ear and hears only a hint of the canyon winds.

The others have woken, and from underneath the Ga-Taga furs they bask in the quiet, smiling at one another in relief. Akelou removes the fur. "Why is it so dark? There should be a good moon tonight, and I cannot see any stars."

Argle walks out into the path and sniffs the air. "What do you smell, Argle?" asks Leotie.

"There is water in the air." Argle looks up into the darkness and sees a flash inside the dense clouds above. Following the burst of light, a loud crack of thunder echoes in the canyons.

"A storm is above us, a nasty thunder cracker. We should find better shelter from the storm."

"There is none better to find, Argle. We will have to wait out the storm here," argues Akelou.

The rain starts to fall, and it comes down hard. The companions rush to protect themselves from the rain, pulling the furs over themselves. Leotie looks down at her feet and notices they are submerged under a stream of rapidly moving water.

"Where does all of this water lead to?" she yells out to the others in a shivering voice.

Suddenly, Argle's ears shoot up, and he turns, looking down the dark path behind them. He takes a few steps and stares into the darkness. "RUN! CLIMB THE WALLS!" he yells as loudly as he can, pushing them towards the side of the canyons. They all try to climb the slippery wall, but the falling water pushes them back. Their hands and arms begin to cramp from the cold. Then a sound like the stampeding Ga-Taga echoes in the narrow canyons. Akelou looks back, and as lightning flashes, he sees a mountain of water rushing toward them. He grabs Tib and Leotie as he prepares for the wave to hit them. Argle, jumping as high as he can, climbs up the rock and avoids the tilting water.

The canyon river sweeps them into its grip. Akelou clenches his fists tightly as the cold water strikes his body. The water's power forces them against the rocky floor and cuts into Akelou's wet, wrinkled flesh. Tib and Leotie cling onto Akelou's neck trying to stay above the surging water. They fight the river, bouncing off the walls and defending themselves against whatever the water sweeps up.

Akelou looks up and sees Argle jumping onto something ahead of them. In another flash of light he sees something splash into the water. Akelou focuses his acute eyesight on what fell and sees a petrified tree racing towards them. Akelou reaches out his hand, grabbing a hold of the wood and pulling Leotie and Tib onto the log raft. They desperately hold onto the tree, trying to regain what strength they can. The current grows as the walls of the canyons close in around them. Akelou hears an unnatural echoing approaching and looks out to see a hole carved into the side of the canyon. Inside the gaping hole he sees the raging water drop and the open sky beyond the canyon's edge. The water has broken through the canyon wall and is falling down its side. Between the flashes of lightning he sees the outline of a rising tower.

He turns to Leotie and grabs her hand. She is exhausted, and her pale face is covered with wet hair. There is fear in her eyes, for she senses what is coming. Akelou begins to hear the crashing water ahead and knows they do not have much time. A shadow passes above, and Akelou sees the outline of Argle floating to the rim of the hole.

"Hang on!" Akelou yells, hoping Leotie hears his voice. Akelou sees the edge of the hole and the water tunneling down and out the side of the canyon. He pulls Leotie and Tib onto the top of the racing log. He knows he has only moments until they are cast into the abyss. Akelou sees the approaching horizon and, knowing what he must do, he lets all of his power build in his chest. His necklace burns and his wrist goes cold. He remembers back to the cliff above the jungle. He sees himself with his arms stretched and his vision around him.

He opens his eyes and sees the golden light around him rising from the carved marking on his back and arms. Leotie and Tib hug Akelou for their lives. He opens his mouth and raises his arms into the air. From his mouth the deafening screech of the Wa-Hone shakes the canyon walls, and water explodes around them. The golden light of his vision fills the cave as they race to the edge of the falls.

Akelou jumps from the log and thrusts his arms, and they shoot out from the opening into the night. He feels the cold wind under his arms as he glides across the storm-filled sky. The deafening crash of the water behind them fades as they soar into the night towards the shadowy tower. A golden trail of light flows from Akelou's arms and necklace as he soars downwards. Argle glides below him with his underbelly flapping in the wind.

Akelou is blinded by the rain and wind that crash against his face. He opens his arms and spreads his fingers, opening his golden feathers that capture the wind, slowing their decent as they come to the wall of the tower. Argle hits the wall with great force, bouncing and skidding down its side as he tries to claw at the slippery rock. His claws spark as he tumbles down the side of the tower. Akelou lifts his legs toward the tower's walls and sees talons of light around his feet ready for the impact of the collision. The talons strike the wall, digging into the rock and stopping them from sliding into a furious river at the tower's base. Argle climbs over to Akelou, struggling to grapple the slippery jagged rock. The rain continues to pour down as Leotie and Tib cling to Akelou's back.

"Where now, Akelou? We can't stay out here much longer," Argle yells over the rain and water below.

Akelou looks down and sees the river that runs around the base of the tower. He knows from studying the map that the entrance to the tunnel is down by the water's edge somewhere. He points to the river, and they start to climb the wet rock.

"Argle, you must search for the opening. Your vision is the sharpest! It will be a small tunnel near the water's edge!"

Argle takes off, exploring for the entrance and leaving Akelou hanging onto the side of the tower while Tib and Leotie dangle from his back above the water. Akelou peers back through the pouring rain to see the massive waterfall exploding from the canyon walls. The sloping edge of the canyon stretches in both directions as far as his eyes can see.

"Ouch!" Akelou hears Leotie yell.

Akelou looks down and sees only darkness. Waiting again for the lightning, he sees a flash followed by a deep crack that shakes the tower. Akelou opens his hands, and he, Tib and Leotie slip down the side of the tower. The lightning comes again, and he sees Argle waving at them from below. Akelou slides down to Argle, "Did you find the entrance?" Argle gives him an awkward look and nods his head. "Then take us to it."

Argle leads them to a flat area on the tower. He points down at the river, which is now dangerously close. Akelou sees the entrance and knows why Argle gave him a look. The entrance is just below the surface of the turbulent water.

Leotie taps Akelou on the shoulder, and in her face he sees her desperation. Realizing that both she and Tib will not survive much longer without shelter, he notices a massive boulder above them. He closes his eyes and thinks about his stepmother and father. He imagines them back at the hut of his youth as slaves-a master whipping his father in the fields, and his mother hunched over a fire, broken and consumed with sorrow. Rage grows inside him, and his brace starts to shine. He turns and strikes the side of the tower with all of his might. His fist slams against the rock, and sparks explode from the impact. A shock wave races towards the boulder. The others watch as the boulder starts to shake, swaying back and forth before falling with a crash against the tower in front of the entrance. The water flows around the boulder, exposing the tunnel below. Akelou signals for them to jump. They all leap for the tunnel and roll onto the hard tunnel floor.

"MOVE!" Argle yells as he pushes them deeper into the cave. The pressure of the water has forced the boulder forward, slamming it through the entrance. The boulder emerges, now the size of the tunnel, and it continues to race towards them. They run deeper into the tunnel and as they run, Akelou picks up Tib whose markings are flashing violently. Akelou looks back and sees that the boulder is moving closer and the tunnel is shrinking.

"JUMP!" he yells at the top of his voice. The boulder slams into the tunnel wall, collapsing the ceiling behind them. They all lie on the floor exhausted and panting for breath in complete darkness.

"We will sleep here in the dark until we have the strength to move." Akelou takes out a vial that Mia-Koda gave him. "Take a small drink of this. It will help warm your body as you sleep." Everyone takes a small chug from the vial and quickly falls asleep. They lie on top of each other, soaked, bruised, and shivering from cold.

Near the eastern rim of the Whispering Canyons, a large group of Daboon has gathered. They sit in a circle, surrounding a pile of satchels filled with sand from the black shores. The powerful storm that passed overhead three days earlier has made the Daboon overly agitated. Their fur is coated with a sandy paste that irritates their skin and eyes. There has not been such a gathering of Daboon like this since the ancient days of their first master.

Grumblings have started between some Daboon in the group. They have been waiting in the cold for something they do not know or understand. They were gathered by Un-Ra, who bears the helmet of Si-Imab. He can sense the Daboons' growing frustration and impatience. He has promised them a new life free from hunger and isolation. He told the leaders of the scattered packs that his master would grant them great power. They have followed him blindly over great distances and endured many hardships and near starvation. If they go much longer without a kill or a purpose, they will begin to turn on each other and fall into chaos-and Un-Ra knows this.

The second largest Daboon, whom Un-Ra named Ve-Na, has been walking among the small groups of Daboon and fueling a rebellion.

"There is no great lord who would give us power. Un-Ra is no leader, he has brought us here under trickery. He means kill us and feast on ar bones and steal our magical black sand."

Although most Daboon cannot understand Ve-Na's poor speech, they feed on his forceful tone. Un-Ra senses this as he looks down at the Daboon atop a formation of rocks. He stands tall and roars out to his mutinous brethren. "I hear whispers of doubt from those I bring. I offer great power and fresh meat to these fool beasts that I rescued from starvation and scavenging, yet they whisper like sheep against my back. My Lord will walk among us soon, and with him will come all things."

Ve-Na walks up to the cluster of rocks, followed closely by the rest of the Daboon. "He lies there is no powerful lord. Ave we not suffered enough doing what the mighty Un-Ra commands like we ar slaves. Many of us die on this long journey. If we fight together we can beat him."

The Daboon behind Ve-Na growl and slam their arms against the ground in agreement.

Un-Ra continues, "Do not blasphemy our Lord in front of me, worm. Our great Lord does not betray his followers. He will grant all that he has promised, but you must prove your loyalty to him if you want to be rewarded. It's your lack of faith that keeps him away. Did I not bring you to the black shores where the great sand was collected? Was it not I who brought you to the hut in the trees where we feasted on the flesh of man and soft fur? The dark Lord showed me the path to these gifts-"

"Curse you Un-Ra ar curse the dark lord," growls Ve-Na, as he picks up dirt, tossing it at Un-Ra and challenging him before all the Daboon.

Un-Ra jumps down from the rocks, landing beside Ve-Na and tossing mud in his face. "I will show the rest of the Daboon what happens to blasphemers."

"Your confusing tongue will taste good," Ver-Na says as he and Un-Ra circle each other.

They both wave their arms at each other in a display of their dominance. Un-Ra arches his back and shows Ve-Na his long powerful quills. He begins to contract his back muscles, and his quills click loudly. Ve-Na does the same, rattling his quills together in an effort to show Un-Ra his strength.

All the Daboon in the small herd now rattle their quills, which fuels the energy and aggression in all of them. Un-Ra attacks first, lunging at Ve-Na. They growl as they attack, exposing their teeth and brandishing their claws, trying to rip each other apart. Another Daboon jumps towards Un-Ra from inside the crowd, but Un-Ra turns and shoots quills from his back at the attacking Daboon. The Daboon falls to the ground shaking as the toxins seep into his bloodstream. Un-Ra tosses Ve-Na to the ground and races towards the wounded Daboon, ripping at him with his teeth. Ve-Na tries to help the fallen Daboon, but Un-Ra is too powerful. Un-Ra grips his jaws around the fallen beast's throat, and the Daboon around them roar with excitement as they hear Un-Ra snap his neck. Un-Ra turns back to Ve-Na with blood dripping from his mouth. He roars loudly with the other Daboon, and in a bloodthirsty frenzy the Daboon begin to beat and molest the slain beast, ripping his body apart and feasting on the fresh meat. Ve-Na tries to flee, but the surrounding Daboon push him back into the pit toward the fight.

"Elp me you fools. He will destroy you all," Ve-Na calls out in desperation.

Un-Ra starts to move toward Ve-Na, when a loud bellowing echoes from above. The Daboon stop roaring and gaze up to the sky. Un-Ra looks back and sees the Hornbill perched on the rocks where he once stood.

"The dark Lord is upon us. You will now witness his true power," Un-Ra yells as he bows before his master.

Some of the Daboon bow, like Un-Ra, toward the rocks. Others try to scatter, but are trapped by a wall of darkness that rises from the ground. Some curl up in fear, exposing their quills for protection, and others try to attack the darkness. From within the wall of shadow a black hand grabs Ve-Na. He screams in pain as the claws of darkness pierce his flesh. The Daboon watch as the dark hand grips Ve-Na. They bob their heads up and down, submissive to the darkness. The hand slams Ve-Na to the ground, breaking his body. From inside the wall Un-Nabus walks beside Un-Ra, and the rest of the Daboon bow.

"You have done well, Un-Ra, my loyal servant, and rewarded you will be."

"Thank you, Master."

Un-Nabus turns to the Daboon and raises his arms. The darkness around him mimics his movements, and the Daboon cower.

"My children, the Atha-Ba, Lord of the Daboon, has come to reclaim your loyalty. In days past, your fathers were forged by the will of the Hhtuno, and to the Hhtuno you are bound. Pledge yourselves to me with the blood and sacrifice of this disbeliever. Defy me, and your fate will be his." Many of the Daboon do not understand, but they feel Un-Nabus's presence and bend to his will.

Un-Nabus walks among the cowering beasts. "If you are to be an army, then you will need to be armed as great warriors worthy of the Daboon."

Un-Nabus points his staff at the boulders, and the darkness surrounds them. When the darkness clears, the Daboon stare with excitement and greed at what is left behind.

"Take what you can carry, for we march on to the tower."

The Daboon pick up the maces, clubs, axes, and armor made from the stone.

"Un-Ra, I promised you a great reward for completing your task, and I shall be true to my word." Un-Nabus raises his hands, and the darkness lifts the last untouched stone before Un-Ra. Un-Nabus walks to the satchels piled in the middle of the circle of Daboon. He takes a handful of the black sand and tosses it into the cloud of darkness. A spear of shadow pierces Ve-Na's slain body, and a blood cloud from the wound combines with the black sand. The darkness crushes the stone, and a firey light begins to shine.

"Rise, Un-Ra, and claim your prize."

Un-Ra rises from his knees and reaches inside the darkness, gripping his hand around cold, smooth stone. He pulls out a hammer from inside the darkness. The stone is now black and is covered with burning markings.

"Take this, Un-Ra, for only the greatest Daboon warrior may wield it."

The other Daboon watch as Un-Ra raises the hammer over his head. The hammer shines in the darkness, and Un-Ra roars. The Daboon gather around their leader and roar and slam their weapons on the ground, shaking the world beneath them.

"Now march, my Daboon, and follow your master, for the glory of battle and the taste of blood will soon be yours." Un-Nabus turns and assumes the form of the dark bird, and the Daboon march behind him to the tower of Ogdah.

CHAPTER SIXTEEN

Deep within the caves under the tower of Ogdah, Akelou and his companions have been trying to regain needed strength. Akelou opens his eyes and grabs his necklace, rubbing it with his fingers to light the tunnel around them. He gets to his feet and wakes the others. They all stretch their aching muscles and begin their journey again. With great effort they have climbed through small gaps in the rock for three days. As they now emerge from the honeycombed foundation of the tower, they come to a deep inner trench. Choking steam rises from the dark below as they circle the pit, following a narrow path. Tib has given up trying to climb and now travels on Akelou's back.

Argle whispers down to Akelou, "I have seen torches over this ridge guarded by three men."

Leotie nods to Akelou and takes an arrow from her quiver. They cautiously creep over the ridge and look down across the dark pit. They can see the guards standing watch.

"That must be an entrance to the dungeons. The princess must be somewhere beyond it," Leotie whispers to Akelou.

Akelou spots two of the guards sitting on the ground, asleep against a wall. The third guard holds a torch and paces back and forth in front of an entrance. Akelou points to Argle, "Climb above us and wait for our signal. When you see it, glide across the pit and attack one of the sleeping guards. We will take care of the others."

Argle climbs up and out of sight.

"What is the signal, Akelou?" whispers Leotie.

"When I strike and Argle leaps across the trench, hit one of the sleeping guards with an arrow. We must be as silent as we are deadly, and not alert others of our presence."

Leotie strings an arrow and waits for Akelou, who looks down at his feet for a small pebble. When the guard turns and begins his walk back

towards the edge of the pit, Akelou tosses the stone into the darkness. As the stone strikes the tower, the guard, hearing the falling rock, turns and walks to the edge of the trench. Akelou swings his axe over his shoulder and then lunges it toward the guard. The axe spins in the darkness, whistling in a lethal silence. Hearing a whisking in the air, the guard lifts his torch only to see a flash before the axe strikes his forehead. The guard goes limp, leans forward, and falls, disappearing into a cloud of rising steam.

Akelou's axe rises from the darkness towards its master, and Leotie wastes no time taking aim and releases her arrow. The arrow strikes the sleeping guard in the chest. The guard wakes from the shock of the impact and looks down at the arrow sticking out from his chest. The arrow has pierced his lungs, and he tries to scream but can only gasp. The sound wakes the other guard, who groggily gets to his feet. He lifts his torch to search for what has woken him. Then, another arrow from Leotie's bow slices through the air finishing off the injured guard.

The remaining guard turns and sees what has happened to his comrade. He lifts his rifle, just as Argle lands on him, driving a thumb claw into his back. His rifle fires, before he drops it into the trench, echoing against inside the silent tower. They both fall and roll towards the edge of the pit. The guard stumbles but gets to his feet with blood pouring down his arm from Argle's claws. He looks back at Argle, who is shaken from the impact, and grabs his sword. The guard raises his weapon and smiles as he looks down, knowing he has the upper hand. Argle tries to shuffle to his feet, when suddenly he hears a loud thud. The guard drops his sword and groans in pain. Leotie has landed another blow, and an arrow sticks in his back. Argle wastes no time and charges at the wounded guard. He grabs the guard and head butts him with his father's helmet, cracking the guard's skull. The guard falls back, plunging down into the depths of the pit.

Akelou looks down across the pit at Argle, who signals that he is alright. Akelou reaches into Leotie's pack and takes out a bundle of Pokwa rope. Mia-Koda knew that to enter the dungeons they would need to make it across the trench. Akelou takes out a grappling arrow from Leotie's quiver and ties the rope to the end. He points above them, showing Leotie where to aim the arrow. She strings the arrow and searches for a jagged ledge. She releases the arrow, and they watch as it strikes the rocky wall of the tower. Akelou tugs on the rope until the arrow is securely nudged in the stone. Then he picks up Tib and puts him on his back. Akelou's hands the rope to Leotie.

"Are you ready?" he asks Leotie as they look into each other's eyes.

Leotie grabs the rope, takes a deep breath, and lunges forward into the darkness. She drops down, racing toward the other side of the pit and disappearing into a billow of rising steam. The rope is not long enough, so

Leotie jumps for the ledge. She lands hard, rolling forward from the impact. Argle helps Leotie up, and they both look back at Akelou.

Akelou reaches out his arm and whispers a chant. A cyclone of noxious gas blows the rope in Akelou's direction, and he leaps from the side of the cliff, with Tib squeezing his neck in shock. Akelou grabs the rope with one hand, and they sail down to Leotie and Argle.

Akelou looks up when he hears the noise made by the stress on the rope. The rope snaps, and Akelou and Tib drop like a stone in water. Leotie and Argle watch in horror as Akelou and Tib falls below the ledge. Akelou reaches out with his arm before they hit the wall with a powerful thud. Tib screams as he loses his grip around Akelou's neck and falls back towards the trench. Akelou reaches out and grabs Tib by his ankle. Tib covers his eye with his hands as he swings upside down, his loincloth draping down over his face, suspended above the abyss of the pit.

Akelou pulls the screaming Wicker up and puts him on his back. Akelou climbs the short distance back to the ledge. Once over the ledge, Argle and Leotie help them up. Tib jumps down to the ground and starts kissing and rolling on the rocky floor. Akelou stands, dizzy, trying to regain his senses after the fall. He notices his back is wet and dripping with some kind of warm liquid. He looks down at Tib and sees that the Wicker's loincloth is soaked in urine.

"TIB!" Akelou yells, with disgust on his face.

Tib hides behind Argle, covering his body with the glider's bushy tail. Leotie and Argle start to laugh as they see the wet stain on Akelou's back. Akelou laughs, too, and brushes some dirt and rocks from his body. They all look ahead into the tunnel leading into the tower and see a few dimly lit torches.

"Arm yourselves. We do not know what awaits us in there. We look for the princess, we find her, we secure her, and then I will open a door back to the canyons. We must be silent and like shadows if we are to succeed in our quest," Akelou tells the others as he tucks in his necklace under his clothes and grabs his axe.

They begin their walk into the tower, weapons in hand: Argle has his father's false claws, Akelou his axe, Tib two small stone knives given to him by the Pokwa, and Leotie her bow strung with an arrow. They continue on their quest, racing past flickering torches as they search for the princess.

Akelou points to Leotie as they come to the end of a tunnel. Exiting the tunnel, they find themselves at the top of the lower tower. The ceiling of the pit is above them, and they can see another tunnel, followed by a rope

bridge that leads to a stone stairway at the base of a wooden door. They begin to hear moans, then the sound of a cracking whip. Akelou watches as a guard emerges from the tunnel and walks to the bridge.

Leotie readies her bow, but Akelou signals for her to wait. Akelou points to the guard, then to himself, then to Argle and the far tunnel. They turn back to Leotie, who is ready, then Akelou and Argle silently charge at the patrolling guard's back, as Leotie aims her arrow. She releases her bow, and the arrow soars past Akelou and Argle, striking the guard center mass.

"Ugh," the guard yells as the arrow hits him.

He turns to see Akelou lunging for him with his axe raised, and a blur of fur and claws soars over his head. Akelou quickly finishes off the guard, tossing his body over the edge into the pit. Tib jumps from Akelou's back and scouts the tunnel ahead with Argle. Leotie exits the tunnel and creeps towards Akelou. They reach the next tunnel, and look into it to see Argle and Tib in a narrow hall lit by torches.

"Can you kill those torches, Akelou?" whispers Leotie.

Akelou nods his head and points at the torches. The stone on his brace shines black, and one by one the torches go out. Once the flames die, the companions huddle together. They hear a creaking echo outside of the tunnel as the large wooden door at the top of the stairs opens. Akelou quickly glances out and sees two guards with long spears walk into the tower.

Akelou looks at his map, then whispers, "We must go into the tunnel, that is where the main dungeons are. The wooden door at the top of the stairs is the entrance into the upper level of the tower. Leotie, you must strike down the guard on the left. I will take care of the other. Argle, once the torches are out and the guards slain, scout further into the tunnel with Tib."

Akelou reaches out, pointing at the torches beside the door. Leotie and Argle watch as Akelou's brace shines. One of the guards looks at a torch as it dies out, and he lowers his spear.

"What is-"

The guard starts to speak as Akelou's axe strikes him in his side. Akelou stretches out his hand, and his axe releases from the guard's body and returns to him. The force of the axe leaving his side pulls the guard into the pit. The other guard is frozen with fear as he watches his comrade descend into darkness. The guard turns and rushes for the door.

"Intru-" he tries to yell, but Leotie's arrow pierces his shoulder. He awkwardly stumbles and reaches for the lodged arrow. Another arrow strikes his neck, and he collapses onto the floor in a pool of blood.

Argle climbs further into the tunnel with Tib riding on his back. They come to a bend and take a quick glance around the corner. The light is poor, but he signals that the path is clear and that they should join him. When his companions reach him, Tib jumps down from Argle's back and runs to Akelou.

"You both must return to the entrance of the tunnel and stay behind and look out for trouble. Tib and I will retrieve the princess. Once you hear my call, come to us, and I will open a door to escape. Argle, climb as high as you can, hidden in the darkness, and wait as lookout for other guards. Leotie, stay inside the tunnel listening for Argle's signal in case any enemies come. Fall back towards the dungeons if you are overwhelmed."

"Good luck, Akelou," Leotie says as she grabs his arm.

"To you, too," Akelou says, before he walks off into the tunnel.

Water splashes against the floor of a dark cold cell. A man laughs as a female Pokwa shivers in the corner of her stone prison. Goito, Columbus former ship cook, the master of the dungeons, drinks from a silver stein and looks at the princess lustfully. He is a bald, thick-built man with a large protruding belly. On his chest hangs a chain of bones from former prisoners. His legs are covered in armor that clanks as he walks. He is as dirty as he is foul-tempered, and his mind is filled with dark and twisted thoughts.

"Move, mutt," Goito says as he kicks his dog, a canyon wolf, before sitting down on a wooden stool. He takes the last bite of meat from a leg bone and taps it against the ground, attracting his wolf's attention. The wolf looks at the bone and begins to whimper. "Come and get it you filthy mongrel," Goito says as he waves the bone in front of the wolf's face. The wolf begs for his long-awaited scraps. "Take this," Goito says as he hits the wolf across the face. The wolf cries in pain, and Goito laughs in amusement. He takes a chug of ale and wipes his mouth as the liquid drips over his mountainous belly. "Aghhh," he grunts, and throws the bone into the dungeons before he passes out. The wolf growls at his master, baring his large teeth, before running off for the bone.

Akelou, followed closely by Tib, has come to another bend in the tunnel. He hears something smash against the rock, and the pair backs into the wall. Akelou peers around the corner of the tunnel and sees something moving in their direction. He signals Tib to step back as he raises his axe. Akelou revels himself and confronts his enemy, but then takes a step backward at the sight of the wolf. The animal's oversized ears shoot up, and it growls when it sees Akelou in the tunnel. The wolf creeps closer to Akelou and wags its tail as it picks up Tib's scent. Akelou can see Tib's fluttering

markings in the eyes of the drooling wolf. He steps in front of Tib and lowers his axe, falling to one knee. He can sense that the animal is stressed and suffers from abuse. He looks deep into the wolf's eyes. The wolf sees no fear or aggression in Akelou, only a welcoming gaze. The wolf stops growling and cautiously walks up to Akelou.

"It's alright, boy. I won't hurt you," Akelou says as he remembers the deep love he had for his dog, Carn. The wolf stops before Akelou and lies down on the ground submissively. Akelou moves to pet him, but the animal raises his head and flashes his teeth. "Good boy, quiet now," Akelou says, as he pets him. The wolf welcomes the affection.

"Open your mind, show me what lies ahead." Akelou places his hand over the wolf's head and looks into its mind. He sees a flash of the Dungeon Master and the princess. His necklace shines as he binds himself with the wolf. He can tell that the princess is near death and knows time is running out. He takes his hand from the wolf.

"Will you help us, friend?" Akelou asks the wolf.

The wolf gets up and licks his face. "Good boy, lead us to your master."

The wolf turns, picking up its bone, and slowly leads Akelou deep into the poorly lit tunnel. As Akelou follows the wolf, he begins to notice prison cells carved out of the stone walls. The first cell is empty, but traces of its old inhabitants can be seen. In the cell there are bits of torn cloth, bone and the reek of death. Cautiously, Akelou and Tib continue further into the dungeon, peering into each cell. Akelou comes to a cell and sees the whites of some creature's eyes. He moves toward the cell, when suddenly he feels claws grip his shoulder. He spins, raising his axe, ready to strike whatever has grabbed him. When he turns, he is shocked by what he sees: thin, rough, and weary-looking Meno and Salali. He lowers his axe and moves closer to the captives.

"Save us, release us, please. We are slaves taken from the Menoli. A few of my kinsmen and I were taken prisoner when we attempted to rescue our brothers. But when we were brought here, we found all but one had perished."

Akelou stares at the glider who speaks. On his face there is a grey stripe slashed across a dead eye.

"Stripes, is that you?" he whispers.

The enslaved men and Salali rush to the stone bars.

"It is I, Stripes of the Menoli city. How do you know of me?"

"Son...is that you?" asks a weak voice from the back of the cell." Gliders and men part as an older, emaciated man is helped into the flickering light. "Taeau, is it really you, son?"

Akelou's throat closes as he sees a shadow of the man he once called father. The old man reaches out from within the cell and touches Akelou's face. He is badly starved, and Akelou can see the signs of many beatings over his body. With tears streaking down his cheeks, Akelou touches his father's cold, weak hand.

"It is me, father. It is your son- "

"Stop making all that noise, slaves, for if you wake me from my sleep again, my whip will tear into your flesh," yells out Goito from inside the dungeon.

Akelou turns, and the wolf starts to growl. Akelou's necklace and brace pulse with energy as the sight of his father consumes him. He has never felt a wrath like this before. His mind feels lost, and the world turns red. Goito steps into the light and sees Akelou breathing and fuming with rage.

"Intruder!" yells Goito, and he snaps his whip at Akelou. Akelou steps away from the cell and faces Goito. He feels no fear, only the growing fury that burns his soul. Flaming light from his brace engulfs his axe as he stares down the Dungeon Master. The wolf and Tib stand true, readied for battle by Akelou. Then Akelou lunges for the Dungeon Master, and the tunnel echoes with screams.

Leotie hears the screams from the dungeons and looks back into the flickering light of the tunnel. Scratching from Argle's claws alerts her to the sound of the wooden door slowly opening. Leotie watches three young, armored men emerge from the entrance.

"Why are the torches out, Verna?" says one of the youths.

"I do not know. How would I know that? Where are the guards? They must have left their posts, the lazy whelps. I will find out their names and have them whipped. Ouch!" Verna yelps as they begin to walk into the lower tower. One of his comrades lowers a torch to see what has stubbed his foot.

"It is one of the guards. He is dead! There is blood everywhere."

Verna looks down at the dead guard. "Draw your weapons. There are intruders, perhaps more tree rats my father can use in the mines."

They draw their swords and run to the wooden bridge. Hearing their footsteps on the bridge, Leotie takes a breath and leaps out of the tunnel with her bow drawn. She releases an arrow that strikes one of the men.

"Ahhhh," he screams, shocked by the blow. Wounded, he stumbles and drops the torch to the ground. The others reach for their companion, but they are too late. He trips over the ledge, screaming as he disappears into the pit. Verna and his comrade huddle back-to-back with their blades drawn. Verna stares at Leotie in the torch light.

"It is just a woman. We can take her! CHARGE!" Verna yells as he and his friend run toward Leotie.

Leotie reaches for another arrow, but she has none left. She kicks out the string from her bow, grabbing its end. Watching Argle land on one of the assailants, her courage grows. Unaware of his fallen comrade, Verna continues his attack, swinging his sword at Leotie's head. She ducks under his sword, striking him in the gut with her bow. She comes up behind him and knocks him across the back of his head. Verna stumbles to the ground and rolls toward the entrance of the dungeons. Leotie drops her bow and draws her blades. She looks back to see how Argle is faring. He is on top of the soldier and is clawing at his face. Verna gets to his feet and points his sword at Leotie with one hand. He reaches behind his head and feels blood gushing from his skull.

"I will kill you both myself," he whimpers. "I am Verna, son of Columbus and Master of this tower. You will soon beg me for mercy, woman-"

Leotie charges before Verna finishes his speech, and he stumbles when their blades meet. Their weapons meet again and again echoing in the tower with each blow. Verna sees an opportunity and punches Leotie across her face and slashes her side with his sword. Leotie limps back and drops one of her blades. Verna starts to chuckle and the wooden door to the inner tower opens. Columbus rushes out to see the slain guard on the floor and his son engaged in a death struggle. Seeing that Verna is distracted Leotie reaches into her chest pocket and takes out the poison laced arrow tip given to her by Oboe. She lunges it at Verna with a painful grunt. The tip just grazes Verna across his neck. He touches the bleeding scratch made by the tip and smiles, raises his sword ready to strike down his enemy. But he hesitates starting to choke as his body begins to react to the poison. Columbus seizes an archer standing besides him, "Shoot them down!"

The archer quickly takes aim and releases the arrow he has aimed at Leotie's back.

"Look out!" yells Argle.

Leotie knocks Verna in the face with the blunt end of her blade and ducks as the arrow flies above her, striking Verna in the chest.

"Father!" he yells as he stumbles back, dropping his sword and grabbing at the arrow.

Leotie does not hesitate and jumps, kicking Verna in his chest. Columbus watches as his son falls into darkness, crying out to him for help.

"NOOOOO!" yells Columbus.

"Argle, cut the bridge! Come on," Leotie yells.

Argle leaves the badly wounded soldier and slices the end of the bridge before fleeing towards the dungeons. Breathing heavily, Columbus rushes to the bridge.

"How will we cross the bridge, sire?" asks a guard behind Columbus.

"FOOL!" he yells before beating the guard with his staff. The end of the staff sparks as it strikes the guard, tossing him into the darkness of the pit. Columbus raises his staff, and the rope of the bridge begins to retie itself. Once the bridge is restored, Columbus yells, "After them, you fools! Kill the rodent and bring me the one who killed my son."

The guards charge into the dungeons after the intruders, and Columbus walks to the edge of the rocky cliff and looks down into the darkness. Columbus grips his staff tightly and approaches the wounded friend of his son. Between his shallow breaths he looks up at Columbus and tries to speak. Columbus lowers his staff just above his face. The young man's body goes rigid, and he cries out in pain, spitting up blood. His body arcs and a light rises from his chest into the end of Columbus's staff. The king lifts his staff and the youth's body falls to the stone floor, cold and lifeless.

Akelou stands above the Dungeon Master. Goito holds his shoulder and looks at the bloody stump that once held his whip. His wolf gnaws on his decapitated forearm, twisting and thrashing at it with its jaws. Akelou reaches down to the Dungeon Master's side and takes his keys.

"Tib, take these and release the princess. We must flee quickly."

Tib runs to the main cell with the keys. Akelou leaves the Dungeon Master and comes to the prison cell and instructs the prisoners to step back. His brace shines brightly as he slams his fist into the ground. The shock wave from the impact shatters the stone bars, and the captives rush out of the cell, thanking Akelou with tears and hugs. Stripes and the prisoners pounce on the Dungeon Master, who cries out for mercy. Akelou takes his father into his arms and helps him walk out of the cell.

"I am here, father. Do not fear, for I will take you home."

Dirty Hands does not have the strength to speak. He just weeps in his son's arms. Leotie and Argle rush to Akelou.

"Akelou, you must open the door. There are guards behind us, we have no time," Leotie yells as she appears out of the dark, panting and holding her wound.

"Leotie, take my father into your arms. Argle, help the princess and tell the others to be ready."

Argle leaps past Akelou to the Meno and Salali behind him. Akelou takes out the Moura stone and sprinkles it with the dirt from the Whispering Canyons. He drops the stone and starts to swing it in circles. A high-pitched ringing echoes in the cave, then a circle of light illuminates the tunnel. Argle runs up to the princess and is stopped by gliders.

"Friend, brother Salali, are you from the Menoli city?" ask Stripes.

"No, but my family was. I am Argle, son of Black Claw, Half Moon, and stepson of Broken Wrist. Now, one of you help me carry the princess, and the rest of you go back to Akelou. He is getting us out of here."

The gliders look at each other when they hear Black Claw's name.

"I will help you, Argle. My name is Stripes, and your family is well known to me." They look at each other as they pick up the princess and rush back to Akelou who has opened a door with the Moura stone.

They can see a star-filled sky within the door. Argle watches as Akelou waves him on as arrows begin to fly around them. Columbus and his men are close, and as they approach Akelou, they see a black void circling in the tunnel.

Argle and the prisoners follow Leotie and Tib diving for the door landing on dry earth. There is a flash of light, then all they hear is the blowing of the canyon's winds. Argle smells the dust and the faint scent of the forest. He looks up to see a clear night filled with stars and a large moon. He has not seen the moon in many days, and he now looks at it as if seeing it for the first time. His body aches, but the relief of escaping with his life numbs the pain. He gets up to see the starved princess, weak prisoners and his friends, Leotie and Tib, whose markings are flashing brightly as he embraces Leotie's leg.

"Akelou, come quick! Dirty Hands is fading," shouts a weak Meno.

Everyone rushes to the side of Dirty Hands side who lies on his back. Akelou grabs his father's hand and moves in close to hear his father speak.

"Akelou, my son, I am all that is left of my father's line..." he sighs as life begins to leave his body. "Your mother...she, she was killed during the uprising when I was captured...she died in my arms. I failed her, my son...I am so sorry...all she ever wanted was to see you again." He reaches into his tethered pants and pulls out a piece of cloth. "She gave me this to give to you if I were to ever see you again." He hands Akelou a torn, blood-stained swatch of cloth. "She ripped it from her dress. It was the only thing left she had to give...it is the only reason I survived so long. She told me to swear to tell you, if I ever laid my eyes upon you again...that she never once...not for one day...did not think of you. She loved you above all things...I have wanted to go to her for so long...now I can, and with peace in my heart...I have miss-ed...he-r...s-o."

With tears falling from his cheeks, Akelou embraces his dying father. "I love you, and I love her. Tell her, father...tell her."

Akelou watches as his father draws his last breath. Akelou closes his father's eyes and looks up and sees his friends. He stands and faces the tower of Ogdah, "YOU HAVE TAKEN EVERYTHING FROM ME...I CURSE YOU, AND I WILL HAVE MY VENGEANCE!" Akelou yells, shaking his fist at the tower.

Leotie puts her hand on his shoulder, "Akelou."

Akelou feels Tib embracing his leg, and he turns to the Meno and Salali. "I know you are tired, my friends, and desire to go home. We must gather wood and send my father off into the spirit world so he can see my mother once again. We will travel to the Noshota swamps and return the princess to her people. Then Mia-Koda will open a door back into the Menoli city."

Everyone gathers wood from the forest, laying it on Dirty Hands' wooden tomb. As Leotie collects kindling, she bends down and notices strange markings on the forest floor. She rubs her hands around the wild imprints. She continues to search the area and finds more of these tracks. She looks up at the others, then back into the darkness of the forest. A fear chills her skin as she stares into the forest. She can sense an evil, an evil like none she has ever felt. She slowly returns to the group and sees all of the Meno and Salali gathered around Dirty Hands' body. Akelou walks up to his stepfather with a lit torch. He lowers his head and clenches his fist, squeezing it tightly before dropping the torch on the kindling. He steps back and joins his friends as they watch the flames climb toward the stars. Akelou feels a tongue lick the back of his neck and hears the dust wolf start to growl. He smiles as he sees Akima and Leotie's horse behind them. Akelou turns and embraces Akima, tightly gripping his mane, and he pets his soft fur.

"Akelou," yells Leotie as she holds up the princess. "She will not make it long in this dry wind. She is near death and needs to go home."

Akelou agrees as he looks back at the dying flames and takes out the Moura stone. He looks down at the dust wolf and pets the tired animal.

"You are free now. Go live in peace and find happiness in the wild." The wolf licks Akelou and sits by his side, standing his ground and nudging his nose into the Akelou's gut. "You are welcome to come, but a tough road lies before us. Ok, then I must name you." Akelou looks deep into his eyes. "I shall call you Jabra. It means, 'with big ears,' in the Menoli speech." The wolf looks up and howls loudly. Akelou nods his head and scratches the wolf's neck.

Akelou opens a door into the muddy shallows of the swamp. They leave the edge of the canyons and return to the swamps in the early morning. The air is much cooler and humid as they slosh in the thick waters. The princess falls to the swamp floor. She begins to roll around in the swamp, drinking what water she can and covering her skin in the lush mud. She gets to her hands and knees and starts to croak in the darkness. Jabra's large ears perk up, and he growls as the torches light the swamp around them.

"They are back, and the princess travels with them!" they hear voices yell, followed by distant croaks.

Pokwa begin to emerge from the trees and to congratulate the princess's rescuers. They offer the weakened Meno and Salali provisions and carry the princess back to the city. The Pokwa soon become quiet as the king appears from behind a tree. The princess falls into her father's arms, and they weep together. Females bring the princess her royal garb as well as more food and water for the heros.

"OUR PRINCESS HAS BEEN RETURNED TO US, MY FRIENDS!" shouts Theopa. "Tonight we rejoice in her return and honor her rescuers with the greatest of feasts. Lift these champions onto your shoulders, my brethren, and lead them to the Choa. Hooray! Hooray! For Akelou and his companions, HOORAY!"

"HOORAY," yell the others as they lift Akelou and his friends, leading them to the city. All the Pokwa sing and celebrate as they march to the Choa. Once they reach the entrance, Mia-Koda is waiting for them holding her staff that glows in the darkness. She raises her arms, and the crowd calms down. She lifts her staff to Akelou's face, gazing at him in the light, then she moves her staff to the others. She lowers her staff and walks towards the weary Salali and Meno.

"I see joy and relief in the eyes of my many Pokwa friends, but I also see pain and suffering in the eyes of these few. Much has been sacrificed for this homecoming, and much still must be sacrificed. White Stripe, son to the Stewart of the Menoli, come forward." White Stripes comes to Mia-Koda side, nervously crouching before her.

"Where once a great city of men and gliders stood, now there is only slavery and suffering. I have been to the realm of the Menoli and have talked to the scattered rebels that live in hiding, including your mate, Whispers."

"You must go and lead them against the Nossa that rule your city. Most of the soldiers that occupy your city will soon be summoned to join the forces against the Pokwa, and they will leave only a few guards behind. You must use this opportunity to take back what was once yours. Once you have reclaimed the Menoli Tree, the city must empty. When this is done, you must meet me at the three stones, where I will bring you back to the Noshota to help defeat Columbus' army."

Stripes falls to one knee and raises his head, "By my claws I pledge to return and fight against Usk-Ka. I will go back to our city and rally what soldiers we can and return in haste. I only hope we have the strength to do what is needed."

The Pokwa stomp their feet and croak a rally cry in response to his oath.

"Good, my friend. Courage is what is needed now. You must all look into your hearts and find your strength, for a battle will soon be at your door, and I cannot promise victory." Mia-Koda walks to Akelou's side and grabs his arm, raising it into the air. "But you will not stand alone as long as friends and loyalty still live...there is always hope!" The Pokwa erupt in cheers and resume the celebration.

Mia-Koda embraces all who have come, and she stops at Argle. She inspects him and stares at his helmet, and an expression of understanding fills her face. "You are the youngest of Black Claw's offspring, are you not?"

"Yes, I have traveled far with Akelou and Leotie, into the darkness and back. My mother has told me of you. She has told me of your power and the good you have done for my family."

Mia-Koda pats Argle on his shoulder, and takes the Moura stone from Akelou to open a door to the realm of the Menoli. "Remember, Stripes, bring everyone that you can, for if we fail, both cities are doomed." Stripes bows to Mia-Koda and walks into the doorway, followed by the Meno and Salali.

"Argle, what are you doing?" asks Akelou as he grabs him before he walks through the door.

"My place is with my people and my sister. I will bring my father's helmet back to the Menoli and return with an army to aid you in battle. We will meet again." Akelou and Argle lock forearms before Argle walks into the doorway and disappears.

Mia-Koda stands before Akelou. "When I was among the Meno and Salali in hiding, I was told Dirty Hands was taken captive. Did you see him alive?"

"Yes, he gave me this from my mother before he left to be reunited with her."

Mia-Koda looks down at the small piece of cloth. "Now, rejoined, your parents celebrate with us from the spirit world. There is no time at this moment for loss and grief. Instead, embrace in the joy of a daughter who has been returned to her family and the friendships you have made."

The celebration rages in the hall of the Choa, and Tib, Leotie, and Akelou are given full honors. Then Akelou slips away and steps out onto the terrace that overlooks the swamp. He stares into the horizon and thinks about his mother. A hand caresses his neck and startles him. He turns and sees Leotie standing behind him. She looks deep into his eyes and smiles. Akelou gazes at her and her long black hair, and takes her into his arms. A slave to his heart, Akelou holds her tight and locks his lips upon hers. The romantic embrace lasts for moments, but the world stops around the young lovers for a lifetime. As they release themselves, they turn and look over the swamps together, holding each other tightly.

CHAPTER SEVENTEEN

The doors to Columbus's chamber bursts open.

"Bring me parchment, you idle fools," Columbus coarsely shouts to his advisors. "My son has been slain by forest savages while you sit here and do nothing." He rips the parchment from a cowering advisor's hand and begins to write.

General Ush-Ka,

I send you this parchment as a grieving father whose son was murdered by a treacherous forest savage. I command you to attack the Pokwa city at once, sparing no lives but one. You will find a girl covered in animal skins and carrying two short blades. The scent of my dead son will still be on her. Bring her to me alive, for her soul I will rape from its vessel for eternity. Instruct Captain Ullace to fall back and reinforce you from the outer swamps. You will lead the first attack on the city. Once the city has fallen, Ullace and his men will lead the assault on the Menoli city, claiming more slaves for our mines. With these new slaves the shard will be discovered, and with it we will have the power to leave this forsaken land and conquer the Eastern Kings. Do not return to me without the girl, or the last shard you crave so dearly will never be found.

Lord Columbus

Columbus wraps the parchment and seals it with melted wax. He walks to a cage next to his throne and hands the letter to a canyon raptor. As Columbus opens its cage, the bird jumps onto his arm and waits for its orders. "Take this to General Ush-Ka with all speed, my servant. Do not stop until his arm you rest on. If you think of seeking your freedom, you dirty savage, or Ush-Ka tells me this letter never reached him, I will have your father boiled alive and your mother ravished before I have her burned. Disobey me, and never again will you take the form of man again."

The birds squawks, takes the letter from Columbus, and exits the chamber through a high window. He sits on his throne and points to his advisors, "Leave me, you wretched cows, and do not disturb me until you have my son's murderer in your grasp. Have every Indian savage expelled from my tower and forced outside our walls. Command the guard that no one sleeps until Ush-Ka has returned." His advisors bow and leave Columbus alone in his dark chamber.

"Akelou, wake up, Akelou," says Leotie as she pushes against his sleeping body.

"What is it?" Akelou responds while wiping his tired eyes, which are thickly crusted over from the long night of celebrating.

"The Pokwa chief has gathered a council in the hall. He wants us to attend."

"Right, well, give me a moment to gather my things. I will meet you by the stairs."

Leotie moves her head close to Akelou, and her silky hair crosses his face. Her smell fills his throat as she kisses his cracked lips. She leaves the room, walking carefully to avoid the snoring Pokwa warriors that line the floor. Akelou touches his lips as he hears the loud sound of someone passing gas in their sleep. He turns to see Tib rolling over and scratching his rear. As he shakes his head, Akelou's mind wanders back to the kiss and the night. Quickly Akelou dresses and kicks Tib in frustration. Leaving the room, he meets Leotie by the winding stairs that lead to the hall of the Pokwa. On their way to the hall, Akelou catches Leotie glancing at him, and when their eyes meet, they both smile and quickly look in the other direction.

Once they come to the door that leads to the hall, two Pokwa guards stop them. The guards, brothers, salute the couple before opening the door. In the hall the king, his court, and high-ranking warriors like Oboe and Mia-Koda have gathered. The princess, dressed in her royal Pokwa garb, sits next to her father. She does not look at all like the naked, starving, and dehydrated prisoner they rescued. Her finely crafted armbands are polished and shine brightly. The princess's loincloth drags behind her, glimmering as she rises from her throne. Over her body there are many painted symbols, and on her head she wears the royal tiara of the Pokwa. The princess approaches Leotie and Akelou, and embraces them in a gentle, aristocratic hug. She kisses Akelou, then Leotie, on the neck and bows.

"I am most grateful to you, my courageous outsiders. The Pokwa will always be your friend and the Choa a home to you."

They both bow, thanking her for her words. The hall fills with the sound of stomping feet and loud croaking, then it quiets as everyone looks up at their king. Mia-Koda motions for Akelou and Leotie to come over and sit beside her.

The Pokwa chief stands and raises his hands. "We come here today, gulp, to discuss the inevitable attack of Columbus' army. Our princess and our future have been saved, gulp, but the time of celebration is over. By the time the moon is full, Ush-Ka will be inside our borders. His army is large, gulp, their blades are long, and their steel is sharp. Ush-Ka is a merciless warrior who will kill everyone in his path if he is able. His men will turn our lands red with the blood of Pokwa. He will come with beasts and savage men who will not stop until our city burns. He will hunt down our children and our mates. No one will be safe." The king lowers his head and rubs his tired, worried eyes. "I ask you who represent the Pokwa families to choose. Do we stand and fight to the end, or flee, scatter, and hope to survive?"

The hall erupts in shouting, "Fight-"

"We stand and fight-"

"This is our land. I would rather die than flee."

The king again raises his arms, quieting the hall. "Yes, yes, but simple battle may not save us. This is the last home of the Pokwa; there are none outside our borders. We have no kin to call for aid-"

"What about the forsaken ones. Long have they dwelled in the shadows, but never have they attacked us. If this is our darkest and most desperate hour, then I say it is time to seek them out once again," says an old Pokwa of the court. The hall becomes silent, and many Pokwa shake their heads, having heard Bacas talk about the dark ones before.

"We do not know if they still survive, or if they do, where to find them. They may try to kill or betray us, for their hearts have become black and their minds wicked," says the King.

"They do survive, I have seen them and I can take you to the bog where you can find their underground dwellings. It is time to find where their loyalties lie. The Pokwa cannot win this fight alone. We must reach out to all our allies and forgive past betrayals and renew old bonds, or the Pokwa may vanish under Columbus' growing cloud of darkness," says Bacas.

The King sits back into his throne. He shakes his head and looks at Akelou. His daughter lays her hand on his and caresses his forearm. Theopa looks at her and breathes deeply. "I will honor the decision of the court. If they believe the mud dwellers should be searched out, then I will send the warriors. If there is any Pokwa that believes this is an ill-fated plan, then speak now."

The hall is quiet, and many in the court nervously whisper to each other. The King stands again, "It is settled. Bacas, assemble a search party to find the forsaken ones. Oboe, have the breeding pools emptied and the word spread."

Theopa raises his hands and closes his eyes as he prays to the Gods. "May our offspring have a home to return to."

Akelou grabs Leotie's hand, and they step down, place their weapons on the ground, and dance the Enopay war dance. The rest of the hall watches

the dance and begins to stop their feet. Croaking and cheers rise from the warriors as they lower their weapons and begin dancing. The king escorts the princess from her throne, lowers his scepter at her feet, and dances.

CHAPTER EIGHTEEN

Un-Ra, shadowed by the Daboon army, crouches below the canyon's edge staring at the moonlit tower of Ogdah. The Daboon are restless as they huddle, gripping their weapons and waiting for their master. Un-Ra watches the Hornbill transform from beast to man, between two pillars at the base of the stone bridge that leads to the tower's gate. Un-Nabus's eyes glow as he looks back at his army.

"My Daboon, glory is at hand. When the gate falls, storm the tower and slay all in your path. Then, my Daboon, you must climb the tower to the Columbus's chambers. There you will bear witness to the destruction of a false king, the reclamation of our tower, and the fulfillment of all I have promised."

The Daboon begin to growl and pound the ground in excitement. Un-Ra looks back to his warriors and raises his hammer. The Daboon roar as one, their eyes filling with fury and their mouths drooling with blood lust. Un-Nabus opens his hand, and from his dark mark the Book of Ixkin seeps out and opens. The Daboon flinch as a thunderous crack explodes from the book and a silver streak shoots into the sky. A misty cloud forms, swirling around the tower. The book closes and seeps back into Un-Nabus's mark. Un-Nabus pulls his hood over his head, and the Hornbill ascends into the mist. A deep bellowing echoes, reverberating against the stone.

"Did you hear that?" says an archer looking out from the terrace above the gate.

"Yes, there is evil riding on the wind tonight. Be on your guard, soldier," says the captain of the gate. "Ush-Ka's army should be attacking the Pokwa by now. We are all that is left to defend the tower since Columbus sent the natives beyond our walls."

"Captain, look," says an archer who points towards the Hornbill that has landed on the stone terrace. Darkness hides the bird, and Un-Nabus emerges from the blackness with his staff in hand. The guards are frozen with fear as they stare at the black sickle on his staff. The captain of the gate yells at his men, "Intruder! Sound the alarm, warn the king!" A soldier

pounds a gong that rings throughout the tower. Torches emerge from openings that look down at the gate.

"Attack the intruder! Kill him!" yells the captain again. The archers release their arrows at Un-Nabus. The arrows soar through the mist, and Un-Nabus raises his hand and they are engulfed in darkness. Un-Nabus lowers his hand and grips his staff, gliding across the terrace and attacking the archers. The captain watches in horror as his men are quickly butchered by the dark figure.

"Reinforcements! We are being slaughtered," yells the captain as he looks down into the inner courtyard. Soldiers have started to gather at the gate, and one points behind the captain. He looks back, but sees only darkness before his head is sliced from its body. It falls, bouncing against the inner wall and landing in the courtyard. Un-Nabus looks down inside the tower and sees the lever that releases the gate. He points his staff downwards, and darkness shoots down the side of the tower to destroy the lever. Chains rattle, whipping furiously as the gate comes crashing down, striking the bridge. The tower's guard has formed a defensive line behind the gate that waits for an attack. A guard that was sent into the mist screams as he runs back from inside the fog. "Beasts, giant beasts are coming!"

The guards gasp and step back as they see a Daboon emerge from the mist soaring through the fog before it land on the soldier's back, crushing him with a stone mace.

"Hold your positions! We must defend the gate!" shouts the leader of the guard. He charges, leading his men to defend the tower. Flashes from the men's muzzles light up the courtyard and Un-Nabus watches as his Daboon slaughter the men in a chaotic blitz of strength and ferocity. The few remaining men retreat into the tower screaming with fear. Un-Nabus opens his arms, again taking to the skies and flying upward to a window high in the king's chambers.

"Lord Columbus, the tower is under attack by an army of beasts! These beasts are like Ush-Ka himself. Our men are being overrun, and we have no means of reinforcing them," says a soldier that kneels before him.

Columbus grabs his staff. "Call my guard and tell them to retreat back into my chambers," he yells. "Fools they are if they think a few beasts with stone clubs can take this tower." He returns to his throne, flapping his royal garbs in noble arrogance.

"Lord Columbus, the beasts will be at your door any moment. We should flee the tower. It is lost, my lord," says the king's closest advisor, Memra.

"Memra, go to the door and make sure all the guards make it into my chamber."

Memra rushes to the stairs and starts shuffling in what guards he can. When the last of the guards have entered the room, they push the chamber doors shut. The doors close with a bang, and Memra looks back from the stairs and panics.

"Lord, let me pass! There is still time...the beasts have not yet made it to the top of the stairs. Help me, Lord, mercy..." Memra slams his fists against the door as he screams. He hears noises coming from the stairs behind him, and he starts to shiver. Trembling, he smells the pungent stench of beasts and the sound of dripping blood. In a frantic, quivering turn, he spins around to see the Daboon. Their dark fur drips with blood, and their grotesque hands tightly grip their weapons. He looks into their eyes and cries out as Un-Ra shoves his way through the Daboon, tossing a mutilated soldier to the ground. Un-Ra slowly approaches Memra and lowers his head towards the cowering man. He roars loudly, showing Memra his long, bloodstained teeth. The Daboon behind him roar in victory, raising their weapons in the air and pounding their arms against the floor. Un-Ra raises his arm, and the Daboon behind him become calm. He looks into Memra's eyes and smiles at the fear he sees. Un-Ra grabs Memra and tosses him back to the blood-crazed Daboon behind him. His screams last only moments.

"The dark master wants this, slurp, door destroyed. NOW BREAK IT DOWN!" he commands. His soldiers ram their weapons and bodies against the door. The guards inside the chamber brace the entrance against the impact of Un-Ra's warriors.

"Stand aside," commands Columbus, and he raises his staff into the air. A burst of light fills the chambers, and the guard watches the wooden doors slowly turn to stone.

Columbus begins to laugh. "No number of cursed beasts will be able to destroy that. My subjects, I have saved us from this doom, and now we only have to wait for the return of my armies that will destroy these devils." The men, exhausted from the fight, begin to cheer and hail their lord, but a new fear grows inside their hearts. A cloud rises from the floor, hiding the door in a thick darkness. A deep bellowing echoes loudly, and the men scream, holding their ears looking at Columbus on his throne.

"What sorcery is this, Lord-"

"What is upon us, King?"

"Protect the king," yells the last captain, arousing his men from their hysteria. Surrounding the king, they point their weapons at the growing darkness.

The black cloud grows, clawing at the walls as it climbs to the ceiling. Un-Nabus steps out from behind the darkness, and the guard trembles at the sight of his black blade.

"Attack, you fools! Kill him, ATTACK!" yells Columbus, pointing to the closest guardsmen.

Two men timidly charge Un-Nabus, discharging their rifles and brandishing their bayonets. Un-Nabus dodges the attack and slays the men in one lethal but graceful movement. The men burst into a pool of blood that rains down on the cold lifeless floor. Un-Nabus voice fills the chamber, shaking it with every syllable.

"You trespass in my tower. Lower your weapons and sacrifice yourselves to me, if you do this your deaths will be quick and without pain. Defy me, and suffer my WRATH!"

"I am the lord here and you have no power, demon," says Columbus, raising his staff. "I shall show you the true power of Columbus, LORD OF THE WORLD!"

The staff explodes into a furious barrage of light. Streaking energy singes the air as it races towards Un-Nabus. Un-Nabus stands calmly as the light approaches. A wall of protection engulfs the light into a wisp of dark matter. Un-Nabus raises his staff and slams it against the ground, and the door behind him explodes. Columbus falls out of his chair, and his guards are blown onto their backs. A soldier cries out as he sees the whites of the Daboon's eyes as they enter the room. Each guard is pinned to the ground by a Daboon warrior. The remaining Daboon circle Columbus.

"P-Please, I have wealth, great wealth. I will give it to you...I-I-I am a son Italy and the hero of Spain. The Queen herself has professed her love for me. She will grant you great amounts of wealth and land if you spare my life. You can rule over these lands alone for all time. I can give it to you, for I possess the power, and I alone know the secrets of this tower."

"He lies. He knows not what he possesses. The Kaah that he has tied to his staff belongs to the Hhtuno. He is a thief and should suffer as a thief," Un-Nabus hears the Ixkin speak to him.

"I-I will grant you my throne. You can rule over this tower. I will give it to you if you spare me-"

"You know nothing of what you speak. This is the ancient watchtower of the Hhtuno. Its purpose you cannot comprehend. As for the relic you hold, I do not need you to understand its power." As Un-Nabus speaks, his necklace falls out from under his robe and reflects moonlight from the window. Columbus looks at the outline of the necklace in shock.

"Y-You are a Delar! That is impossible, your line is dead-"

"I am a Hhtuno. How dare you speak of me."

"You must stop his lies. Take the Kaah from him and destroy this peasant!"

"Un-Ra, come!" Un-Ra obeys his master's call. "Turn and expose your quills." Un-Ra turns and bends his neck. Un-Nabus plucks a poison-laced quill.

"My Daboon, it is time to finish what we have started this night."

Un-Ra looks at his men and roars, raising his hammer. The Daboon thrust their weapons down upon the surviving men, crushing them all but one sniveling guard by Un-Ra. Un-Nabus looks at Columbus, and the quill shoots from his hand, striking the defeated king on the shoulder.

"Ahhh," the Columbus yells as he drops his staff. Once the staff hits the ground, the Kaah breaks free.

"That, thief, is a poison quill from a Daboon. The pain will be great as the toxins seep into your blood." Un-Nabus raises his hand, and the Kaah, a piece of black stone chiseled into a spear point, comes to him. Once he holds the Kaah, he hears a loud crack. Everything becomes black and the floor vanishes under his feet. As the darkness fades, he can see a small stream where a woman is kneeling and holding two small boys in her arms.

CHAPTER NINETEEN

Akelou stands in Theopa's hall marveling at the hieroglyphs painted on the walls...stories of battles and acts of heroism in Pokwa history recorded by the elders. His mind drifts as he stares at the shadows that dance on the stone and begin to take shape. Trees sprout into a forest, and among the trees, a hut reveals itself. He sees the outline of his mother sitting on a stump and husking corn collected from the fields. Akelou stares at a shadow of himself sitting by her side; he is listening to her sing. His shadow turns and runs, followed by his old dog, Carn. He runs to his father who is kneeling, waiting for Akelou to run into his arms. Akelou jumps into his father's embrace, and Dirty Hands tosses him into the air squeezing him with love. He tilts his head and walks up to the wall and tenderly touches the shadow of his mother.

"You will always be with me mother," he whispers as his fingers run down the wall. The sounds of Pokwa horns wake him from his dream.

"Akelou, it is time. You must come with me," says Theopa. "Ush-Ka is at our door and calls us to battle. My warriors are in position and await our signal. The Pokwa are ready, gulp, to defend our home till the last of us stand. I ask you, my friend, kin of the Delar, are you ready to die by my side defending what is not yours?"

Akelou takes a large breath, blinking at the wall before he turns to the king. "By the axe of your forefathers...forged by mine...it is victory or death, my king."

Akelou stands tall and locks arms with Theopa. "TILL DEATH," they say to each other.

Tib, wearing a nut helmet and gripping two stone blades, stands proudly beside Akelou. He looks up at Akelou with his bulbous eye and points towards the horns with his blades. His markings flash as he leads himself to battle. They walk through the door, and Theopa grabs Akelou's shoulder as they emerge onto the terrace. They gaze down from the stone terrace at the legions of Nossa warriors standing behind General Ush-Ka at the edge of the swamp. The Pokwa warriors blow into their bone horns and raise their weapons at the sight of their king.

The two armies face each other, separated by a short stretch of open swamp. The Pokwa warriors brandish their weapons, stomp their feet, and croak loudly. Akelou catches a glimpse of Leotie waving her blades as she stands beside Oboe. She looks up at Akelou, and their eyes meet. He wishes she would have agreed to stand by his side, but she would not leave the warriors. She is a proud and stubborn woman. His heart pounds with fear and with love for her.

The warriors ready themselves for the king's words. Leotie stares at the Nossa across the battlefield and takes a deep breath. She examines their greater numbers and superior weapons. Their spears are tall, their armor thick, and their iron-clad shields stout and solid. She knows the Pokwa are mighty warriors, but their armor is made from bark, the shells of giant turtles and their weapons from wood and hand-cut stone.

Oboe places his hand on her back. "Do not be afraid. The Pokwa have faced mightier armies before. If we are all to die today...then we die together and with honor." Leotie looks up at his face, and courage enters her heart.

"GENERAL USH-KA, INVADER OF LANDS AND SLAYER OF THE INNOCENT, gulp, I COMMAND YOU, LEAVE OUR BORDERS, OR THE BLOOD OF YOUR MEN WILL STAIN OUR SWAMP RED. I GIVE YOU THIS LAST CHANCE, gulp, TO TURN YOUR ARMY AROUND AND FLEE, OR I WILL UNLEASH THE STRENGTH OF THE POKWA AND CRUSH YOU!" Theopa yells down from his muddy terrace.

The Pokwa roar and splash water at the words of their king. They grow quiet, and all eyes look at Ush-Ka and his men. Ush-Ka bellows out in his cracked, wicked laughter. "You dare threaten me, soft-back, your empty threats are wasted and unheard. I give you no means of retreat or terms of surrender. I will destroy your cursed city before the sun sets...and the Pokwa will be forgotten like the ancient kings of men." Ush-Ka lifts his stone mace into the air. The Nossa warriors standing in tight formations begin to part, clearing a path.

The Pokwa move back and gasp as men appear holding chains attached to grey crocodiles. The crocodiles snap at everything around them and thrash their thick armor-covered tails with excitement at the sight of the Pokwa. Leotie looks at the water's surface and watches as it begins to bubble and ripple.

"ATTACK!" roars Ush-Ka, signaling his men to charge. His warriors break out in a run, splashing through the swamp.

"HOLD!" Oboe yells to his men as he extends a large stone rod. The Pokwa are jumpy at the sight of the crocodiles and nervously grab their weapons, ready for a fight. "HOLD!"

"NOW!" yells the king, and Oboe slams his stone staff against a rock under the water. From beneath the water's surface half of the Pokwa army splashes up with their dart blowers, firing poison darts. A wave of darts descends on the Nossa as they charge. The warriors fall into the water, shaking in pain and drowning as the poison paralyzes their bodies. The Pokwa continue to fire their darts as the army moves closer. Many of the crocodiles are freed from their masters and now dive under the water, racing toward their prey.

"FIRE!" yells Ush-Ka, and from the cover of trees a wave of arrows flies toward the Pokwa. The dart blowers dive back into the water, crawling into underground shafts to avoid the attack. The rest of the Pokwa army leaps into the air, curling into tight balls protected by their armor. The Pokwa land on the Nossa, spearing, crushing, and bludgeoning all they can. Oboe leads his warriors into battle with unmatched fury and courage. He lands on a crocodiles back, driving his spear between the beast's shoulders and through its body.

Leotie charges, breathing deeply as arrows soar past her in all directions. Beside her, Pokwa are being swept under the water by submerged crocodiles. The screams of the Pokwa echo in her mind as the crocodiles' death spins tear flesh from bone. The adrenaline and the ferocity of the battle overwhelm her, and the only thing she can feel is the pounding of her racing heart. She breaks the battle line and stops the long sword of a Nossa warrior with her crossed blades. Through his screams Leotie pushes his blade to the side and slices him across his neck. She looks over her shoulder and sees a bladed staff coming down at her. She side steps to safety and waits for his staff to break the waters surface. Seizing the moment she runs up the wooden staff, leaping over the warrior, spreading her legs and reversing her body, cutting his back as she comes back to the swamps floor. A flash of steel knocks Leotie to her back. She hears the crunch of her nose breaking as splashing water blinds her to her attacker. Through her blurred vision she sees a Pokwa engaged in battle with the Nossa that struck her. The Nossa drives a blade into the Pokwa's chest. Leotie cries out, and her nose gushes blood as she charges the Nossa and drives her blade into his belly. She pushes him back screaming, spitting blood in his face. The warrior falls, and she tries to catch her breath.

Her teeth slam shut as a blinding pain races up her back. Her legs go numb, and she falls under the water's surface. She looks up and sees a shadow through the water. A massive hand lifts her up out of the swamp. Through blood and water she looks down and sees the top of Ush-Ka's head.

"This battle will soon be over for your friends, and you will watch them die helpless and broken in my arms," Ush-Ka roars, lifting Leotie over his head for everyone to see.

Akelou looks down, and there is Leotie in the grip of Ush-Ka.

"Leotie!" he yells, then turns and begins to run into the hall. He takes but one step when his necklace explodes with light, and the world around him disappears.

A new world materializes around Akelou. He can neither smell nor sense anything, but through the darkness he recognizes the Black Forest. A voice startles him, and Akelou crouches in a defensive position.

"My end is near, take what life still beats in my heart and use it to save that which is dearest to it," echoes a woman's voice.

A light begins to shine through Akelou's chest. He stares at it in wonder at the light passing through his body. He sees a woman kneeling in a rising stream, and in her hands a light illuminates the forest. Akelou walks into the stream, feeling nothing as his legs dissolve into the water. He approaches the kneeling woman and looks into her eyes. Something familiar stares back at him.

"Who are you? What has happened to me? Answer me!"

The lone woman looks at him, and Akelou at her. Her luminous brown eyes pierce his soul, and he falls to his knees. He cannot feel the water or the wind, but in his heart he knows who she is. Akelou reaches out his hand to touch her, but his fingers pass through her like a soft breeze. He looks down and sees his infant self, sleeping peacefully with a thumb in his mouth. He looks at the face of his twin brother for the first time since that very night.

"I have a brother? You are my mother? What is your name? Tell me, where can I find you? Why are you here?"

In a burst of light the satchel holding him and his twin brother is gone, and his mother is alone. He follows her as she climbs the bank of the stream and stands next to a tree whose roots strangle the muddy shore. She takes a sword from under her robes and touches it to her face. Akelou watches as she drops her dark necklace to the ground. He stares at the dead amulet and grasps his own necklace.

She turns and swings her sword, and a flash of azure light slices Akelou across the chest. He stumbles back, holding his chest in shock, then a Nossa warrior falls to the ground besides him. He watches helplessly as his mother is attacked by Columbus's men. Akelou stands in awe as she defends herself, gracefully wielding her sword against her enemies. Never in his life has he seen such swordsmanship. There is no fear in her eyes, and she does not hesitate to strike down her foes. His mother slays a finely armored warrior and tries to lift her sword from his body. Akelou looks back when he hears a rustling in the forest. He approaches it, and comes face to face with Ush-Ka. He jumps in front of his mother, trying to block the quills that strike her in the back.

"YOU!" he yells as he confronts the beast. "You again? You, you have haunted me my entire life. It is you, beast, who has taken everyone that I have loved."

Akelou tries to attack Ush-Ka, but his fists fade through the beast. He watches as Ush-Ka lifts his mother against a tree, and in the beast's other arm he sees his father's dead face. Akelou screams. He hears something new approaching his mother and Ush-Ka. A figure covered in robes emerges, and he listens to this cloaked figure tell his mother how she will die. Akelou hears the soft dying voice of his mother speaking in the language of the Delar, and understands her words.

"Tonight, I die. You have murdered my lover, and I have abandoned my children to the wild, ancient beast and coward of a different land. But I have fooled you. Both my children will survive, and they will grow into men of the Delar. I have foreseen your doom. Each of you will be slain by a blade wielded by my sons. My body of flesh may soon turn to dust, but the seeds of my fathers live. I curse you both, and you both will be cursed. My love and I will watch you suffer, and together, standing beyond this world from the shores of death, we will rejoice in your destruction."

Tears streak down Akelou's face as his mother's soul is stripped from its human shell. He watches as his mother's and father's bodies are cast to the ground and abandoned on the bank of a small stream. Akelou crawls to his murdered parents and kneels by their side. The world around him fades, and soon there is only darkness. He looks out into the void and sees a figure in tethered robes staring down at him with two glowing eyes. He can sense its power and tries to move towards it. His body is almost gone, but his necklace shines, rising from his chest. He can see the figure's necklace rising towards him, and Akelou reaches out to him. Each necklace is shaking with energy, and then a blinding flash turns everything to white.

Akelou opens his eyes and finds himself inside Theopa's hall. His senses have not yet returned as he looks around the room. Tib and the king are trying to wake him from his dream. Akelou looks over the terrace, and his insides burn with hatred at seeing the beast once again. The King and Tib step back, startled by Akelou's sudden movements. Akelou sprints towards the terrace with supernatural speed. Then he leaps over the edge, spreading his arms and screaming the call of the Wa-Hoon. His necklace and brace burn, leaving a trail of light behind him as he rises over the battlefield. Golden wings of flame rise from his markings. Akelou flaps his arms, and in a blur of speed and light he lands by Ush-Ka in an eruption of water.

Ush-Ka is thrown to his back from the shock of Akelou's landing. Ush-Ka uses his stone mace to lift himself from the swamp floor. Akelou stands face-to-face with Ush-Ka's belly and yells, "TIME TO DIE, MONSTER!"

Ush-Ka laughs, "And who is this worm that cries for my destruction?"

"Do you not know me, foul beast? For our paths have crossed before. I am a child whose mother and father you murdered and left to rot on the forest floor. I am Black Claw's nephew, who I watched you murder along with his son, who was like a brother to me. You have made me an orphan many times over, and today I will have my VENGEANCE!"

Akelou lifts his necklace toward Ush-Ka. "Recognize this? My mother wore one as well. Today I shall fulfill my mother's prophecy."

Ush-Ka looks at Akelou and now understands he has not destroyed his ancient enemy as his master commanded him to do. For two and a half thousand years he waited, transformed to stone, to be awakened to kill the last Delar. He raises his mace before Akelou. "I will crush you as I crushed your whimpering father, half breed. I brought him to his knees, took his head, and tossed his body into the flames of his burning home." Ush-Ka laughs loudly and raises his mace higher. Akelou looks up at the beast's neck and sees a string lined with many trophies. At the center of the necklace is a large black claw.

"Yes, I took his thumbs and laughed as I walked over his rat son. Now, today, I shall laugh again after I destroy you and this pathetic city. My master will soon walk this world again, and when he does, you will all again be slaves." Ush-Ka swings his mace towards Akelou.

Ush-Ka's weapon is met with a thunderous crack. When the water settles, Ush-Ka looks down at Akelou who has stopped the weapon with his brace. Akelou waves his arm, and Ush-Ka's mace is tossed back into the swamp. Ush-Ka steps back, and his men watch with fear at the power of Akelou. Ush-Ka looks around and recognizes the doubt in his warriors' faces.

"Cowards, do not look at this child with fear." Ush-Ka takes a sword from his belt that is dwarfed in his hands. "This is the sword of your witch

mother, boy. I thought I had rid the world of your cursed race that night, but now I shall finish what I started. I have not endured an eternity of solitude to fail my master, so come to me, half breed, and meet your doom."

Ush-Ka grips the sword, and it swells and twists in his large claws. It no longer shines but becomes dull and lifeless. As the weapon morphs, Akelou can hear a soothing ring coming from the blade. Akelou listens to the sound and yearns to hold the Namid himself.

Dropped from Ush-Ka's grip, Leotie has been swept up by a wave of water. She washes up on a Pokwa home. Leotie opens her eyes, but her body is numb. She lies helplessly on her back as water crashes over her limp body. With menacing agony she moves her head and watches Akelou facing off against the beast that broke her. Leotie's heart goes cold as Ush-Ka brandishes the massive blade toward Akelou. The man she loves now faces a great danger alone, and she can do nothing but whimper as she tries to move. Her lungs begin to fill with liquid as the poison from Ush-Ka's quill races through her body.

Leotie cringes as Ush-Ka swings his claws at Akelou. Akelou narrowly escapes the blows, diving to his side and rolling on the surface of the water, tossing his axe at the beast. Ush-Ka ducks under the axe laughing as it soars past him, but the axe circles back and strikes Ush-Ka in the back. Ush-Ka roars as the blade digs into his flesh. Smoke rises from the blade as Ush-Ka's black blood pours from the wound. Akelou leaps into the air, flipping over Ush-Ka. He reaches out his hand and his axe returns to its master.

Leotie can smell the swamp mud as her body slowly slips towards the dark water. Tears fill her eyes and her cries go unheard within the chaos around her. Choking, she stares at Akelou as he fights, and a memory comes to her. She is back in the great hut and is dancing with Akelou on the night he returned to the Enopay. Leotie closes her eyes, and when she opens them again she is staring up at Akelou from his lap. She watches his lips as he speaks about his time in the jungle. His smooth, amber skin reflects the moonlight from the opening of the hut.

"I love you, Akelou," she whimpers.

She looks back to Akelou, who is surrounded by Nossa warriors as Ush-Ka recovers from his wound. The warriors circle him with their swords drawn. Akelou tosses his weapon and strikes the first Nossa with his axe. He ducks, and his axe leaves that warrior, flying back to Akelou and then striking a shocked Nossa behind him. Akelou dodges a blow and punches the swamp with his fist. The ground shakes as a body-crushing wave engulfs his attackers, sending them away screaming.

Ush-Ka attacks Akelou from behind, swinging his blade at the young man's head. Akelou dives into the water and emerges behind him. He tosses his axe at the beast, striking him three times. Each time his axe drives into Ush-Ka's back, it releases itself and returns to Akelou's hand. Ush-Ka falls to his hands, blood pouring from his deep wounds. Ush-Ka raises his sword and swings it at Akelou with all of his strength. Akelou faces the blow and lifts his axe to meet Ush-Ka's arm. Leotie watches as Ush-Ka's limb falls into the swamp, and then the beast falls to his knees.

Blood-filled waves splash against her face. She watches as Akelou grabs the beast's neck and takes something from him. Akelou stands in front of Ush-Ka and raises his arms; his vision rises from his markings. He opens his mouth and expels the scream of the Wa-Hoon. The scream releases a great ball of energy, and a wave rises towards her. Through the oncoming wave she sees Ush-Ka roaring back with his ears gushing with blood, until he falls into the water. The wave crashes over Leotie, and when she opens her eyes all she can see is darkness. She struggles as the cold of the water enters her lungs. All her pain and the sounds of the battle fade as her eyes shut and her body floats to the surface.

Akelou stands above his enemy and takes back Black Claw's claw from Ush-Ka's necklace. He looks into the water, and there is his mother's sword shining through the water in majestic waves of light. He reaches into the water and grips the sword. A chill blows over him as the cold steel of the Namid embraces its new master. He raises the blade from the water and faces his new companion. The sword changes in Akelou's grip, growing to a new length. Akelou watches as the markings begin to resemble water running down the length of the blade.

The Nossa have pulled back, hesitant due to the loss of their leader. The warriors stand at the edge of the swamp and stare at the Pokwa. A captain of the Nossa shouts at his men, ordering them back on the offensive. A rally of arrows cover his charging men, and they begin a new assault.

"Akelou! We must fall back. We are being overrun. Retreat to the Choa," says Oboe, drawing Akelou's attention from the Namid.

Akelou turns to Oboe, waving at him to fall back as arrows rain down around them. Akelou starts to retreat, when he sees eyes emerge from under the swamp. Akelou yells out, but it is too late. A grey crocodile lunges out of the water, clamping its powerful jaws around Oboe's leg. Oboe tries to fight off the beast, but the crocodile spins, thrashing its tail and ripping apart his leg.

"Hang on, Oboe!" Akelou yells, and he runs to help his injured friend. He fights his way through the charging Nossa, trying to reach Oboe

before the crocodile takes him under. He sees a smaller Pokwa jump on top of the crocodile.

"TOE, NO!" Akelou yells in horror as Oboe's son tries to save his wounded father. Toe rubs his hands over his skin, then puts them over the crocodile eyes. The crocodile releases Oboe, thrashing and bucking from the poison that has blinded it. The youngling is thrown into the air and lands hard in the swamp. The crocodile, blinded and in pain, swims towards Toe, chomping its teeth wildly. A terrified Toe curls into a ball, shivering and awaiting his doom. Akelou throws his axe at the beast, striking its side. The crocodile closes its mouth and spins in the water, trying to free itself from the axe. Akelou leaps into the air with his sword drawn. He lands on the crocodiles belly, plunging the Namid into its throat. The beast goes still, and Akelou looks down at Toe.

"Save my father. He is hurt."

Akelou grabs Toe and tosses him back towards the Choa and away from the charging Nossa. Once he sees that Oboe's son is safe, he rushes to Oboe's side and lifts him from the water.

"My leg...you must use your sword...it is beyond help."

"But-"

"Do it!"

Akelou looks down at his friend's leg that has been torn apart. He rips a piece of cloth from his pants and ties it around Oboe's thigh. Akelou raises his sword and cuts off Oboe's leg. Oboe screams in pain, then passes out. As Akelou lifts him over his shoulder, he feels the warriors closing in behind him. Another barrage of arrows rains down, and he hears them hit Oboe's shell armor. He looks at the Choa, where the remaining Pokwa defend the entrance. Toe has gotten the attention of the Pokwa guard, and he sees the mouths of the Pokwa as they shout to him.

"DOWN!"

Akelou dives into the water as a barrage of poison darts race towards the Nossa. Akelou quickly gets to his feet, dragging Oboe behind the Pokwa lines. The attacking Nossa hit the Pokwa guard, and the fighting continues.

"Thank you, son of the Delar, for saving my father. Thank you," Toe says as he cries and hugs his father, who is still unconscious.

"Make ready for a direct attack," Theopa yells from inside the tower.

CHAPTER TWENTY

Behind the battlefield Captain Ullace leads the reinforcing Nossa forces. Ullace is a Nossa chieftain, commander of an elite group of Nossa warriors. He is a stout and burly man worn by time and scarred by battle. His long, golden hair and beard hang down over his shoulders. He wears a fur patch over the eye that was gouged out by a rival clan of Vikings, and he carries the ancient sword, Bergthor, forged by the forefathers of the Nossa.

"Inon, my son, Ush-Ka will crush these long legs swiftly. Once the Pokwa are defeated and Ush-Ka's men are tired from battle, we must ride against them."

"What! Our fellow brothers...why, father, will that not sit well with the men."

"They will do as they are commanded! Ush-Ka must be destroyed, and I must be named General of Columbus' armies. Ush-Ka's men will be reduced in numbers and tired from battle. They will be easy to defeat, but it will take the rest of us to destroy that cursed beast Ush-Ka. Sacrifices must be made...the men will understand, knowing the spoils they will receive if we succeed. Once I become general, I will get closer to the king, and when I have gained his trust, I will slay him with the blade of our people. I will become king, and the Nossa will multiply and prosper in these lands." Ullace and his son begin to laugh as they discuss their plans.

A Nossa soldier turns his head when he hears a rustling in the trees. He looks up and sees the branches swaying softly in the calm breeze. He elbows his friend and points to the treetops.

"What? What do you want?"

"I think there is something in the trees, brother."

"There is nothing in the trees. It is just the wind. I cannot wait to get out of these stinking swamplands. My feet are rotting in this muddy hell. Once we kill these freaks, we will have first rights to the Menoli city. I will take a wife, and settle down in the forest and raise a family. Ullace has personally promised me at least one woman and my choice of land."

"Ullace has never spoken a word to you, lying fool-"

"You calling me a liar, you ugly woman?"

"I will call you worse than that-"

"WILL YOU?" the soldier yells, as he jumps on his friend, striking him in the face.

The two soldiers start to fight, and a circle of cheering men encourages them. The commotion breaks the ranks of the Nossa warriors. Ullace and his son look back to see what has stirred the men.

"We must get the men back in rank, father."

"No, let them get a little fire in their bellies. They have become restless from all of this waiting. It will help them on the battlefield."

"You are a wise and great leader, father. It will be a great day when you become king." Ullace and his son watch the men fight and cheer.

As an archer from the rear of the ranks pushes against those in front of him, he hears a rustling behind him. There is movement in the trees. He takes a step closer trying to get a better look, when an arrow knocks him to his back. He opens his mouth to warn his fellow warriors, but his warning is drowned out by the screams and taunts of the men. He lies on the ground and sees men covered in dark paint and armed with arrows and spears. In the trees, eyes stare down at him from within the branches as he takes his last breath.

"We are under attack!" a Nossa screams as a spear drives into his back.

"Arm yourselves! Fall back into rank," a Nossa spearman yells, but the men are confused as they are being attacked from all sides. The Nossa warriors charge after the painted men who have fled back into the swamp.

"Pursue the attackers, form a defensive barrier around the captain," shouts Inon as he tries to regain control of his men.

"Wait for my signal, Argle. We must catch them by surprise. Together we will take out the leaders. I will handle the smaller one, and you, my brother, can have the honor of killing the Nossa leader."

"Thank you, Stripes. Our lands will again be ours, and I can bring my mother back to her true home."

Stripes looks over his shoulder towards other Salali, hidden in the trees, and scratches his claws against the bark of the tree. The treetops begin to echo with scratching. Salali leap from the branches, attacking the remaining warriors. The trees unload with gliding Salali that float down toward the unsuspecting men.

"FATHER, LOOK!" shouts Inon as the gliders attack from above with their false claws open.

Ullace turns to see Stripes tackle his son from his horse.

"INON!" he yells, and he raises his sword to save his boy. He aims his sword at Stripes and yells, "RODENT SCUM!"

Argle leaps onto his back, driving his large thumb claws into his shoulders. Ullace falls from his horse screaming. He hits the ground and rolls away, grunting in pain. Argle leaps onto his belly.

"Many years ago, you and your men destroyed my home and murdered my father. Today we will avenge those who fell under your swords and were taken as slaves." Argle raises his false claws and takes the head of Ullace. He grabs the head of the Nossa leader, leaps on the back of Ullace's horse, and holds it out for all the men to see, "YOUR LEADER HAS FALLEN, YOUR LEADER IS DEAD!"

The Nossa turn in the direction of the voice and see Argle holding the head of their beloved chieftain. "Ullace has fallen! Fall back! Save yourselves!" yell many of the Nossa.

The men scatter and run off into the woods in retreat.

"We must fall back to the city and help Akelou. Come, brothers, leave the defeated men to run and hide," yells Argle.

The Meno and Salali warriors cheer as they charge toward the city and to the aid of the Pokwa.

"Theopa, we will not be able to hold them for long. Their numbers are too many, and we must get to higher ground, away from the crocodiles," Akelou shouts.

The king agrees and tells the Pokwa to sound the horn of retreat and follow him into the hall of Eol. Akelou, with Toe's help, carries Oboe up the stairs and into the hall. A few Pokwa warriors stay behind and defend the stairs behind them. Akelou makes it into the hall and places Oboe on the floor. He goes to the door and looks out as the last of the warriors comes up the stairs. He waves at the last two Pokwa to hurry into the hall.

The remaining Pokwa are brothers, guards of the hall. They look at each other, then to the stairs, and back to the door they have guarded all their life.

The eldest brother speaks, "The Nossa are close, and the last of the Pokwa warriors behind us have been slain. We must defend our home and protect the king."

The brothers embrace each other. They butt heads and raise their weapons, charging down the stairs. The brothers leap to glory, killing many Nossa and martyring themselves for their brothers.

"Find what you can and bar the door," Theopa tells what few Pokwa are left. The king sits down on his throne and lowers his head, taking off his crown. Then he feels a hand grip his shoulder.

"This may be the end, my king, but do not lower your head, for your Pokwa look to you for courage. My Lord, I weep for the loss of the many Pokwa who have died here today. My friend, Leotie, whom I love, is nowhere to be found, and I fear she has fallen. If we are to die, then let us meet death with courage, so we can be reunited with our kin without shame," says Akelou.

The Kings stands proudly and speaks, "release the door and let them come, and may we meet our destiny with the pride of our people. Let it not be said that in our darkest hour we died as cowards, but rather united and worthy of being called Pokwa warriors."

Theopa raises his weapon, and the Pokwa cheer. They stomp their feet, rallying the last of their strength and courage for the final battle. They walk away from the door and stand next to each other, tall and proud, as the door shakes and cracks under the beating from the Nossa.

"Son, look at me," Oboe calls out. Toe wraps his arms around his father and sobs. "Do not weep for me, son, for I die with honor, and I will see my father again soon. I have missed him and will have no shame when we meet. You, my son have made me proud, and have become a true warrior. I shall tell my father and his fathers of your deeds. You have earned the right to carry our family's name. You must survive, Toe, and take care of your mother. Do not feel shame in fleeing the warriors here, gulp, you have already proved yourself in battle. You are young and can fit into tunnels and hide from the Nossa. Go to the swamp's edge where the princess leads our women and children away and help them survive."

Toe's skin begins to fade as he shakes and sobs, "I love you, father. Don't go. I need you. I am afraid, I am not strong like you, FATHER!"

"You are stronger than you thi-"

Oboe takes his last breath in the arms of his weeping son. Akelou reaches down and closes Oboe's eyes, lifting Toe from his father.

"No, he is not dead. I must stay by him. LEAVE ME!" But Akelou forces Toe from his father and shakes him.

"Your father is gone, Toe. He would not have wanted you to die crying over his body." Akelou holds his axe in front of the youngling. "Take this and fight by my side, and when the time is right, climb that wall if you can and escape out a window."

Toe wipes his eyes and stares at the axe. He grips it with both hands and stands tall by Akelou's side. The axe begins to glow, and Toe shakes as he holds the weapon.

"Theopa, look!" yells a Pokwa warrior as he watches Toe.

Toe's bright youngling colors fade. His size and stature change as he matures into a young adult. The warriors and the king watch in wonder as the axe shines and Toe morphs into a man. The axe fades, and Toe falls to his knees. Having witnessed this before on the day the axe chose him, Theopa walks to the crouching youth and removes his crown.

"The great axe of our people has chosen a new master. All hail King Toe, son of Oboe, and the future of our people!"

The room full of Pokwa fall to their knees and honor their new king. Theopa lowers the crown onto Toe's head and kisses him on the forehead. "You, son, are now the leader and the future of our people. You must flee. Survive and take my daughter as your queen. If the Pokwa are to have a future, it will rest on your shoulders now, for you must see them out of this darkness."

"Yes, my Lord," Toe says.

They all stand and face the breaking door. Akelou raises the Namid and takes a deep breath.

"I am sorry, Leotie, that I could not save you. I will see you and my families soon. I loved you...I never told you, but I do."

The door pounds, and the wooden boards crack. Everyone waits for the last assault of the Nossa. They stand ready, but it does not come. The pounding on the door stops, and they hear the men screaming and running back down the stairs. Fresh cries are heard from the swamp below, and they rush to the king's terrace and look down at the swamp. They cheer as they watch warriors on painted horses ride out of a door opened by the Moura stone. Akelou sees Alo leading Enopay warriors on horseback against the Nossa.

"Mia-Koda has succeeded. Let us go to our allies from the plains!" yells Theopa. He points to the Salali and Meno warriors who are surrounding the Nossa army.